A Novel

Bart Bare

Canterbury House Publishing

Vilas, North Carolina

Canterbury House Publishing, Ltd.

225 Ira Harmon Road,
Vilas, NC 28692
www.canterburyhousepublishing.com

For information about permission to reproduce
selections from this book, write to:
Permissions
Canterbury House Publishing, Ltd.
225 Ira Harmon Rd.
Vilas, NC 28692-9369

Book design by Aaron Burleson, spokesmedia

Library of Congress Cataloging-in-Publication Data

Bare, Bart.
 Girl : a novel / Bart Bare.
    p. cm.
 Summary: After her mother dies, Loren Creek, a precocious
fourteen-year-old, flees the Tennessee foster-care system for North Carolina
where, with the help of a curmudgeonly mountain man, she evades detection by
pretending to be a boy, even becoming place-kicker on the high school
football team.
 ISBN 978-0-9825396-4-4
 [1. Runaways--Fiction. 2. Sex role--Fiction. 3. High schools--Fiction. 4.
Schools--Fiction. 5. Foster home care--Fiction. 6. Mountain
life--Appalachian Region--Fiction. 7. Boone (N.C.)--Fiction. 8. Piney Flats
(Tenn.)--Fiction.] I. Title.

PZ7.B250263Gir 2010
[Fic]--dc22

2010008569

Caroline

Chapter 1

"Your Honor, I can live by myself. I don't need anyone."

"Loren Creek, you are fourteen; a precocious fourteen, but fourteen nevertheless. Even if I agreed that you were capable of doing so—which I do—the statutes forbid it. In the eyes of the court you are a minor, and as such, you must be under adult supervision."

"We've tried that twice, and it didn't work." Loren felt Mattie's sharp elbow in her ribs, then added, "—Your Honor." Loren shuddered as she remembered the groping hands waking her in the dark. Hastily whispered entreaties, promises, and then threats. Only her quickness and strength saved her. The second foster placement was as bad as the first. *You little slut. You tryin' to snake-eye my man from me. I seen how he watches you. I seen the looks you give him.* As soon as that "foster mother" stomped out, Loren went to her bedroom, packed her bag, and was out the window. She hitched a ride to the only home she had known; the modest frame house in the hollow where her mother raised her. Police searched her out two days later. When they returned Loren to her second foster placement at nine in the morning, a slatternly woman appeared at the door dead drunk. She was the only adult there. *I just don't know why the child up and left—we been kind to her.* The officers returned Loren to Mattie in Piney Flat, and then saw to it that the inebriated woman's name was removed from the list of foster care homes.

"Your Honor, those people just want the money. They don't care about me, or helping kids with no place to go. They just want some drink money."

The judge glanced again at the police reports, her eyes rested on the precisely written accounts of two failed foster placements. Once again, she was struck by the clarity in Loren's penned statements included in the reports.

"Your Honor. I started taking care of my mother and our house when I was nine. I been payin' the bills, doin' the cookin' and cleanin' since mother had to stop work and come home. I kept up things as well as Momma had—she said I did it better." Loren paused to see if the judge was attending. "I know how to run a house and a farm. I been doin' the accounts and checks—signin' Momma's name. I been doing repairs and painting. I garden. I mow the lawn and trim the bushes. You could go to my house right now and you'd see it clean and orderly." She recalled her mother's repeated admonition, *Don't give in to sloth, Loren. Sloth is the playground of fools.* "There's nothing I can't do around a house. By the time I was twelve, I was head of the household, and have been since. Momma showed me how to do things, and I did them. We didn't need any help." She paused, and then quickly amended. "Neighbors pitched in some. Folks around Piney Flat are good. But they didn't help me any more than I helped them—we do for each other. Someone'd bring me a sack of taters—Loren knew her mother would have cringed at her country dialect—and

I'd keep their kids when they had to go somewhere. We trade off. Eggs for taters, cheese for side meat. It all works out. All it takes is folks with a notion of fair play. 'Point is, I don't need any *adult supervision*—especially the kind I been getting from Foster Care."—another jab in the ribs.

Judge Edythe Tilson looked from her documents—health records, birth certificate, school records—and into the determined gray eyes of the slender girl across the table. *I can't even get my girls to clean their rooms.* "I visited your house last week. I found it clean and comfortable. The outside grounds have apparently been well-cared for…"

"Your Honor—sorry for interrupting—but I'm worried about my Alice. She wants milking twice a day, and I know that ain't happening. And the chickens— they can only live on their own for a while, then they'll go to the wild, and the foxes'll get em. I worked hard to build up that flock of layin' hens. No one's looking after them like they need. Neighbors are trying, but that's askin' a lot. It's been two weeks now since we started trying foster homes, and neighbors have kept up my farm. I'll bet Alice's stall ain't been mucked out more'n once or twice. I don't keep a dirty barn—Your Honor."

God, there are times I hate this job. "Your animals will be sold off by the state and the funds placed in escrow for you. The money from the sale will be yours."

"You'd sell Alice? She's family. I've lived off her milk most of my life, and you'd pass her off to some stranger—who might…" Finally, the girl broke, and tears glistened on her cheeks. "Alice is my friend. I clean and groom her every day. She loves it and pays me back with gallons of rich milk. I make butter, clabber, and cheese. You give away my family—Alice, the cats, the hens, and my rooster, Attila—and I'll hate you as long as I draw breath. You can't do that. It ain't moral. It's cruel."

"Miss Creek, I don't have a choice in the matter."

"That ain't so, it can't be, it just cain't. My mother told me that we're a country of law, and that our courts are just. This ain't just. It's evil." Loren broke free of Mattie's firm brown hand on her wrist and stood at the table, leaning toward the judge. "You must be evil."

Immoral, cruel, evil. Judge Tilson, fighting back tears and anger, responded softly. "I was raised on a farm, Miss Creek. I'll personally see to it that your animals go to good homes."

"They got a good home. They got me. We're family. I tend Alice, she gives milk that feeds the cats, they kill the mice that would eat the chicken feed. I sell the chicken eggs and buy good feed for Alice. We ain't just a bunch of critters—we got a home." Loren could feel Mattie shaking beside her. She knew Mattie was choking back tears.

Even Mattie, soft-spoken nurse-maid and mid-wife to dozens—even Mattie, strong as she is—knows the unfairness of this. Loren turned to her anguished friend. "Mattie, I'm sorry."

"Loren Creek, having listened to your argument, it is the decision of this court that you must be returned to an appropriate foster home. Another home has been selected for your placement. Should this placement fail, the court will have no alternative but to place you in a state institution until you are eighteen years of age. Bailiff, escort Miss Creek to the office of the court for further disposition." The judge's face was devoid of any display of feeling as she gathered her papers and dropped them into the file box on her desk.

At the doorway, Loren broke free from the bailiff's grasp and spun about, facing the judge, who was watching her exit. "Damn you. Damn you to hell, you unfeeling witch—Your Honor." The bailiff regained his hold and led her from the room.

The judge rose and exchanged looks with the stout black woman who had sat beside Loren. "Mrs. Hooks, would you please accompany me to my chambers?"

Judge Tilson seated Mattie Hooks in front of her desk and took a chair beside her. Mrs. Hooks, I have reviewed this case several times now, and it occurs to me that you are a major part of Loren's life. I've checked into your background and found it to be excellent.

"Thank you, Your Honor, I've tried to live a Christian life."

"Yes. I want to ask if you would act as Loren's temporary—I don't want to say guardian—temporary family member until her mother passes away and the Child Protective Services are able to find a truly suitable home for her. The next time I will over-see and inspect the placement myself."

"Your Honor, I would be proud to take her in permanent myself, but as you know I live with my daughter and her husband in a small house, and... Well, he's bad to drink."

"I understand Mrs. Hooks. I would be satisfied to let Loren stay at her house and have you check on her on a daily basis. You will need to call the child protective officer of record each day and report on Loren's progress.

"I can do that, and will be glad to."

"There is the issue of transportation."

"I have my own car, Your Honor, and can take Loren wherever is needed."

"The court will reimburse you for..."

Mattie raised a silencing hand. "Excuse me, Your Honor. No need of such a thing."

Judge Tilson nodded in acceptance. "If you need anything, or have any problems in this matter please call me—here or at home." She handed Mattie her card, on which she added her home phone number. "Can you think of anything else?"

"No, Ma'am, Your Honor."

"Do you have any ideas about how we can satisfactorily place the animals?"

"Yes, Ma'am, I can take two of the cats, and some of the chickens. I have neighbors who can take the rest of the chickens, and the other cat. I don't know about Attila. I don't think he's catchable, and if he was caught, I wouldn't want to be the one to let him out. A neighbor—a good family with children—will take Alice."

"The court will release some funds to help in the placement of the animals. Will you call me next Wednesday morning at eight o'clock, just to check in?"

"Yes, Ma'am."

"In the meantime, the court will issue you the sum of one hundred dollars for food and care of the animals."

"No disrespect, Your Honor, Ma'am, but I don't want no money for takin' care of my child or her belongings. I helped raise her from birth. Her house, and the things inside will be taken care of like she was there. I'll see to that even if'n I has to go there every day until it's all settled. No disrespect."

"None taken."

Rising, Judge Tilson extended her hand. "Please stay in touch with me, Mrs. Hooks. I don't want this spirited child to get lost in the system. Let's go get Loren so you can tell her of our plan to let her stay in her house until…"

"Yes, Ma'm, Your Honor."

The judge accompanied Mattie Hooks to the office of the court down the hall, and then returned to her chambers.

In her chambers, Judge Tilson slammed the door shut, opened it, and slammed it again, shaking the wall with the weight of the heavy wood. Her frustration came out as a guttural growl, forced through clenched teeth as she pounded both fists on her oaken desktop. Her shoulders shook and her stomach muscles convulsed as she choked back the need to cry.

Dammit. Damn it to Hell. This is not fair. The girl was right. This is evil. And I'm a part of it. I'm evil. The Honorable Edythe Tilson dropped into her chair, slammed her elbows onto the desk and propped her chin over her tightly clenched hands. *I wish to Hell I'd never heard of Piney Flat.*

Weekdays at noon, many good citizens of Elizabethton—accent on the fourth syllable—Tennessee drive north on Old Hwy 19E to a restaurant nestled in a deep cut through a hilly valley of some five miles. If they were to continue on another dozen miles they would drive past the huge grandstand of Bristol Speedway. However, most stop at the large roadside parking area of The Ridgewood Barbecue and join the midday lineup to pay reverence to efforts of Jim and Grace Proffitt. The Proffitts began pleasing palettes at that location in 1947, and have kept up one of the few remaining outdoor barbecue operations in the state of Tennessee. Outdoor barbecue lost state approval some time back, but Ridgewood was grandfathered in.

No less than two national magazines accord Ridgewood barbecue fixings as the best in the nation. There are scores of traveling salesmen who drive far off their route to pay respect, driving through pastureland, forest, and by modest dwellings with large gardens in the back. If asked the location of Piney Flat, most would respond with "who?" and a shaking of the head, not realizing that Ridgewood Barbecue lies at the northern edge of Piney Flat, a rural community scattered among the Western foothills of the Appalachian Mountain chain that borders Tennessee and North Carolina. Loren Creek was raised up a couple of good-sized pastures from Ridgewood's carefully screened and maintained cook shed. If the wind was right, eating lunch at home was out of the question. Residents of northeastern Tennessee, southwestern Virginia, and northwestern North Carolina set aside regional differences to gather and pay homage over plates of western style barbecue, fresh hot fries, and small pots of the world-class baked beans. The vittles are served up by smiling ladies who appear to eat where they work. Eyes glaze over as the daily congregation savors their favorite dish, justifying the trip. Businessmen, lawyers, carpenters, and farmers, all shared in this democracy of excellence. It was the only restaurant meat that Loren's mother would permit.

From her front porch, Loren could smell Ridgewood's evening offering. Her thoughts drifted to the noon-day walks that she and her mother took there to eat among friends and strangers. She remembered the wildflowers along the way, the spring violets, summer ragweed, and the towering Joe Pye and Iron Weed in the Fall. Evening dark closed in around her as she slowly worked her rocker. *This is my home.*

That evening over supper, Edythe Tilson confronted her two teenage daughters with Loren's problem. Both of the girls wore braces, both were dressed casual chic in Old Navy blouses and studiously ragged jeans, and both girls sported carefully disheveled hair.

"She was right, Mom. You should have left her alone, that's what I would've done. The law is wrong, real wrong."

"I couldn't, Tara. It would violate the state statutes. I pushed the envelope as it was by letting her stay at her home alone while her mother was in the hospital. A nurse had brought her situation to the attention of Children's Protective Services, and that started the ball rolling. Loren's mother has been shuttled between hospital and home care for almost three months now, while Children's Protective Services has developed Loren's case and sought a suitable placement."

"Suitable? They sure don't sound suitable to me." Meredith stated flatly. Sounds like the placement homes need family care more than Loren does."

"I've done everything I legally can to help Loren. I've bent rules, and ignored the routes of action ordinarily taken, in order to accommodate myself to this truly exceptional young lady. I've let her live at home with no supervision, I've tried temporary foster home placement in order to see how she would adjust."

Meredith broke in, "From what you've told us, all I can say is that it's a good thing for her that she *didn't* adjust to them."

"Because of her history of self-sufficiency," Tilson said, I've given Loren much more freedom and autonomy than is normally accorded people her age. I've stuck my neck way out for this child."

"She's not a child, Mother." Tara snapped.

"You're right, Tara. And that's why I've taken the risks for her."

"Aren't those foster families screened?" Meredith asked.

"Yes, they are, but do you have any idea how over-burdened the people in Child Protective Services are—and how hard it is to find potential foster homes? They just don't have the time to do an adequate screening in all cases."

"That's not right," Tara interjected. "Why is it that way, Mom? How can it be so wrong?"

"Money; it comes down to money. It always comes down to money. We have wonderfully talented, hard-working people doing the job, but they are asked to do way too much. I see it every day in dealing with the legal aspects of their work."

Tara, the same age as Loren and some twenty pounds heavier with baby fat, looked at her mother. "The law's wrong, Mom. Isn't it supposed to be about justice? Fair play? Isn't it supposed to represent decency?"

"Justice, yes. Fair play, not necessarily. Usually, yes, but sometimes, no. And I guess sometimes we miss the justice target too." She cut wide slices of whole wheat bakery bread and handed them on a plate to her daughters.

Meredith said, "Looks like you missed both of them this time, Mom."

"Well, let's talk about it, girls, and see what we can do to set things right."

Meredith, ever the defiant one, said evenly. "Okay, Mom, but you're on the side of wrong so far."

Cell phone music came from an adjoining room. Tara's choice of rings. "Sorry, Mom. I forgot to turn it off."

"Sounds like you and Meredith volunteered to do the dishes again, Tara." Judge Tilson answered with a smile. Meredith shot a dark look at her sister.

The following Wednesday, Mattie Hooks drove Loren to the courthouse, and sat in a waiting room as Loren went to Judge Tilson's chamber. A pitcher of milk and some cookies sat on a small table that separated a pair of comfortable chairs.

Judge Tilson poured two glasses of milk. "Loren, I have two daughters—fourteen-year-old Tara and sixteen-year-old Meredith. I took the liberty of discussing your case with them last night over supper, and we came up with an interesting possibility." The cookies and milk sat untouched. "I—that is we, my girls and I—thought it would be a good thing—a right thing—if you were to come live with us. You could finish high school as a member of our family. You would have your own room, your needs would be taken care of, and you be as free as my own daughters." Loren didn't move or react. "What do you think?"

"What did your man say?"

"I—we divorced almost ten years ago. There's just the three of us."

"You couldn't keep a husband?"

Edythe Tilson reflected a moment. "He and I weren't happy together, and we thought it best to go our own ways."

"The girls think that was best too?"

"No. They were quite upset, but got over it."

"Got over it?" Loren reflected on the thought. "I've done without a father for all my life. I can't count the number of times I've thought on how good it would be to have such. And your girls 'got over it'?"

"Yes. After a period of adjustment. What do you think? Would you consider giving my offer a try?"

"Charity? I want to keep what's left of my family together; I want to live in the family home where I grew up, my mother grew up, and my grandpappy built from timber he cut and milled. When my mother—passes," Loren took a deep breath. "I'll own the family home. I'll have more than enough insurance money to pay my way, and see me through college—my mother's dream. Everything—everything that you and the foster care people have offered me are nothing more than obstacles. I want to make my own way, and you're offering me *charity*? You're not family, you're not even a neighbor. Me and my neighbors—we exchange kindnesses. We

10

don't take from each other. I don't take from them. You're nothing but a stranger putting her nose in my business. You don't care for me, my ways, or what comes of me or my git."

"Not at all. You're a fine young lady, in some ways you're more mature than my girls, who are pretty mature on their own. You're intelligent, disciplined and self-starting, and you are willing to take responsibility for yourself—more so than many young people who are four or five years older than you, in fact more so than many adults I've seen. I would be pleased to help you out as a person whom I admire and want to help. This is not just simple charity I'm offering."

"If you want to help, you'll get out of my way and let me live my life, my way. I don't need or want help—from you or anyone else. I have a family home. I have place. My mother's near death in the hospital. You want to take away my home, my family—my animals are family—and offer me charity. You call that *help*? You can take your charity and your cookies and go to hell—Your Honor." Loren rose from her chair. "I want to go. You've insulted me enough for this day."

CHAPTER 2

The only color in the room came from the mason jar of Fire Pinks picked that afternoon from a sun-dappled bank behind the farm. Their angular red faces reflected sunlight from atop the dresser, their wild beauty shouting at the walls of the austere hospital room.

"Gal pal—I guess we're close—to the end—you and me." The voice was tired as worn denim.

"Mother, don't talk such foolishness. There's no end to us—there's no me without you, and no you without me."

"I know. And one of us not being here doesn't stop that. When—I'm gone—now don't hush me—I'll still be here—in you. Just like when you're in school—you're right here in me—heart and head. When there's this much love between two people, no one ever goes away. It's a comfort to know I'll always be—in you."

The girl smiled through her sadness. "When I've got hard choices, I ask myself, what would Momma do? And you have the answer for me. It usually looks to be the difficult path, but in the end, it turns out to be the right—and easy—way. It always happens like that. I—I can trust what I know you would want. I guess that's what faith is about. I guess it's what love is about—someone we can have faith in, someone we can trust like you and I trust each other. Faith—love—trust, they go together, just like you told me. I love you, Momma, I trust you, and I have faith in you; I always have, and always will. All the really important things I know—about life and people—they come from you."

The woman's eyes closed and she smiled around her pain. Her daughter's words were balm to her last hours. Even breathing was hard. She opened her eyes. "Remember, there's insurance—big insurance." She seemed to grow stronger. "Don't let anyone take that from you. Mattie is the executor, and I told her what to do. It's in writing in my will. The lawyer has a copy, the clerk of court has a copy, you have a copy, and Mattie has a copy. Everything's notarized—right and proper. That money is yours. Don't let the lawyers nickel and dime it out of you. You do like I told you. I want you to promise me a—some things."

"Yes, Momma." The girl knew what they were.

"Get that college degree."

"I will, Momma."

"Don't let man nor beast, nor personal demon, keep you from college."

"I won't, Momma."

"When you—when you're standing in the sun on that stage, in your—in your black—your black robe." She stopped and caught her breath. " — with that piece of paper in your hand—I'll be smiling down on you, and thinking—we done it—we did it."

"I promise."

"And—when you—get—degree." Breath was precious now. "Remember to use—it. Use it to give, not—to get. We'll be—be—remembered not for what we—got, but what we—what we gave." Her breathing labored and she closed her eyes. "You and me."

"We will, Momma."

"One more thing. Never forget—we're on this—earth—to create—to create beauty. This is so because—because love grows out of beauty."

"I love you, Momma. You are beauty."

Late that night Loren lay beside her mother. The mother's head was cushioned and framed by her daughter's thick locks of auburn hair. *She feels so frail—there's almost nothing to her.* At dawn her mother took a deep shuddering breath, exhaled long and slow. Then the next breath didn't come. Loren didn't move, but lay there with her mother's head pressing her shoulder. The nurse came in, wordlessly turned off the electronic monitors, and left the mother and child to a silence that bound the edges of the room.

CHAPTER 3

Friday afternoon. All of Piney Flat was there. One of their own was gone, and the entire community came to pass before the open casket laid out in Reverend Burke's spacious sitting room. The kindly man of the cloth had spoken eloquently during the service held in his front yard. His elevated porch served as pulpit. The weather was kind. It was as though Spring tipped its' hat in honor, flooding the valley with gentle warmth and a bounteous blue sky that sighed white mounds of cloud.

"Sarah Creek was a woman-child," he spoke softly, "when I came to Piney Flat. I remember her like it was yesterday. She came to services with her mother, Zalene. She was a faithful follower. We knew her on Sundays, at the Wednesday evening youth group, and whenever she was needed. During her teens she volunteered—more than others. I could always count on Sarah." The short, spare minister paused to look over his pulpit at the assemblage seated on his lawn. "Many of you," he continued, "remember Sarah as friend and schoolmate. She was one of us. Her family was known. Her grandfather helped build our chapel, timbering some of his land to supply the lumber. We worship under timbers and siding from that family's land and hand."

A lone warbler provided music. Loren remembered them as her mother's favorite, her saying, "How could something so tiny make such music beauty?"

The reverend continued. "Sarah finished school here and high school nearby. She was a hard worker, studious and learned. Her good grades earned a scholarship to the university." The preacher's face darkened slightly and his voice went deeper as he continued his recollection. "Midway through her last year of college, Sarah met a young man from Indiana. She turned to more worldly pleasures and was soon lost to us. I remember her mother asking for my intervention because Sarah was considering withdrawing from school. It was futile." The reverend pulled a large white handkerchief from his coat and ran it over his forehead. "We lost our Sarah to the young man from Indiana. Years later, when she returned to us, she came with a daughter in her womb, and a sense of bitterness I had not known in her. Sarah left her Loved one to his prodigal lifestyle. She would not speak of him. Sarah Creek took over the family farm and helped her mother and father live out their lives." The good reverend paused and gazed into the young leaves of the huge maples nurturing his yard. The only sound was Sarah's warbler. His gaze returned to his flock gathered on folding chairs. "Sarah's daughter grew into the fine young lady we have with us today." Reverend Burke nodded to Loren seated in the front of the congregation. "Then came this illness, a darkness that would not be denied or turned aside..."

The talk lasted for nearly half an hour as people wept and remembered, nodding in sympathetic recollection.

The better part of the next two hours was taken up with the removal of the casket and the community to the graveside service, and then the return to overflowing tables at the home of Reverend and Mrs. Burke.

Food was out of the question for Loren who sat receiving neighbors and friends in the parlor, accepting condolences, expressions of sorrow, and hearing promises of help. By late afternoon, most people, having performed their community duty, left for home, business, or shopping. Loren went to the window to watch some of her departing friends. When she turned back to the room she was faced with Judge Tilson and two teenage girls.

"Your Honor." Loren nodded at the Judge.

"Loren, these are my daughters, Meredith and Tara. We've come to express our sympathy for your loss." Loren nodded acceptance and acknowledgement to the mother and her family. She gestured to a circle of parlor chairs.

The judge began as soon as they sat. "I know you're angry with me, Loren, but I want to tell you, once again, that I'm pledged to do everything in my power to help you—in ways you find acceptable."

"Your Honor, it's my mother's funeral, and I won't speak my mind, and not in front of your girls. I thank you for coming, but I know what you call my 'best interests' aren't the same as what I call my best interests. That's all I'll say."

Judge Tilson sat forward on the edge of her chair, hands tightly clasped in her lap. "I don't want you to leave this community. I've been trying to find neighbors who will take you in as your foster parents, but I haven't had any luck."

"No, and you won't. They know how I feel, and they know what I want—and what I don't want. I know families here who would take me in tomorrow, if they felt that was what I wanted. But no one—not a soul—in Piney Flat will lift a finger to help you take me away from my family home. They respect my wishes. They know I refuse to be taken in by anyone. They will take and hold my animals for me. They will mow my lawn, protect my property, and wait for me to return. Family and neighbors is everything to the people I know. My neighbors and me, we don't trust the government—some purely hate the government. They've watched the government hunt down and jail their moonshiner relatives. The government has taken their family lands so they could make dams. Whole communities were put underwater—and are mourned to this day. The government forces these independent people to its will with no say so. The government and its rules have never helped these people in the long run. They—we—are mountain people, and we look out for our own, we respect other's ways, while we go our own. Everyone in Piney Flat has turned their back to you. That's how it is, and that's how it's going to stay. Now I don't want to talk about it any more—I've already gone on longer about it than I should. I want you to respect at least that wish of mine." Loren clenched her jaws and looked into the judge's eyes. She sat erect, knees together, hands on lap. Meredith and Tara, who had remained silent and composed while Loren spoke, exchanged looks. Each nodded slightly.

The judge was taken aback by the candor, intelligence, and resolve of this slip of a girl. After expressing her condolences and a brief observation on the fine qualities of the people she had met that day, Judge Tilson and her daughters excused themselves.

15

Loren watched from the window as they left in the judge's green Audi sedan. Tara, from the back seat, turned and watched Loren as they pulled away. Loren saw that the girl was crying as she gave a slight wave of the hand.

By four o'clock the community had gone home, leaving a half-dozen ladies and a couple of teenage boys to clear and clean. Over the ladies' protest, Loren remained to help.

In the following week Loren carried out the tasks she had known all her life. As agreed with the court, Mattie Hooks stopped by for twice-daily visits. But now it was different. Loren Creek was alone, and acutely aware of the fact. On Sunday of that week she attended church, and was again hugged, bussed on the cheek, and witness to a river of tears. That afternoon she did her bills and penned thank-you letters. She answered e-mails well into the evening, going to bed just before midnight.

The following day she did the usual chores, she milked Alice for the last time before a neighbor came to get her, fed the chickens, and weeded the garden, then tended the flower beds in the front of the house and alongside the walkway leading from the road to her porch. She put fresh cut flowers in vases and jars around the house. That afternoon she visited her mother's grave with fresh flowers and a spray of sweet-pea which she used to adorn the gray-green stone that had been selected by her mother, and quarried and cut by a local man who had gone to school with her. No bill was sent. The sod had been returned, leaving only a slight mound to settle. Loren mused over the words carved under her mother's name and her birth and dates. *Out of Beauty—Love.*

She walked the mile from the cemetery, waving to passing friends who slowed, but knew better than to offer a ride at this time. She paused at the beginning of the flagstone walkway leading to her tidy frame house. It looked so big now, empty and deserted; asking not to be forgotten. As agreed earlier, Alice had been taken away while Loren was at the cemetery. She didn't want to see Alice riding off in the back of a truck that would take her away from the only home she had known.

On Monday she called a local shelter and asked that they come and pick up the bounty of surplus food that crowded her refrigerator and kitchen counters. She asked that they bring containers so she could return plates and serving dishes to their owners. By late that afternoon her kitchen had returned to normal, save for a large stack of clean dishware waiting to be returned. Loren knew what pieces went where by their patterns.

On Tuesday, Loren mowed the lawn, hosing down the small riding mower before putting it into the barn next to the farm tractor. She cleaned the animal stalls and added fresh hay where needed. She gathered eggs and talked with the hens who listened closely. That afternoon she replaced the water filter in the pump house—there seemed to be more silt than usual clogging the filter. It had been a wet spring.

The week passed quickly—as it does to those who know industry. On Thursday, Loren cranked up her grandfather's immaculate old Ford pick-up and drove the hollow, returning dinnerware to neighbors. She had taken care to note which food went with which dish so as to pay compliments accordingly. When she returned home the house seemed even emptier. She parked the truck in the barn, went into the house and set to vacuuming—one last time.

She took a late afternoon walk to the cemetery, enjoying the kind spring warmth.

She wore her mother's favorite yellow dress in honor of her mother and the spring daffodils. Again, she studied the grave stone. *Out of Beauty—Love.* That evening, Loren walked home slowly, noting more than usual, the common sights along the way; fence post knots, certain large trees, clusters of spring flowers. *Maybe they will leave me alone. Maybe they will decide.*

CHAPTER 4

Just as she walked up her driveway, a small, bright red car approached from the direction of the reverend's house; it slowed and pulled into her driveway. Meredith and Tara Tilson stepped out of their Ford Focus.

Loren beckoned the Tilson sisters to join her on the porch stoop. The girls gathered like friends, legs tucked up under chins as they sat gazing at the valley below the cabin. After a while, Tara broke the silence. "It's beautiful here. I can see why you don't want to leave. If I had a place like this I'd never ever want to leave."

"Yes, it's beautiful. Momma and I used to sit on this porch of an evening and read to each other. When it was too cool or wet, we'd sit by the fireplace and read. Sometimes we'd stay up—on the weekends—all night, just readin' out loud or to ourselves. We'd go to sleep of a morning after the cow was milked, and the chickens put up. It's the only home I know—or care to know. Have you ever stayed up all night and read with the—with your mother?"

"No," Meredith replied, "but it sounds nice."

"It was, and now your mother wants to take that memory away from me."

The two girls looked at each other. It was apparent they weren't sure where to start. Meredith moved closer to Loren. "We want to help you, and we think we have a plan you might like."

"Mother would ground us for a month if she knew we were here. I mean, we'd be in serious trouble," Tara said.

"She'll not hear it from me," Loren answered. "But why do you want to help me? We just met last week and we don't know each other."

"Because it's wrong. That's why." Tara said. "It's wrong for the law to try to put you out of your house and make you live with strangers. That's a bad law—and Mother has told us enough about you that we kinda feel like we're friends. She never talks about her cases—almost never—but she has talked about you every night over supper. I mean, it really bothers her."

"I don't like being felt sorry over." Loren said quietly.

"That's not why we are here." Meredith countered. "We're here because we think you're getting the shaft, and we want to keep it from happening."

"Okay, what do you two think I should do?"

Meredith continued. "We have an idea that we got from a couple of boys we met at your mother's services. They jumped our case as soon as they found out that our mother was the judge, but when they realized that we were on your side, mother's and not our, they opened up about you and your family. You really have a lot of friends here."

"The boys were cute." Tara giggled, covered a smile with her hand, and then she blushed furiously.

Loren sat erect and poised, unwilling to extend herself to the children of the woman who would remove her from her home.

"Sam Hightower and Jason Pike think it would be a good idea for you to move to North Carolina or Virginia," Meredith said softly, and then added, "I think it's a good idea except for the money problem."

"Money problem?" Loren asked.

"You need money to live on." Tara said, "If you got a job you could pay the rent and buy food. We could probably take up money from the people in Piney Flat to help out. It wouldn't be easy but you might be able to make it."

"I have money. There's the insurance. I'm supposed to get $250,000 on a policy my mother has—had."

Tara looked at Loren with wide eyes, her mouth slightly open. "Two hundred and fifty…"

"Yes, but I can't have it 'cause I'm a minor. The money has to be managed by somebody called an executor."

"Who's that?" Meredith asked.

"My mother put it in her will that it should be Mattie Hooks—she's an old friend of the family. She knew my grandmother, and helped birth and raise my mother. She's sort of a local midwife and herb doctor to a lot of folks hereabout. She's like family."

"What's she like—do you trust her with all that money?"

"She's the best friend I've got, Tara; of course I trust her. She saw to it that there would be no wait at all for the insurance claim. The day after Momma passed she was at the insurance man's office with a death certificate."

"You can't get any of that money?" Meredith asked.

"I can have some of it. Mother told Mattie, and put in the will, that I can have up to thirty thousand dollars a year until I turn eighteen, then the money is all mine."

The girls watched as a dusty grey Taurus came down the road, slowed, and then turned into the driveway and pulled in next to the Focus.

"Darn."

"Who is it?"

"It's that foster agency man. He watches me like a hawk. He's creepy."

A figure eased out the partially opened door of the Taurus. As the man rose to his full height of five eight, the first thing noticed was a jutting paunch that belied his slenderness. The next thing apparent was the lack of color; Aldrich Herms was gray. His hair was gray, his clothing, and his complexion. Gray. Herms leaned on his car door, smiling. He raised his Fedora in greeting.

Tara whispered, "He looks like he's got a bowling ball under his belt."

"Evenin' Miss Creek, you ready to try your new home?" He asked in a nasal high-pitched voice.

"I've got one more day, and I plan to use it. The court says I have until tomorrow. I'll go then. Judge Tilson and I talked about this and she agreed to let me have another week—'to get my affairs in order'."

"You need to go now, young lady." Herms walked up to the side of the porch stoop and stood eye-to-eye with Loren, who was seated on a step.

"Court says tomorrow, Mr. Herms. I'll go tomorrow."

Herms reached out and took Loren by the wrist. "There's folks waiting. Decent folks. You might want to learn some respect, young lady, and you might consider trusting others a little."

Loren struggled to release her arm from Herms' grasp.

"How 'bout if we go to your new home? They're waitin' for you right now. I told them I'd fetch you."

"You can just un-tell them, Mr. Herms. I'm staying until tomorrow evening. The court says midnight and I'll stay until midnight if I want to."

"I think not, Miss Creek. We're going now."

A low voice spoke from behind Herms. "Let her go." Herms looked back over his shoulder at Meredith Tilson, standing with a shovel raised over her right shoulder. "You let her go right now or I'll put you on the ground with this spade—I'll do it, I will."

Herms dropped Loren's arm and turned to the tall, stern-faced girl. "Miss, you don't know what you're doin'. You're threatenin' an officer of the court, and you are in a heap o' trouble."

"The only trouble I'm having right now is getting you off this property until you're legally able to enter it—which right now you're not. Get in your car and leave."

"Miss, I don't want to…"

Another voice came from the porch above Herms. "One button; all I have to do is press one button and you will be the one in trouble. Leave." Tara was holding her cell phone in one hand and a stout fence picket in another.

"Mister Herms," Loren said softly, "please come back tomorrow evening this time, and I'll go with you—no problem. I'm sure you'll respect the wishes of someone who has just buried her mother." Loren lowered her eyes and turned away.

Herms saw this easy way out and took it. Removing his gray hat from his thinning, slicked-back hair he said, feigning confidence, "Yes, of course I will, Miss Creek. I see you are busy entertaining friends." He turned and walked away in a rolling shuffle, limping slightly. At the car he turned back to the girls and mouthed a grin. The only part not gray was his tobacco-stained teeth.

"Evenin', ladies."

The girls watched Herms drive slowly down the road to town, leaving a slight trail of blue exhaust.

"What an ugly, ugly man," Meredith said after taking a deep breath.

"Yes, he's a sad creature," Loren said.

"Sad? Bad, I'd say. He just seems to give off evil in his breath. Go wash your hands, Loren. Wash where he was grabbing you—where's Tara?" Meredith turned, looking around. Just then she and Loren heard someone retching around the corner of the house. They moved quickly to Tara who was leaning by her hands on the wood siding. She looked up at them and said, "I'm sorry." She'd been crying. "I've never been so angry and felt so helpless at the same time."

"Helpless? Sis, you put the fear of God in that wicked man. You sent him packin' with that cell phone of yours."

"Think so? Really?"

Loren added, "I wish you could have seen yourself. You looked like some kind of warrior with that fence picket in your hand. I know that I wouldn't mess with you. Thanks, Tara."

Loren and Tara washed up at the spigot coming out of the foundation. They shook the cold water from their hands then wiped their face with them. Loren gave Tara a gentle hug. She turned to Meredith. "You have a plan?"

Meredith gestured a return to the porch stoop. "Yes, we think you could escape from foster care by going across the state line. You could go to school over in North Carolina or Virginia and Mr. Herms would never find you, and you'd be no more than fifty miles away."

"I don't think that would work," Loren said, adding, "Also, where would I live? I'd need to enroll me in school, locate a place to live, and find an adult to vouch for me in a zillion ways."

"How about Mattie, wouldn't she do it?" Meredith asked.

Loren looked down at her work-worn hands. Their condition made her self-consciously glance at Meredith's well-manicured, polished nails. "Yes, she would, but that's a lot to ask."

"Wouldn't hurt to ask. I'll bet she wouldn't mind being your adult cover, or at least finding someone in the community who would do it," Meredith said.

"It just won't work. They're not stupid. They'd come looking for me. All they'd have to do is check with the schools for any new student that answers my description. There aren't that many high schools in the region. They'd find me in a week."

"They wouldn't if you were a boy," Tara said, grinning.

CHAPTER 5

"A boy? Do I look like a boy?"

Loren and Michelle looked at Tara like she had just uttered a profanity.

Tara sensed that her idea was about to be attacked. "No, you don't look like a boy right now, but you're tall, lean and strong. You have a strong face—it's not that you're not pretty, it's just that…"

Loren cut her off with a hand wave saying. "No offense. I've been a tomboy all my life. There are no girls my age around here. Also, I spend a lot of time outdoors working the farm."

"If we cut your hair," Tara continued, "and put you in boy's clothes and some clodhopper shoes, you would almost pass. Then, if you worked on the way you walk and moved your body…"

"It's crazy," Meredith said.

"No, it's not," Tara answered angrily. "It's a good idea, and one that'd keep Mr. Herms from finding her. He'd never think to look for a boy. How tall are you?"

"I'm five feet ten inches. Momma said my—my father was tall. She says I look like him.

The girls fell silent in the fact of this omission from Loren's life.

"Breasts," Meredith said with finality. "You're fourteen, and due to start getting breasts any day."

"She could wear something that would flatten her," Tara said.

"Momma was flat-chested until she started college." Loren placed her hands over her breasts. "I've seen pictures of Grandma when she was in her late teens, and she was flat as a fritter."

"You are athletic," Meredith said, almost to herself, then added quickly and with more energy, "How did you get to be in such good shape? You've got muscles in places where I don't even have places."

"Come with me. I want to show you something in the barn," Loren said, rising from the stoop. The girls followed her around the house and down the path to the barn.

"Mother was a dancer and a gymnast until she met my father. He ran a band that traveled from one gig to another. All that moving about kept her from working out on a regular basis, so finally, she gave up trying." Loren stopped and quickly looked away.

"What is it?" Tara asked.

"I've never told this to anybody before. I think I've wanted to have someone to tell about my Momma and me—but I've never had anybody, and I don't know how to do it. It feels strange—but good too."

Meredith took Loren's hand. "Just tell it like it happened—we'll listen. We want to know." Tara nodded in agreement with her sister.

Loren took a deep breath, and resumed walking. "Well, when Momma moved back here she wanted to get back into dance and gymnastics. She said it made her feel powerful."

They reached the barn and the girls followed Loren into a side door. Loren hit a light switch and the girls found themselves in a spacious modern gymnasium/dance studio. They were standing on a solid maple floor under bright lights. The walls were finished with wood paneling and large mirrors. There was a set of parallel bars, uneven bars, rings, a balance beam and a hanging bar. The room was well equipped for dance and gymnastics. Overhead lights concealed the raw wood siding and structural beams found in barns.

Meredith and Tara stood in the doorway, mouths agape. "Wow," Tara jumped into the room and spun around on the polished floor. Loren turned on a sound system that rested on wall shelves, and music came from all four corners of the room. Then she shed her dress and shoes down to lycra body suit. She moved to an exercise bar fastened to a wall, where she began stretching exercises. Tara and Meredith watched as Loren went from stretching to a floor routine with the poise and confidence of an accomplished athlete. Grace, suppleness, strength, and confidence; it was all there. The sisters exchanged looks of astonished awe as Loren began a series of exercise activities. She went to the parallel bars and then to the uneven bars, finishing off on the balance beam. When finished, she walked with cat-like grace up to her new friends. She was breathing deeply, and sweating from her efforts. She moved with the feline grace of an accomplished athlete. It was as though her body had become a poem.

"What do you think? Could I pass as a boy?" She was breathing deeply and sweat was starting to form on her brow and body. Slender muscles outlined her lean form, and she displayed the shoulders of a swimmer.

"That was awesome," Tara exclaimed. "Could you teach me to do that?"

Meredith, who was standing closest to Loren, looked her directly in the eyes. "You know, it just might work. You've got the physique of a slender boy. If we cut your hair…" She paused, reached out and pulled Loren close, hugged her, and then pushed her away at arm's length. "Tara's right, that was awesome. I don't think I've ever seen anyone our age do *anything* that well."

"Thank you. I owe it all to Momma."

"The two of you must have been close—like you said."

Loren frowned and thought for a moment. Tears started to well. "We were all we had, or needed—or wanted. We were a team, and then Mother started fallin' ill when I was eight. Huntington's Chorea. She had just finished building the workout room when the sickness came on and she couldn't control her body. By the time I was ten she was unable to dance or work out at all. For a time, she did some stretching exercises with me, but even that wore her out, so she put all her energy into teaching me the movements and routines. It was a labor of love—for both of us." Tears filled her eyes, rolled down her cheeks and fell on her chest. "This is hard."

Tara reached out and pulled Meredith and Loren into a loose hug. "Can we be friends? I know that you're mad at Mom…" Loren nodded. Tara continued, "But—but, I—*we* want to help you live the kind of life you want—not in some foster home or as some charity case."

Meredith added, "We don't want you to lose this place, especially now, after you've shown us what it means to you. I know there are ways, there must be. I'll look into it."

"We've already talked with Mom about it," Tara said, "and all she's told us is that the law is 'unreasonably inflexible' in cases like yours. She doesn't like ruling the way she has, but told us that if she tried to do anything else, the protective care people would have another judge take your case—one that might not care as much about you or your situation."

Meredith spoke up. "Let's go back to the house, sit down with a paper and pencil and see if we can draw up a plan. I think we can pull it off—boy." She smiled and tilted her head at Loren's flat chest.

"Okay, but first I want to show you around the barn." Loren slipped back into her dress and shoes, then led the girls through an inside door that opened to the rest of the barn. The barn was built of old fine-grained chestnut—a wood that, given a good roof, can last for centuries. There was a clean, straw odor in the place. "This is—was—Alice's stall. The roomy stall was made from eight inch planks, one inch thick, polished in places where the cow had rubbed. "She's a Jersey and is real sweet. I groom her down almost every day. She loves it and gives me gallons and gallons of great milk and cream. Mr. Phipps has her now, and he's promised to take good care of her until I can."

Loren made a choking sound followed by a quick sob, then she caught herself, took a quick breath and went on. "I tried raising pigs, but I couldn't stand selling them off for meat, and hogs are useless unless you want to sell them off or butcher them. They are smart, cute, and a lot of fun but useless. After I sold them off, I couldn't eat pork for a long time. I kept chickens in the coop next to the barn, but only for eggs, which I bartered with my neighbors for vegetables and meat. I don't mind eating meat, I just don't like gettin' too personal with who's going to be my supper. I can do it, but I just don't like doing it. I've got agreements worked out with neighbors. They're good neighbors—they're not rich in money, but they are in spirit or sense. Mother used to say that they had everything but money. She read me a book by that name and it made good sense. *Everything But Money*. It's about a Jewish family in Brooklyn, but I reckon there's folks like us all over the world."

Loren placed her hand on the fender of an old gray tractor. "And this here's Henry. You can't run a farm without a good tractor. Henry here plows and pulls and lifts and hauls; he's my right-hand man." Loren stroked the tractor's fender like it was a pet horse. "The Oakes family, next door to preacher Burke, agreed to keep Henry running and in good shape in exchange for the use of him. He's to stay here out of the weather when he's not being worked."

Loren pointed at some smaller stalls that had been recently added. "I'd planned to get some goats, now that I'm older and stronger. Goat milk brings good money, and they're intelligent animals—fun to have around—and they don't have to fill people's dinner plates to earn their keep."

"And here's Momma's pride and joy." Loren pulled the canvas cover off a bright red truck. "It's a 1951 Ford pick-up. Momma's dad, my grandpa, bought it new, and kept it clean and running right. That's the original paint; it's never been left out in the weather, and never will be if I can help it. I was allowed to drive it when Momma thought it was absolutely necessary. Sometimes I crank it up and pull it out into the sunshine to just sit and listen to the engine tick away. I puts me in mind of Grandpa. He used to let me drive it some when he went into town. I'd sit in his lap and steer while he did the gas and brakes. That's how I learned to drive. I'll never part with this truck or the tractor. I know how to keep them running right, and I intend to do so. Mr. Oakes has been a big help showing me how to mechanic."

Loren stopped and looked around the barn. "This wood is so beautiful. I've climbed over all the rafters and beams in this barn. I used to look for funny faces and magical creatures in the grain and knots of the wood. My favorite is an elf face on the top of that middle beam—you can't see it from here, you have to be on the beam. He's wearing a pointy hat and showing a big-tooth grin." She stopped and looked around the barn one last time, and then said with finality, "Let's go to the house." Tara and Meredith exchanged glances. They joined hands and fell in behind their guide.

About halfway back to the house, the girls heard a cat meow, and turned to see a large, round-headed tom following them on the path. He was black except for a white diamond on his chest

"Oh, BC, what are you doing here old tom? Don't you know you're a member of the Slagle clan now?" Loren scooped up the grizzled veteran of many fights and held him, purring, to her chest.

"That's some motor he's got," Meredith said.

"Yes, he wants some milk—don't you, baby? Well, this one last time…" Loren turned and hurried up the path to the back porch. She placed a small bowl of milk on the porch stoop for the cat, then stood back and watched as he walked up, sniffed it, and looked up at her before drinking. "He's like me, he don't much care for store-bought. I guess I'll have to call the Slagles and ask them to come get him. He'll probably come back here a time or two before he realizes this is not…" Both of the Tilson daughters were beyond red-eyed.

Seated at the kitchen table the three girls huddled over a pitcher of iced tea and a note pad that Loren brought from her room. Tara acted as the secretary.

Meredith led off. "As I see it, you're going to have to leave tonight."

"I cain't leave tonight."

"Why not?"

"I told Mr. Herms I'd be here tomorrow."

"So what? He's a jerk." Tara said.

"He may be, but he trusted me, and I'll not lie to him. I don't go back on my word or break trust. Not to mention, I'd put Mattie in trouble. Your—the judge trusted her to keep an eye out for me. Besides, I feel sorry for him."

"How can you say that? The man is evil." Tara raised her voice in disbelief.

"I think he's an honest, man in a nasty job, and I'm not going to make him look any more foolish than he already does. I'll go through with the placement, and then run away. That way he can share the blame with the placement family. Besides, if they're anything like the people I've been placed with so far, I won't mind running away."

"That's okay," Meredith said. "It gives us more time to plan. You go ahead and move in with the foster family, and you can leave after we've got things put together. Actually, it works out better that way. We've got to get you some identification—and that isn't going to be easy. I've got a friend—a freshman at King College in Bristol—who's a computer geek. There's nothing he can't do over the Internet. I'm sure he'll help. You've got to get some money, decide where you should go, and…"

"I like Abingdon, Virginia." Loren said. "That's a nice town. Momma and I used to go there to visit the antique stores.

"That is a nice place, but it's small and you'd stand out." Meredith said, and then continued. "I'd say Boone would be better. I'm going to school there this fall at Appalachian State University."

"I thought you were just sixteen." Loren queried.

"I'll be seventeen in two weeks, and I skipped second grade."

Loren thought a moment, frowning. "Boone would work. It's in North Carolina, but just across the state line. Momma used to take me to all kinds of concerts and plays and things there—when she could still get about. We went there once to see the Alvin Ailey Dance Group. They were amazing. I floated in my dreams all that night. That was when I knew that I wanted to be a dancer. Also, there's Appalachian State University with lots of students, and a large high school. I'd be just one more teenager in a crowd. It's a big tourist town, and there are thousands of strangers coming and going all the time—hiking in the summer and skiing in the winter. Boone would be an easy place to get lost in. If I'm in Boone, and you're in Boone, we'll be able to see each other once in a while."

"Better than that. I'm in a summer program that's scheduled to begin in a week. This fall I'm enrolling as a freshman, but Mom and I decided I could get a head start on my course work this summer. Anyway, I'll have an apartment for the summer before I move into the freshman dorms in the fall. During the regular school year, freshmen students have to stay in a dorm room, but anything goes during the summer. Wait a minute; this is starting to come together! You can stay with me until we find a place for you. There's plenty of room in the apartment. It's got a hide-a-bed couch. No problem. This is working out okay."

Loren frowned at this. "So far, everything looks too easy. Nothing works this well."

"No," Meredith answered. "It's not going to be easy. But if we work together on this we can make it happen. There are so many details to work out. Making you into a boy, getting some funds for you, finding a place for you to live. Getting you an ID. Maybe you can get a car. I wonder how old you have to be in North Carolina to buy a car—and to get a driver's license."

"Transcripts," Tara said.

"What?"

"We've got to get school transcripts from a school or she—he," Tara smiled, "won't be able to get into school. That's going to be tough."

"We'll work on it," Meredith said. "I think I know how we can make this work."

"Okay, but in the meantime, I've got to leave here and go to another foster home." Loren said, scanning the familiar setting of the kitchen as though trying to commit it to memory.

CHAPTER 6

Forge and Ellie Rose had moved into town so they could be near the school where Ellie taught sixth grade. Forge managed the Mountain Feed and Seed until it shut down in the early nineties. Ellie retired two years after the Feed and Seed store shut down. Forge took up carpentry and 'hit a lick' now and then. Childless, they lived frugally, saved their money, and were more than pleased to take in a "needy orphan girl with a solid Christian upbringing," as Mr. Herms had presented his youthful case.

Loren, with her one suitcase, was brought to the Rose home, introduced, once again told the rules according to foster care, and left to adjust to a new life.

Herms took Loren aside as he was leaving and spoke softly through yellow teeth, "I told these folks that you were from a fine Christian home, don't disappoint." As he shook Loren's hand she became aware of kindly eyes and a look of genuine concern. He turned to his car and was gone with a wave from the window.

Mrs. Rose was beside herself with the joy of finally having a child in the home. Mr. Rose was amused with his wife, and took on a grandfatherly demeanor, which pleased Ellie all the more. Loren inquired as to chores.

"Child," Mr. Rose explained, "there are no chores to be taken on here. Our water is piped-in city, we cook with electricity, and heat with oil. We own neither stock nor chicken, and our food comes from the grocer."

Loren took this in, looked long at Mr. Rose, and then asked, "What do you do with your time?"

"Why, we do the Lord's work. We read the Book, we visit with those in need, and attend church regular. The missus and I take evening walks when the weather's fair. We walk along the river, and bring food to the ducks at the dam. Folks visit, and we visit them. Ours is a quiet way. I know you'll like it here, once you've grown to know it."

"Mr. Rose, I've been running a working farm since I was nine. I tended and milked our cow, fed the chickens, gathered eggs, grew and tended a big garden, and did most of the cookin' and puttin' up. While I was doing that, I went to school and looked after my ailing mother. If something broke, I fixed it. If there was a need, I took care of it. I paid the bills, and managed the house because my mother could hardly rise from her bed since I was twelve. These last three months she's been in the hospital, waitin' to die. Last week the Lord brought her home, and I rejoiced to see her suffering end. So please don't tell me there's no chores to be done—I don't know how to do that."

The Roses looked on in thought. Mrs. Rose sat upright in a worn rocker with her Bible in her lap. She stroked the cover of her book as though it was a pet cat. Loren knew it to be a gesture of love and adoration. Her rocking grew slower and slower as she prepared to speak. Finally, she stopped rocking altogether.

"Loren, child. You have been visited with the trials of Job, and have stood the test and prevailed. Your life has been marked with hardship and deprivation. That is ended, and you are safe and secure with us. Your days will no longer be days of toil and sweat, but can be filled with the sweet joys of young womanhood."

"My life was not hard. It was easy—because I was hard. My mother taught me how to work, and to work at work. She taught me that to live without discipline is to die without honor, and that if I wanted to be young when I was old, I would have to be old when I was young. I believe my mother was truthful. I don't know boy nor girl who can do what I can do—I'm not bragging, I'm just saying what is so. Mother also taught me that the weak are takers—only the strong can give. She said to be able to give is a privilege and an honor."

Mrs. Rose sat still and quiet with her lips slightly parted as Mr. Rose rocked and smoked his pipe.

"I can't come here and live off you and not do something in return." Loren said tersely. "I need chores."

Three days later, at 9:30 in the evening, a red Ford Focus stopped at a darkened street corner near the Rose house. In less than three minutes, Loren and her single suitcase were on the way out of town. In thirty minutes the three girls breathed sighs of relief as they crossed the state line into North Carolina.

CHAPTER 7

"I had a key made for you." Meredith handed a key ring to Loren and flicked on the lights to a modest apartment.

"The little key on the ring is to my bicycle lock. The bike is chained to the rack downstairs behind the apartments; it's great for getting around town, use it as much as you want." Meredith moved around the apartment turning on lights, adjusting the thermostat, and opening closet doors. "You can use the sofa sleeper. Let me show you how to open it, and where the linens are."

After showing Loren around the apartment, Meredith left her on her own, saying, "Stay as long as you need; Tara and I will come by on Saturday afternoon. That'll give you a few days to find your way around town and learn where everything is. Mother won't be with me because she's already helped me pick out the apartment and put most of my stuff here. If she changes her mind I'll call and let you know. I'll call you anyway—the phone's already connected, and you've got our cell phone numbers."

"Meredith, if your mother finds out what you're doing she'll be furious. Are you sure you want to do this?"

The sisters looked at each other. Tara said, "We're sure."

"How can you two just come and go as you please?"

"Don't worry Loren. We have an agreement with Mom. We follow her rules and stay away from drugs and booze, and the wrong crowd, and she trusts us to do the right thing. We learned pretty quickly that if we tried to get away with something the whole darn Elizabethton police force would be on our case. Mom gives us a hard time about helping out around the house and keeping our rooms neat, but that's about the only grief we have. We laugh and joke a lot, but Mom's not one to cross. She can go from *Mom* to *Judge* in just under one second." Meredith looked at her watch. "We gotta go, Sis—curfew. You look funny, Loren. Did I answer your question?"

"Yes. No. I—I was just thinking. You and your mom seemed to have worked things out."

"It's a trade-off. Responsibility gets us freedom. Some people never learn it," Meredith said as Tara nodded in agreement.

As the girls started to leave, Tara said, "I think we have a relationship with our Mom that's a lot like you had with your Mom."

"Wait." Loren walked up to Meredith and put her arms around her. "How can I ever thank or re-pay you for all you are doing for me? The risk you two are taking for me—a near stranger—is scary to think of."

Meredith thought a moment. "Thank us by making it work." She turned and left with Tara in tow.

The following afternoon, Loren tried out the new cell phone she'd purchased earlier in the day. "Mattie. It's me. I did it. I've left Piney Flat." Mattie was silent. "I can't tell you much right now but I will call later, and we'll have a long talk after I've settled in. In the meantime, I've got a cell phone and can give you the number."

"Are you okay, chil'?" Mattie asked softly.

"Yes, I'm fine."

"Where are you?"

"I don't want to tell you just yet because they'll probably be asking if you know my whereabouts, and I don't want you to have to lie for me. If you don't know where I am, you won't have to lie."

"Do you have your money? I deposited it in your Bank of America checking account two days ago. There's $30,000 in checking and the rest in savings, but the savings account can't be drawn on for a year. Then you're allowed another $30,000."

"That works out good. There's a Bank of America nearby. It's a good thing we did the paperwork before."

"It was your mother's idea, honey. I don't know how, but she seemed to know you would strike out on your own. Maybe she realized how much like her you are. She told me to give you all the money I could after she passed, no questions asked. It seems she was right. I know that $30,000 must seem like a lot of money to you, and it will go a long way, but it won't keep you going more than a couple of years, no matter how tight you go with it."

"I know, but next year I can draw another thirty, can't I?"

"Yes. It's in the will that way, and your mother gave me those instructions, too. But, child, it'll take some doin' if the law's watchin'. Your mother's lawyer is willing to work with me if we be discreet. He don't agree with that judge, but he can't break law."

"Okay. Be careful what you tell the foster care people. The less they know about my insurance money, the better. Don't let them see the will unless they make you."

"I won't. They'll have to law me to see it."

"Mattie, don't go getting in trouble on my account."

"Honey, I'm seventy years old, raised my children, buried my husband, and am just waitin' for my maker's call. Livin' here in my daughter's husband's house—and them childless—is plumb empty. Looking out for you gives me sump'n to live for."

"Thank you. I feel you're all I've got."

"Don't feel that way. There's folks here in Piney Flat who care about you and will do whatever it takes. They won't steal for you, but they won't have any trouble misleading the law—and they have. Remember that, and remember to call me if there's anything you need, or if you just need a body to talk to—someone who cares about you."

"I will. I've got to go now. I'll call you in a couple of days. Is this time of day a good time to call?"

"Yes, three's a good time, everybody's gone off to work."

"Good. Before I hang up, tell me about my house. Is everything okay there?"

"Yes. Don't worry about it. I've got folks helping me look after it. The animals is took care of. The hens is placed with a good lady. But that rooster of your'n - I tell you—that critter wants a pot."

Loren laughed out loud and thought how good it felt to do so. "Now Mattie, don't you go cooking Atilla."

"Cook. Lawd, I can't even catch him.

"Well, leave him be. When I find a good roost, I'll find him one too. In the meantime, I hope the foxes don't get him."

"Foxes ain't dumb, honey. That bird is safe."

"Okay. Thanks for everything, Mattie. I love you."

There was a long pause. "I love you, Child." Mattie's voice went up in pitch and was filled with emotion. "Bye." She hung up quickly.

Loren stood looking blankly at the phone before she hit the "end" button.

By day's end Loren had walked the length of King Street, the main downtown street of Boone, in both directions on both sides of the street. She toured the campus of Appalachian State University, and was impressed with the new dining hall and library. She located the courthouse, the Boone Chamber of Commerce, the high school, and the shopping mall. She collected county and city maps, a copy of the Appalcart bus schedule, and local newspapers—*The Mountain Times*, *High Country Press*, and the *Watauga Democrat*—named after the county of Watauga. Newspaper ads and Chamber of Commerce brochures detailed the wonders of Appalachian living from the perspective of local realtors and merchants. The university had a terrific cafeteria, The Rivers Street Café, where a student could find food to suit almost any palette. Loren spent a good part of the afternoon browsing the shops on King Street. Later that week she would discover that Boone Drugs on King Street was the best place in town to get a home-cooked country breakfast. That evening she studied rental ads, and made up a list of tasks.

Become a boy
Buy clothes and shoes
Find a place to live
Get false ID
Get false transcript of grades
Get a false birth certificate
Find a job
Join a gym
Rent a house with a barn in the country

The next day she biked around town, shopping thrift stores for boys' clothing. By day's end she had washed and dried two laundry loads of cast-offs, and purchased a used book about human behavior and body language. Before going to bed she took scissors to her hair, and sheared it to what could pass for a shaggy boy's cut.

She put on a pair of boxer undershorts, then pulled on a pair of faded jeans, still warm from the dryer. Shirtless and barefoot, she stood before the full-length mirror in Meredith's bedroom. Light from a table lamp slanted across her body, shadowing and highlighting her lithe form. She moved deliberately and flexed her torso and arms, watching the play of her muscles with pleasure. *I can pass.*

The following morning a young man in jeans and red t-shirt walked out of Meredith Tilson's apartment and strode to the barbershop, where he had his shaggy hair shorn to a crew cut while listening to the barber exchange *sexploits* with a couple of elderly male clients. After biking around Boone that morning, Loren found that the Earth Fare grocery on King Street had a terrific organic restaurant.

Loren Creek was poised to enter the murk of maleness.

CHAPTER 8

"OhMyGod!"

"OhMyGod!" Tara repeated as she approached the handsome boy on the walk-way of her sister's second floor apartment. Neither she nor Meredith recognized the boy standing on the second floor walkway. Tara whispered while they were heading to the stairwell that led up to second floor. "He's cute. I wonder if he lives on your floor."

"I don't know, but I'm sure going to find out." Meredith answered.

"Don't forget who saw him first. I got dibs."

"He's too old for you."

As they approached the boy, he broke into a wide grin, and they realized that neither of them was going to date him.

Meredith and Tara went into squeals and giggles over their misperception. Loren, standing with a wide hands-on-hips stance, laughed a husky boy-laugh, bringing more squeals and giggles from the girls. Meredith shooed them inside be-fore they attracted too much attention.

"OhMyGod!" Tara exclaimed. "You look…"

"Like a boy?" Loren asked.

"Yes. Definitely, yes."

"Turn around, let me look at you," Meredith demanded. "Let me see you walk."

Loren strode across the room, using just a little too much swagger and shoulder movement. Then she stopped, turned, and scratched her crotch—an act that sent the girls into peals of laughter.

Inside the apartment the threesome settled on the couch over Cokes as Loren related the events of the past week—laughing over the conversation in the barber shop, picking out boy's clothing, learning to move like a young male, doing away with make-up that she rarely used anyway and adjusting to a crew-cut. The girls listened with such intensity that Loren would have been self-conscious but for the gales of laughter. She put a veggie pizza in the oven, and by the time it was ready, the merriment had crested and tapered off to friendly chatter. As the girls settled into comfortable positions on the living room carpet, Meredith asked, "Any inter-species activity?" Loren turned crimson, causing the intensity in the room to rise again.

"Don't tell me you've got a girlfriend," Meredith said.

"Believe me, it'd be easy."

"I'm jealous," Tara burst out, and followed with, "Tell us—tell it all."

"Don't worry, Tara, no one can take your place—I'll always be yours." It was Tara's turn to elicit laughter as her face glowed bright red.

"Well, I've been spendin' a lot of time on the ASU campus watchin' the students. I wear sunglasses, which lets me stare without bein' noticed."

Thoughts of pizza vanished as Meredith and Tara sat like statues, Tara with her legs crossed and Meredith with knees drawn up under her chin.

"I get hit on most every day; it's purely funny. I'd heard that boys were obvious, but they couldn't be more obvious than those girls. I been invited up to *party* at one girl's apartment, and tonight I'm expected at someone's house. It's like this every day."

"The handsome prince," Meredith joked. "With that build of yours, and your angular face you can pass for eighteen."

"There are kids on campus who look younger than me."

"How does it feel?" Tara asked.

"It'd be funny if it didn't make me feel plumb weird. In some ways this is a easy thing to do, in others it's hard. At night when I'm alone in my room and I start thinking about it, I feel that I cain't do it. I've cried myself to sleep more than once. And I really miss my Momma." Loren said as her eyes filled with tears. "I'm all alone, I'm fourteen, and I'm homeless. I've always had Momma, even when she was sick, but now I don't have a soul. I'm homesick for Piney Flat. I miss my farm and my animals. I miss Alice a lot—she has the most beautiful eyes. This just ain't right."

Tara pushed aside the platter of pizza and slid next to Loren, where she was joined by Meredith, who wiped Loren's wet face and kissed her on the cheek. "You're not alone, you'll never be alone. You've got me, and you've got Tara. I feel like you're one of the sisters—brother." This brought smiles and hugs.

"Me, too," Tara added.

"Thanks, I'm sorry to be such a wimp, but sometimes…"

"I know, I know. Listen, Tara and I both have cell phones. Call us whenever you want, call us every day, and remember, I'll be moving in soon, so you won't be all alone."

"I've thought about renting my own apartment," Loren said.

Meredith frowned. "Why would you want to do that?"

Two reasons. I don't want to get you in trouble with your mother, and I'm a right private person."

"I understand. We've both been raised to be independent. I can never recall not having my own room, although sometimes I've had to share it with this brat of a kid sister."

"Oh!" Tara exclaimed in mock hurt. "Let me tell you sometime what it's like growing up with a bossy, boring…"

Loren laughed. "There's another reason, too. What would happen if you got a boyfriend and you two wanted to be alone?"

"Isn't that the kind of bridge we cross when we get to it?" Meredith asked. Let's keep things like they are. It's complicated enough without you trying to rent an apartment with no ID. It'll be like having a brother around. I've always wished for a brother—but look at what I got instead."

Tara crossed her arms over her chest in a feigned huff. "You just don't know how lucky you are, Sis."

Loren smiled at the bantering between the girls she had come to like. "I still have to be out of here by the end of the summer, because the apartment is already rented, and the complex owners will be here. And, the pizza's getting cold."

They slid the pizza platter back into their reach as they talked about what Tara labeled as 'The Plan.'

As they were polishing off the pizza, Meredith noted that Loren had eaten only one slice.

"Yes, I have to be *very* careful about what I eat if I want to keep my manly figure. It's a true discipline. I also work out at the college gym every day, and I run and bike. I can't lose my muscle tone or it would take weeks to get it back. This lean, hard body that turned you two on when you pulled in the parking lot comes at the price of constant effort. I fix my own meals. About the only things I eat in restaurants are salads, fresh veggies, and lean meat or fish. A lot of the restaurants around here serve what Mother called *brown food*. There are some real good ones, but the students tend to for those that serve mostly brown food."

"What's *brown food?*" Tara asked.

"Look at a menu next time you're in a fast-food restaurant. Have you noticed they use colorful pictures of the dishes they serve? What's the main color? A nice golden brown because almost everything is fried, or breaded then charred or fried. It's all brown in color, and it's all bad for you."

"Pizza?"

"Isn't too bad if you get the right kind and don't have it too often or eat too much of it. Momma was an athlete who believed in a natural diet. She taught me how to stay in shape, and how to eat right. She was fierce on staying healthy through good diet and exercise. I've been doing gymnastics, dance, and competitive swimming ever since I can remember."

"I sure would like to do gymnastics like you." Tara said.

"You could do it, but it would take a lot of work."

Meredith took the last piece of pizza. "Yes, it would, Tara, and right now we have to put our energies into keeping our 'brother's' identity a secret. Incidentally, Loren, I'm almost positive that I'll have a really good set of ID for you in the next few days."

"That soon?"

"Yeah, like I said, my friend—his name is Craig—at King College is a whiz on the computer. Right now it looks like you're going to be Lorne Land—Loren."

Loren's eyes widened. "Lorne? Isn't that way too much like Loren?"

"Craig says it's a great way to hide an identity—right out in the open. He did a lot of searching before he landed that name. It's the real name of a real person who moved away from the school system in Blacksburg, Virginia—which is a good thing if the Watauga County schools decide to check on your background.

"I like the name fine. It's just that Mr. Herms is sure to come looking for me, and I'm worried it'll catch his notice. Mr. Herms is good at what he does." Loren added as an afterthought, "Tell Craig thanks for me, and I'm proud to use his work."

Aldrich Herms was at his desk shortly after sunrise and nearly two hours before everyone else in the office. As always, he had a plan—a plan that he had drawn up on paper. He had learned from a physics teacher that if a problem can be stated it can be solved. He put his daily and weekly activities on paper in order to assure that he had a clear statement of the problems that pertained to his job. The result was a placement record of which he was proud. Herms generally made a listing of pertinent items from which he formulated problem statements, which he used to drive his plan of action. This list he titled "The Loren List" He read:

The Loren List

Smart but inexperienced outside of her home.
Very Independent, private.
A mountain girl who won't stray far from home.
No transportation—must remain close to where she lives.
Values schooling and will try to get into a school.
No ID.
She'll probably get a cell phone to call those she knows—Mattie Hooks.
May try to contact those people who have her animals.
Probably doesn't have much cash money (??)
May try to visit her home at night.
Locate any relatives in the area who might help her hide.
What are her finances? Banking?
Locals will try to help her. Who? How?

His list was long and growing longer with many items crossed out. This day he was going to look at her finances. *Show me the money Loren Creek. Show me the money.* He went to "Banks" in the yellow pages

CHAPTER 9

Loren didn't know how to explain what she was looking for in the way of a house, but she knew she would know it when she saw it. *The Mountain Times* was a good source for realty of all sorts, rental and sales. She quickly learned that a minor couldn't enter into contract; she could buy a house, but she couldn't—solely under her name—rent or sell one that she owned. She could buy a car, but not finance or sell it—nor could she legally drive it.

By mid-June Loren was getting anxious in her search for a suitable farm home she could rent. Doubt was weighing heavily. *This is crazy. I can't buy a house, and I don't even know how I'm going to work it out with the rent. What do I think I am doing? I'm a fourteen year old girl who doesn't know how to do what I need to get done.*

She responded to want ads but consistently came up short; she either didn't like the house, the location, or the people with whom she had to deal. She was everyday on the road, cycling about the county in search of a place where she could settle—a place below the radar..

Loren had replaced Meredith's bicycle tires twice, and gone through five tubes.

She told the girls over a Sunday pizza, "I've been chased by nearly every dog within five miles of Boone—three or four times by some."

"I can drive you around some on Sundays," Meredith pointed out.

"Thanks, but on Sunday folks are in church in the morning and having a long lunch in midday. That doesn't leave much time."

Tara picked up a second piece of pizza. "I wish we could help. I know this is starting to get tiresome."

"Yes, it's tiresome and it's tryin' too. Most folks are courteous and helpful, but I've actually been run off of people's property four or five times—once by an old woman wavin' a shotgun at me. I'm not used to people treatin' that way. All that's bad enough—but I'm running out of time too. Meredith's lease on this apartment will soon be up, and I got no place to go. This is really hangin over me."

Meredith stood up and walked to the window of her apartment, "I don't think that's such a problem. With the fake ID you've got you should be able to rent an apartment somewhere."

"You're probably right there, but then there's the problem of gettin' into school. Just for starters, they're going to require a physical."

"Oh hell, that's right." Meredith said in resignation. "We're screwed. There's no way you can fool a doctor." She returned to the coffee table the girls were seated around and plopped down next to Tara. Loren laid back on the floor and stared up at the ceiling. Minutes added up as the girls silently turned over the problem in their heads.

All of a sudden Tara said. "I've got it! We don't have to fool the doctor. Here's what you can do, Loren. Get a medical form from the school. Make a copy of the blank form, just in case you need a spare. Put the form on a clipboard and carry that to the doctor's office. Now—here's where it gets good—clip your pen to the clipboard so the doctor will use that pen. When he's finished examining *Miss Loren Land* you take the form with you and change it to read Lorne Land and change where he marked sex as F to sex as M. You can do this because the pen attached to the clipboard is an erasable ink ball point."

Meredith broke a long period of silence that followed with, "Sis, when did you decide to embark on your life of crime?" After the laughter subsided, she added. "That's a great idea, but it will take some courage. Think you can pull it off Loren?"

"Meredith, what have I got to lose by trying?"

One hot afternoon a week later, Loren was pedaling Meredith's bike down an unfamiliar back road west of Boone when she came to a small white house set back in a hollow. She pedaled up to the house, got off her bike and walked the high grass around the house, and then she took the steps up to the front porch. *This is the seventh house this week.* A glance in the window showed the place to be empty. The front door was unlocked, so she entered and inspected the compact tidy building. There was a set of steps leading into what appeared from the doorway to be a large attic, but she didn't go up.

Less than fifty yards down the road stood a neat, well-kept brick house. Loren pedaled to it, climbed the porch steps and started to knock on the door, when she felt a wetness on her left hand and, looking down, she saw a large, white bulldog mix. She patted the massive head and was pleased when the fierce-looking animal responded with wags of its stub of a tail.

"Hello there, big feller—you the owner of this property?" Loren sat on the porch floor at the top of the steps and let the animal put his head on her lap. She stroked his back, and the dog melted into a limp pile against her. The dog's name and rabies tags were secured to a stout collar. "Let's see what your name is… Sugar. Perfect; you're the color of sugar; though, they could have just as well named you Snow." The dog responded to "Sugar" with a wag of his stub tail, and a *phht*, then he closed his eyes to Loren's gentle strokes. Loren leaned against a wooden pillar and simply enjoyed the experience of a front porch, a friendly animal, and the feel of a home. She closed her eyes and took in the countryside sounds and smells—crickets and honeysuckle. She was just starting to feel sorry for herself when a voice came from behind her.

"Can I help you, Miss?" Loren turned to look over her shoulder as an elderly man opened the screen and stepped out onto the porch. She moved Sugar's head, and rose to meet the man. The dog sighed big and closed its eyes again.

"Yes sir, I—Sir, I'm a boy, not a girl."

"I see." The man paused and looked at Loren with a pair of pale eyes that seemed to crinkle. "My mistake. All you young people look so much alike nowadays; it's hard for us sorry-sighted mossbacks to tell the difference. Didn't mean to offend."

"No offence taken, sir."

"Can I help you?

"You can if you can tell me who owns that house yonder." Loren said, pointing.

"I own that house. It was built by my daddy, and I lived there man and boy until I married."

"Sir, I'd like to rent it—if you'd consider so."

"Never rented it before. Never wanted to."

"I'm looking for a place to live, and that looks just right. I'm looking for a place in the country where I can keep chickens and a cow. Is that barn out back sound?"

"I reckon it is. Been kept under a good roof goin' on seventy year. Where's your family?" Fields Gragg looked down the road toward town. "Seems your pa or ma'd be the one doing the rentin."

"Got no ma or pa. I'm looking for me and my grandma. She'll back my choice."

"Never rented it out. Don't much care to."

Loren stuck out her hand. "Sir, my name's Lorne Land."

"Fields Gragg." He took her firm grip. Fields Gragg was lean and weathered. He stood straight as a stick at a good six feet. Loren reflected: *Here's a man who's worked hard all his life.* His cover-alls were clean, faded, and smelled of baking soda.

"Mister Gragg, I'd be pleased if you'd let me rent that house. It's almost exactly what I've been looking for—nigh on a month now, and I'm plumb tuckered from lookin'. You won't be disappointed."

"Don't need the rent. 'Sides, you're not old enough to contract, I reckon."

"I'd strike the deal, my grandma will do the contract. She'll stand with me."

"You seem mighty sure."

Loren took a deep breath and stepped back. Sugar rose and stretched mightily, then put his head into her hand, hanging by her side. She stroked the head.

"Fine dog you got here, Mr. Gragg."

"Thank you. Had him as a pup. His mom, and her mom too. They's a good line."

"What breed is he?"

"Just a bull mix. Comes from a town in Florida called Steinhatchee; hit's spelled like a beer stein, but spoke like *Steenhatchee.* I was stationed near there during the war. I visited in the eighties, and came back with a couple pups. The breed is common there. I guess it could be called a Steinhatchee Bull."

"He a good watch dog?"

"He is. Can't tell it from the way he's taken to you. Reckon if'n you'd come burglin', he'd point you to the silver."

"See, Mr. Gragg, he's a fine judge of character."

"He *is* a fine judge of some things. "

"Now, Mr. Gragg, that house of yours—the home you were raised in, and no doubt care a lot for—needs a hand. If it doesn't get tended soon, it's going to start coming down. It needs paint, in and out. There's some wood rot starting on the

40

back stoop, and weeds are taking the yard. I could tend to all those things. I don't know about the roof..."

"Roof's new—a body can see that."

"It may be new galvanize, but it's coming loose on the wind side. A good blow and it'll come away."

"You have a sharp eye, and a quick tongue, Miss."

"Mr. Gragg, I told..." Loren was shushed by the man's raised hand.

"If you're a boy, then I'm a trout."

Loren chewed on her upper lip as she and the old gentle man stood eye to eye. Then she asked, "How'd you know?"

"That sweet dog you're pettin'—If you was boy, he'd have a piece of you in his mouth right now. Sugar takes to women and girls, but he won't abide men and boys. Don't know why—it's just his way. Never have to lock my door though—not many female thieves in these parts."

Loren knew she was blushing in her lie.

"Now, why don't you and me take up these rockers," he pointed, "while you tell me what you're up to—young lady."

"Seems I've got no choice."

"You do. You can get on that bicycle of yours and take on down the road."

"No. I can't do that. Not after you've caught me in a lie. I can't go off without explaining myself."

"That's fair."

Loren explained her plight—in its entirety—as the man listened, never once interrupting, but he never once took his eyes off her. When Loren was finished, he rocked and thought for what seemed a long time. Finally, she rose as to leave.

"Would you like a glass of water?" he asked.

"That would be fine, sir."

Mr. Gragg went in the house and returned shortly with two tall glasses. "Take a seat."

The water felt fresh and cool after her lengthy explanation. "This is good water. You have a well?"

"Springbox. Comes from the slope above the house. It's shared by both houses."

"It's fine," Loren said.

"Runs bold all year, clean and cool. Thought you might want to know. It's always a good thing to feel right about your water."

Loren cupped some water in her hand for Sugar, who lapped it noisily. She leaned back in the wooden rocker and said, "Mr. Gragg, you are a case."

"I've been called that—and worse."

"How come you to change your mind?"

"Never had my mind made, no change needed."

"You said..."

"I said I never rented, and I didn't need the rent. Both true. Didn't say I *wouldn't* rent."

"That doesn't answer what I asked."

"Needn't be so quick; it's not becoming," Gragg said.

"Sorry."

"I trust Sugar's judgment. He hates men, and will tolerate women—seems he's head over heels for you; a good dog deserves respect."

"I've been taken in by a *dog?*"

"There's more. In my younger day I was a little wooly. I been known to run 'shine now and then. Out'n this *occupation*, you might say, grew a mutual disregard between me and the law. I put them out of mind when it suited, and they put me behind bars when it suited. Well, I learned a lesson from all that truck—that a man's not worth a damn unless he's worth damning. Miss, it's been years since I've been damned at, and I miss it more than you could know. I'll not pass this one last chance to thumb my nose at, or—as you young people today might say—*moon*—the damned, 'scuse me, gov'ment. Young lady, if you'll have me, you've got a partner."

Loren sat muted by the out-pouring from what she felt was a normally taciturn and private man.

"You got an answer?" he asked.

"*Now* who's quick?"

"I need be. I'm so old, I don't buy green bananas—minutes count."

"Mr. Gragg—I can't begin to—you don't know." Loren was near tears. "Yes. Yes, I'll accept your help; yes, I want to rent your house; and yes, I want us to be friends."

"Grand! We've got a lot of work ahead. If you want to do what you say, there's a lot of misleadin' and prevaricatin' to be done. Now, I pure hate a liar, but prevaricatin' with the law and outlanders must be God's solace for a body's' bein' money poor."

"We have a deal then, Mr. Gragg?"

"*Lorne*, from now on, just think of me as *Grandpa Gragg*."

CHAPTER 10

Three days after their agreement, the first thing Loren looked to was the yard. She borrowed Field's mowing scythe, a sharpening stone, and took down the brush in the front yard. With Sugar in tow, Fields came to watch from the porch of the rental property. He finally asked to take a turn at the scythe. Loren watched in growing amazement as the shoe-leather-tough man made short work of one entire side yard, hardly breaking a sweat.

"Mr. Gragg,"—*Grandpa* didn't sit quite right yet—"you're wicked with that brush blade."

"Thank you, Loren. It's all in keeping a keen edge, pacin' yourself, and working the slope of the land." He paused, and came up with a sly grin. "Course, knowin' *how* helps some. You're a sight better hand at it than I was at your age—which, by the way, you never…"

"I'll be fifteen come November 28," Loren said, holding the scythe handle next to her body as she commenced to stroke the blade expertly with Gragg's well-worn stone.

"Sayin' it that way makes fourteen sound older?" he said, watching the stone pass over the blade.

"Does to me."

"Well then, Near-fifteen, what do you plan to do for furniture?"

"Thought I'd go to the thrift stores in Boone, and see what I could find."

"You goin to fill my home with broke down, college student cast-offs?"

"That's not my plan, I know how…" Loren said, turning red just as Mr. Gragg shut her with a wave of his hand.

"Let's go look in the attic, we might find some things up there you can use. Can't have you haulin in K-Mart Danish Modern. It's not fit for such a house."

"Mr. Gragg…" Loren was cut off as Fields turned and headed to the house. She followed him up the porch, and carefully hung the scythe from a nail there. By the time she got to the bottom of the stairs, an angered Loren could feel the blood pounding her temple. Then she noticed that the stairway and the attic were lit up.

"I had the electric turned on—in my name, of course. Seems that minors can't contract." The lilt to his soft voice let Loren guess that he was smiling when he said it.

"Thank you. I'll pay the bill to you, then," Loren said, climbing the steep steps. "How much was the deposit?" Loren stopped as her head cleared the top of the attic stairwell. She looked around. The attic was filled with carefully packed and covered furniture pieces, that showed themselves to be well made and carefully tended as the coverings came off.

"Mr. Gragg, you've got a fortune in antiques here."

"I suppose. But the money's not what matters. Some of these were brought over by my great-grandparents. But how come you know about such, bein' near-fifteen and all?"

"Momma had a stall at an antique store in Johnson City. I used to go to auctions with her, and help arrange her space at the shop. Some of these have worth beyond money." Loren paused and ran her hand over a table top. "Your children should have care of these. They shouldn't be stuffed away in an attic like this."

"War took our son, a drunken college driver took our daughter, and a broke heart took my wife. These ain't *stuffed away*. They been carefully wrapped and stored. I come up here once a week to see to them and to renew memories."

"Oh, I'm sorry. I didn't know." Loren softened her voice, and could feel her eyes misting.

"Now don't go getting all soft and teary on me again. If you're goin to be a man, be a man. Easy tears ain't becomin' on a male."

"I won't use this furniture, Mr. Gragg. It's too valuable, it means too much to you."

"I know its worth, and I'm beginning to find yours, *young man*. You can use it if I say you can—and I so say. Now, wipe you eyes; they need be clear to work these pieces down the steps."

Loren was amazed at the slender man's strength as they carefully maneuvered the furniture down the narrow stairwell and about the house. A bottle of expensive lemon furniture oil was produced along with several clean cotton rags. Fields Gragg spoke of the history of the furniture as he and Loren polished the handsome chestnut, cherry, and walnut wood to a fine luster.

One evening that week, Fields came over with a couple of kerosene lanterns and a handful of long tapers. "I just wanted you to see this furniture the way my ancestors saw it, and like I knew it as a boy." They drank coffee and caressed the warm smooth surface of the wood pieces. Loren fell in love with her new home and the leather whip of a mountain man with eyes that crackled and hands that said "I can do it." as they moved with sureness over the objects of his childhood.

By mid-July, Loren had a furnished house, a cleared and clean yard, flowers, and the start of a late vegetable garden—with Field Gragg's help. Greens, lettuce, radish, carrots, even summer squash—some of the fruiting plants came from overgrown potted plants that had failed to sell at Wal-Mart and Lowe's. There were even some cherry tomatoes. The man and the girl made a good team. They worked with a minimum of talk or instruction, and no disagreement because they listened carefully to each other and made well-thought observations.

Fields Gragg saw to the enrollment of his grandson from "up north of here." Meredith provided a transcript with a Blacksburg High School letterhead and medical shot records from a small clinic in Blacksburg. Her friend at King College knew what was needed to satisfy the perfunctory glance of school administrators going through hundreds of freshmen documents. The paperwork in the Watauga County Board of Education showed that Lorne Land from Blacksburg, Virginia was an *A* and *B* student, with no black marks on his school record, and excellent attendance.

Aldrich Herms was busy—he was working on a case that he now took personally. Grainy black and white photocopies of Miss Loren Creek were sent to nearby towns in Tennessee, Kentucky, Virginia, and North Carolina. They were copied, circulated, pinned on corkboards, and would have been forgotten had it not been for rigorous attention to detail paid to his job by the good state employee.

Herms was a frequent visitor to law enforcement agencies, schools, country stores, and government agencies in his tireless quest to find missing children. Unmarried, he lived with his two spinster sisters, Sally and Bertha, and was the doted-on head of the house. He had the best placement success record of any rural county in the state of Tennessee. Aldrich Herms was a man proud of his work, and he took the deliberate flight of Loren Creek as a black mark on his name. He had gone lengths to find a suitable, decent home for Loren Creek, and then to have her run away after four days. It wasn't just a job. It was personal.

Herms visited most every home in Piney Flat at least once. The people he met were quiet, not inhospitable, and some seemed willing to help, assuring him that the minute they "got wind of Loren's whereabouts they would give him a call." It wasn't until after the fourth Piney Flat resident had used that same phrase that he began to suspect more than was being told. So he tried all the harder. He realized he was up against a community—"And they mountain people," he told his sisters one evening over creamed corn, fried squash, and pork chops. His sister Bertha shook her head in sympathy as she passed him a plate of cat head biscuits. Aldrich Herms took to going in an hour early every morning so he could work up his plan of investigation. He was sure Loren wouldn't leave the mountains, and if the community thought that much of the girl, he felt confident that she would be within an hour or two drive. He met with Judge Edythe Tilson.

"I put out flyers in country stores, public buildings, and school bulletin boards in near locations. I got em in Tennessee, Virginia, North Carolina, and even a close town or two in Kentucky."

Tilson listened over her desk. "You know your jurisdiction ends at state lines."

"I met with officers in the counties of border states and they said they'd help. They know how to get me."

"You've put a lot into this, Mr. Herms."

"I'll find that girl and bring her back. This ain't no ordinary case."

Tilson, talked about the case—and Herms' efforts—with her daughters, who were interested listeners.

A week before school started, Fields Gragg and Sugar dropped by one evening to visit Loren, who was sitting on the porch, shucking sweet corn she had traded for eggs.

As the spare, handsome man climbed the steps, Loren asked, "You like creamed corn?"

"I do."

"Your hens are laying near as well as mine did in Piney Flat. I'm pleased you let me take up their care—it feels like I'm earnin' toward keep."

"No keepin' up necessary, Gal. You know that by now.

"I'll pay you with good eggs for your breakfast."

"No payment due. What's a grandpa to do if not let his children keep up his poultry."

"You are a case—grandpa."

"That's been said. I'll tell you what now—you make the arrangements with your friend Mattie have Alice brought to your barn and you and I can slip by late of an evening and get her. They's plenty room in our barn, they's good pasture, and the fence is up. I'd take kindly to havin' a milk cow about."

"I wish I could get Attila here, but catching him is an all-day job. Anyway, that's a good hen house your daddy built. Don't seem to be any foxes hereabout—I reckon Sugar has a paw in that, don't you?"

"It's all in good wood, and it has a good roof. Keep the rain off—it'll last two or three lifetimes. Sugar does run the varmints. Not had a coon around for years. Almost miss em."

"I doubt that." Loren held up a golden ear of corn. "I traded Mrs. Williams for some sweet corn, and she's promised me some shelleys." Loren dropped a cleaned ear into a pan of water and picked up another. "I'll put up some cut corn, if I can use that freezer chest of yours."

"That'll work. I favor cream corn, and I do like shelleys, how do you fix 'em?"

"I soak them with a pinch of soda, then wash them, they cook with a piece of side meat, onion and a clove of garlic. I don't eat them without a cornbread though."

"Sounds right."

Loren stripped an ear, scrubbed away the silk and dropped it in the water saying, "You look like you're not here. Are you okay?"

"I overheard an old friend of yours today over at Wilson's Store—fellow by the name of Herms."

Loren stopped with an ear of corn in mid-strip, saying nothing.

"Seems he's looking everywhere for a young lady name of Loren Creek. He left a poster at the store." Mr. Gragg withdrew a folded sheet of paper from his bib pocket, unfolded it and handed it to the girl.

Loren's hand shook as she looked at herself with nearly shoulder-length hair. She read about her description as a "Missing Person."

"How does he know I'm here?"

"He don't. He's spreading these posters all over. Says he's focused his search on the mountain regions within two hours of his county. Says he's sure the girl won't travel far from her roots. He's dedicated to his line of work, and he don't seem foolish. I went back to the store later and light-fingered the poster. I doubt it'll be missed. Miz Wilson says he's been by twice this summer. Says he visits country stores and eatin' places, and he believes someone's bound to recognize her from the poster. Need some help with that ear?" Fields said with a slight grin.

Loren shot her "grandpa" a hard look, and pursed her lips tight.

Fields sat next to Loren, took up an ear, and started stripping it as though doing it slowly and deliberately would somehow improve the flavor. After they had done a half-dozen more ears he said in an easy voice, "I tell you, son, you've got to learn to appreciate this prevaricatin' more. If you can't enjoy it, why do it at all?"

CHAPTER 11

It's said there are two opposing schools of thought regarding public architecture: hard and soft. Hard architecture is made impervious to vandalism through the use of concrete, brick, steel, and stone, with no ornamentation that could be easily destroyed. Soft architecture protects itself by being inviting and lovely, causing people to not want to destroy it. Prisons are perfect examples of hard architecture, while the cathedrals of Europe model the other point of view.

High Country High was a perfect example of hard architecture masquerading as soft, through the use of color, large glass openings to the outside, and sweeping designs that are out of reach. Red brick, with a shiny green metal roof, it reflected the design most commonly accepted by parent and teacher organizations around the nation. Interior walls were concrete. Floors were tile and terrazzo. It would have made an excellent bomb shelter—albeit with cheerful painted hallways and walls. Failing to appreciate the inherent thrift of well-built, handsome aesthetics, modern educational systems had elevated cheapness to a virtue.

Watauga County was finally able to find an almost affordable and acceptable location for its newest high school addition. The search had been long and difficult, real estate prices being what they were due to exploding growth. This increase of expense by a factor of twenty was of little concern to developers and realtors who, having packed local government bodies with their own, found it easy to convince the public that they were interested in the public good. They then found license to force-feed one apartment complex, condominium, or housing development after another into a limited and fragile environment. Watauga County, North Carolina was Quick Money, a place where land speculators get to heaven without the inconvenience of a funeral. The result of this was pollution, congestion, and skyrocketing land values and taxes. One more pristine area mugged by developers. And then there was more of this-and-that, which brought more of them-and-those with something to sell. They had children, and the children required educating. High Country High School and Lorne Land shared the common excitement of a first year—a beginning.

Due in large part to the county system's desire to justify its new high school, "Grandpa Gragg" had successfully leveraged his youthful tenant into the Watauga County school system as a transfer student, and then stood back to watch the fun. He wanted to drive her to school on her first day, but good sense prevailed and she followed the instructions contained in the mailer sent to her "grandparent." She took the bus. One hour and fifteen minutes of screaming chaos later she was deposited at the bus drop-off in front of the school. Her bus was the second to arrive; Lorne Land ascended the walkway to the main entry and entered a nearly empty atrium. She checked the letter that had been sent by the board of education and followed its instructions to what was to be homeroom for the year. New school, new year, new identity, and a new gender.

New teacher. Mrs. Willis proved to be comfortable and pleasant in the midst of the turbulence to come that day. A rock in a raging stream, she was ever smiling, even-tempered, and welcoming to students who she knew would be confused and frightened by their situation. Mrs. Willis was balm to the fearful and timorous; she was oil on the waves, a member of the thin gray line, and a shrewd judge of character.

"Welcome to High Country High, Mr. Land," she said to the tall, handsome boy standing before her desk. "Lorne, I need your help with something. Here's a map of the school. Would you study it for a moment, and then stand in the doorway and help those who are lost or looking for their room?"

"Yes, Ma'am."

"It will be a little confusing at first, but you'll get the hang of it. Just place your papers right there," she said, pointing to a front row desk.

Loren studied the map long enough to get her bearings then moved to a post in front of the door to assist. Mrs. Willis, being farm-raised, referred to her new students on the first day of school as biddies. She was pleased as she heard Lorne instruct the students entering her class to form a single line to present their paperwork.

That afternoon Fields Gragg and Sugar watched from the porch as Loren got off the bus and waved a greeting.

"How'd it go?" Fields asked before she reached the porch.

"It worked. Everyone thinks I'm a boy."

"Well, good. But that wasn't what I was askin'. I meant how'd you like the new school and all."

"Oh, it's fine. Everything's new and clean."

"It oughta be, as much as it cost the taxpayers. Want some buttermilk? I made cornbread."

Loren nodded, and smiled a wide *yes*. It was near to being home; Loren, Fields Gragg, and Sugar sat on the afternoon porch enjoying the cornbread, cold buttermilk, and the last of summer. Sugar rested his head in Loren's lap, eyes closed, and breathing softly. Some don't need speech.

After a while Gragg said, "I been strainin' on what you're trying to do here. I mean, passing for a boy and all."

Loren waited.

"I think you can do it—mostly."

"Mostly?"

"Yep. That haircut works good, and you got right bushy eyebrows—I like em."

"Thank you."

"You got good strength and quickness. I'm curious—how'd you come by such? You don't move or motion like ary girl or woman I've known."

Loren took a deep breath and exhaled slowly as she recalled her childhood—and her mother.

"Well, you remember I told you about growing up alone with my mother in Piney Flat?"

Fields nodded. "I recollect you tellin' about coming up a farm girl, and having a lot of responsibility and doing hard work since childhood, but that don't account for your muscles and quickness. You're more boy than girl in that way. No offense."

"None taken. When I was coming up there were no girls close by, but a lot of boys my age, so I ran with them. I played baseball with them—I could run as fast and hit a ball as far as any. I could even out-fight some of them. I hunted and fished and swam—even skinny-dipped once or twice with 'em—til my mother got wind of it. I was one of the boys, even played football with them. You ought to see me kick a football or a soccer ball. Momma loved it, but she said that I should enjoy it while I could 'cause before long I'd not be able to do such. She taught me gymnastics, dance, and drove me to Judo lessons, until she couldn't drive anymore. Then I'd pedal my bike the five miles there and back twice a week. Everybody in Piney Flat knew me for a tomboy, but all my life I been getting ready to be a girl, and later, a woman, like Momma."

"Judo lessons?"

"After the third time I came home with a black eye, mother decided to take what she called a frontal approach to the problem, and enrolled me in judo."

"How'd that work out?" Fields asked.

"I didn't get any more black eyes."

"I regret not knowin' your momma," Fields said. "She sounds like the kind of woman I'd want for a daughter. You sure you don't want to make a go of it as a girl?"

"Too late now. Besides, Mr. Herms would find me for sure if I did."

"How come you can't just be a girl and let me guardian?"

"I don't need a guardian." Loren flushed in anger. "I haven't had a guardian since I was ten or eleven. I made all the family decisions since I was twelve. I've had years of independence, and I don't want to be anyone's baby. I've been an adult for more'n two years, and I'd find it a hard go—to be someone's dependent child." Loren felt herself warming.

"Wouldn't have to be that way with us."

"Thank you, but it would seem such to me." She added very evenly, "It's a matter of right or wrong. If I was to want to be someone's dependent, I couldn't pick a better person than you—and I mean that."

"You always been this hard-headed?"

"Only since I had you to copy, Grandpa."

Sugar moaned and rolled over. Loren rubbed his stomach, he took her hand between his paws and gently his jaws around it. She shook him by the muzzle. "Silly mutt."

"Well, just don't go makin' yourself such a tough row to hoe. You got nothin' to prove."

"I got nothin' to prove, but I plan to live like my mother showed me—as my own woman. Strong."

Gragg thought a while then answered, "I'd not call that strong. Strong people need and want others, and are wanted and needed by 'em. Ain't no one person stronger'n family."

"I don't have family, and so I'll do the best I got with what I got."

"I don't agree with what you're tryin', but you know I'll stand behind you."

"I do. Thank you." Loren stood and started gathering the glasses and plates. Sugar barely stirred as she shifted his head to the floor. "I got chores, and homework. You want to fix supper with me later?"

"You do your chores and school work. I'll fix us some vegetables and such later. Come by around six. Just leave them plates."

Sugar rose and followed Loren to her house. Fields called out. "Don't go thievin' my dog." She waved over her back and took off running with Sugar at her heels.

Fields Gragg watched through softening eyes.

Chapter 12

"Hey."

"Hey." Loren put down her book and watched the tall blond-haired boy ascend the path leading up to her porch from the road. There was a flash of white at Fields' house. She dropped her textbook and gestured at the boy. "Hurry, get up here, quick. Hurry!"

The boy, hearing her urgency leaped up the path and made it to the top of the steps just ahead of Sugar. "Damn," he said from behind Loren, who had hold of the collar of the growling dog.

"Down, Sugar, down."

"Yeah, please, down. Sugar?"

"That's right."

"He don't seem sweet. He always this friendly?"

"No. Sometimes he gets peevish."

"Good dog. Good dog," the boy ventured. Sugar growled.

Loren sat on the porch deck with her feet on the second step. "Sit over there," she said, pointing at the column opposite her side. "I'll hold him, and maybe he'll get used to you."

"Maybe. My name's Bryce, Bryce Trivette. Excuse me if I don't reach out and shake, but I want to keep my arm. I live up the road about a mile, yellow house."

"I'm Lorne Land. I've seen your house. Pretty yard. I do like the way your momma has with flower beds."

"Thanks, I'll tell her. She says it's her therapy. What do your folks do?" Bryce asked.

"My folks are dead. Fields Gragg is my grandpa, actually, he's my grand-uncle—but I call him grandpa." Loren knew that Fields Gragg had no living children who could have been her parents; she made a mental note to tell him about this conversation.

"Sorry about your folks. Mr. Gragg is as good as they come."

"Thank you."

Bryce looked out over the meadow across the road. "You play any sports?"

"Yeah, a little, but I'm no good. I play a little baseball, some soccer, and I've kicked a football around some, but I'm terrible at the game—I don't like getting hurt that much."

Bryce laughed. "Sounds smart to me. I like football, but I've played it since I was five, and've sort of gotten used to the bumps and bruises. I saw you on the bus first day—I was sittin' in the back and decided to come meet you—and Cujo here. Hey, Sugar, still want a part of my leg?" Sugar sat on his haunches and cocked his head at the interloper.

Loren stroked his back saying. "It's okay, boy—he's a friend. Friend, Sugar. Friend." Bryce held out the back of a hand, which Sugar licked.

"I think he likes you."

"You sure he's not just tastin' me?"

Loren laughed. "Good dog. Good Sugar." The dog flopped down and emitted a loud *Pfft*. "I think we're okay now," she said, letting go of the collar, but keeping her hand on Sugar's heavy neck.

"Goin out for any teams at High Country?" Bryce asked.

"No, I don't plan to—I'm not that good."

"You don't have to be good to go out for em. The coaches are paid to make you good."

"I've got chores, and homework. Grandpa says I've got to make all A's or he won't let me have a car until I graduate. He thinks sports are a foolishness," Loren fibbed.

"They haven't hurt me any," Bryce said, evidently a little miffed. "Anyway, want to play some set-back? I brought a football." He said, pointing at his bicycle. A football rested in the back carrier.

"Okay, but I've got to get back to my homework before long." Loren held Sugar as Bryce rose slowly. "Good dog." Sugar gave no signs of aggression. "I think he likes you."

"I must have tasted good," Bryce said as he descended the steps. "Let's go to the field across the road. It's level down by the stream." Loren and Bryce casually flipped the football back and forth as they crossed the road and went down to the meadow. Loren made sure she put a little extra effort into the tight spirals she drilled at Bryce.

Loren knew the rules. She'd played the same game with the boys in Piney Flat. A player throws or kicks a football to the other player who tries to catch it. If the receiver catches the ball he takes five steps forward, and it becomes his turn to throw or kick. If he fails to catch the ball the sender takes five steps. The first to reach mid-field wins. The agreement on boundaries was centered around an unspoken honor system. Loren had heard that big-city boys couldn't play setback.

Bryce had an arm, and he knew how to use it. He unleashed a mighty throw to the corner behind Loren, who futilely tried to catch the long-range bomb.

"Good throw," Loren said, returning the ball.

Bryce let go with another—which Loren missed.

Loren caught the third throw, way behind her boundary line. It was her turn.

"Wow!" Where did you learn to kick like that?" Bryce shouted as he ran to retrieve the ball that had sailed way over his head.

"I played soccer some, and I was kicker for neighborhood football games."

"Well, buddy, you got a leg."

Bryce missed the second kick, but caught the third as Sugar alertly watched from the side of the field.

After an hour of back and forth with Bryce winning most of the games, the two retired to Loren's porch and glasses of water. Draining his glass, Bryce said, "I gotta go. See you on the bus tomorrow. You got a heckuva leg, but I have to tell you, you throw like a girl."

CHAPTER 13

When Loren got on the bus the next morning she saw Bryce's shock of straight blond hair at the back of the bus and she went to join her new friend.

"Hey, Leg," Bryce tossed out with a grin as Loren approached. "I was telling my buddies what a great leg you got, and how we got talk you into tryin' out for the team."

Loren was introduced to Buddy Sayles—roly-poly with youthful fat; Ellis Winebarger—sandy-haired with a wide grin; and a pale-complexioned, black-maned mountain boy named Council Teague, who stood over six feet and seemed to be all gangly hands and feet. The talk quickly turned to the 9th grade junior varsity football team and the high hopes the boys had for the season. Bryce was the quarterback, and apparently, the team leader.

"Where you from, Lorne?"

"Virginia."

"They play football up there?" Buddy asked, sniggering to his friends.

"No, we're too busy fightin' bear and catamount bare-handed to play childish sports."

"Childish sports? Oooowee. Listen to the boy. He is baad," Ellis came back, smiling.

Loren knew that the banter was a proving-ground activity for her, and that she had to give tit for tat. The bus trip passed a lot quicker with friends on board.

When they got off the bus at the school, the five friends fanned out and sauntered toward clusters of students who stood talking while waiting for the bell. Bryce and Loren found their way to a noisy scuffle going on, and as they approached, they saw three older boys pushing a younger, smaller member around inside their encircling arm span. The young kid had already been on the ground and was starting to show some wear. His clothes were smudged, his longish hair tousled, and he was fighting back tears. After watching the boy being pushed to the ground the second time, Bryce stepped into the melee and helped the boy up, saying, "That's enough. He's had enough."

"Yeah, who says so?" asked a largish pimple-faced boy who was apparently the leader of the pack.

"I do. Why don't you pick on someone your own size? And why can't you do it one at a time?"

"He's a damned Yankee." A skinny boy with bad teeth snickered.

"Seems more like he's one small feller against three, bigger'n him."

"Yeah, well now it's three against two, ain't it?" Asked Pimples.

Loren joined her friend, saying, "Three against three—Zit-face."

"Four against three," from a pretty dark-haired girl who came to stand next to Loren.

"Damn, we get to fight Yankees and girls. This should be easy."

The dark-haired girl said, "Any mountain girl I know could take you jaybos single-handed in a fair fight. That's the way it is with people who have to gang up on one man to whip him."

Pimples made a move toward them when Loren spun once and leg-whipped the boy's legs out from under him and then fell on him, pinning his throat with her knee. Pimples was turning purple when the bell rang.

On the way to classes, Bryce came alongside Loren and said, "Damn, boy, you ain't one to mess with. Like I said, you got leg."

"The guy was a jerk," Loren said through her anger.

"Remind me to stay on your good side, neighbor."

"Who was the girl?" Loren asked.

"That was Jo Mae Butler—and apparently no one to mess with either. I believe she was about to light into Ollie."

"Ollie?"

"Yeah, Ollie Miles, he's the one you called *zit-face*, the one with the pimples. He's going to hate you for life."

"With enemies like that, I'd say that makes me a good guy," Loren said.

"Well I reckon that's one way to look at it. See you later," Bryce said, clapping Loren on the back before he vanished into his home room.

At lunch Loren took her tray to a far corner table so she could sit with her back to the wall and watch. She was soon joined by the youth that she and Bryce had stepped in to help.

"Hi. Can I join you?" Loren signaled him to sit. "My name's Gentry Starr."

"Hi, Gentry, I'm Lorne Land, pleased to meet you."

"I was really pleased to meet you and your friends this morning. Just call me Gent."

Bryce and Jo Mae joined the small group. First name introductions were made all around, followed by criticisms of cafeteria food, returning to school, and finally, school bullies.

"Where you from, Yank?" Bryce asked.

"Ho-ho-kus, New Jersey."

"Ho-ho-kus? You're puttin' me on, right?"

"No, it's a place, a big place, in point of fact."

"*Point of fact?* Hey, we got us a scholar." Bryce said, leaning back in his chair. "You play football, Yank?"

"My name's Gent, and I'd like to be called that."

"No offense meant—Gent, but I think I'll call you Yank anyway, and whip anybody else who does."

Gent looked sharply at Bryce and then broke out into a smile. "I think I'm going to like you—Goober."

Bryce reached a long arm across the table and the two boys shook. "Fair enough."

Gent looked over at Jo Mae and said, "You're the prettiest girl that's ever come to my rescue—and I've been rescued by a lot of them."

"Really? Why?" she asked. This brought a round of laughter.

"They always told me it was because I was pleasing to have around."

"We'll see about that."

"I sure do hope so. Maybe you can teach me to fight—mountain girl style."

"Knowin' *how* to do a thing, and knowin' *to do it,* is different," Jo Mae quipped.

"Ouch, I believe I've been put in my place. You on the football team, too, Jo Mae?"

"I was thinkin' on goin out for it, but I didn't care to shame the boys so. After all, they're young and impressionable." This brought guffaws and head shaking.

The foursome talked, joked, and laughed as they stabbed at their food, pretending to hate it, and then took empty trays up front to be washed.

Gent and Loren had a class together the next period, and as they walked to it, Gent said, "I think I'm going to like it here."

"Hope so. Sooner you fit in, the better off you'll be."

"Do you fit in?"

"I don't know yet, but I hope to."

CHAPTER 14

It was the third week of classes when Council Teague showed up with a plan for the school mascot.

"The Red *what?*" Gent asked with a puzzled frown. Loren grinned at Gent's ignorance.

"Red *Eft*. Here, look." Council Teague held out a paperback opened to a picture of his choice.

"That's called a Fire Newt where I come from," Loren said.

Gent cackled. "A *lizard*, you want our school totem to be a fuckin lizard?"

"It ain't a lizard, it's a newt, a kind of salamander, and such language, is ugly and not necessary."

"Okay, a newt. And that's somehow better? Sorry about the language, I'm an Army brat, and you wouldn't believe the language I've been around in my fourteen years. I know you're a deacon's son, and I respect that. Respect is important. Anyway—Reverend—you got great hands—you caught every pass I threw your way at practice, and I'm bound to respect anyone with hands like yours."

"They're easy to catch when you put em right where they're supposed to be. Anyway, Gent, I want you to back my choice."

Loren said, "I will. I've always thought they were the prettiest critter on the ground. Findin' one is like discovering a jewel on the forest floor."

"The Mighty Efts?" Gent said. "You lean heavy on friendship. Everybody else wants eagles, tigers, lions, you know, the kind of things that kill things, but not you. No—you think we should be known as some kind of salamander. That's sure to strike fear in the hearts of our opponents."

Council held up the book. "Look at the picture. These things are pretty. They got great color—blue-green spots on bright orange."

"It gets worse. You want our school colors to be orange and teal. I'm thinking about changing friends," Gent said.

"I came to you because I thought you had the most open mind of anybody here at school, and would give me a listen. And Fire Newts would be a great name." Council looked at Loren. "Besides, there's a three hundred dollar prize for the winner," he said over his shoulder as he started to walk away.

Gent called out, "Wait a minute now—Your Grace. I'm just giving you what you're going to hear from everybody. I'm making you strong. Hey, remember this; your friends tell you the truth. Aren't we friends?" Gent took hold of Council's arm and pulled him back.

"Yeah. Yeah we are. Good friends."

"Alright then. I like your idea, but it's going to be a hard sell. No one, I mean *no one* at High Country is going to like what they're sure to call your red lizard."

56

"It ain't red, and it ain't…"

"Hel… Heck, I know that, and you know that, but who else—other than maybe the biology teacher—knows it? Lemme see that book again. Gent opened it and the two boys sat on a bench, studying the picture. Gent leaned back, looked at his friend and said, "*Fire Newts* is a good name, but we need a plan."

Loren said grinning, "I think I know what might help."

A few days later, students started bringing brilliantly colored "lizards" to the biology teacher, wanting to know what they were. They were being found all over the campus grounds. After a week of telling students they were holding the Red Eft, a harmless salamander common to the Appalachian Mountains, the biology teacher placed colored posters on all bulletin boards. The students were informed that the school was apparently located on land where there was a large population of Red Eft—"Beautiful creatures peculiar to the Appalachians. Attend to the striking coloring of these unique specimens, and try not to harm them. In fact, all Red Efts should be returned to the small stream behind the gymnasium." This request made collecting of Red Efts much easier for Council, Bryce, Jo Mae, Loren, and Gent who had been laboriously gathering Efts in the forest and placing them in strategic campus locations where they would be seen. They subsequently succeeded in establishing a large Red Eft population in a region that previously had none - and familiarizing every student in the school with a species of salamander, bright orange in color with iridescent teal spots.

At the end of the week, Council Teague, popular ninth grader, son of a long line of local farmers—and promising tight end—submitted his entry for school totem, reinforcing the appeal of the critter by pointing out that it came with "ready-made school colors." The Red Eft made it to the final selection along with the Peregrine Falcon and the Catamount, the latter being favored by members of the football team, and prospective members of a future basketball team. The Falcon was the favorite of most members of the senior class—who felt sure to win because "Seniors Rule." They failed to see that there were nearly twice as many ninth graders as seniors. And then there were the ladies: modern girls were more than a little tired of seeing macho totems that were meant to aggrandize an inflated sense of toughness and meanness. They were sophisticated enough to know that truly strong men don't need to display.

Gent excused himself from openly campaigning for the Eft, but he wrote Council's arguments, and penned his rebuttals. It was Jo Mae, aspiring cheerleader and track star, who clinched the vote with the students when she coined the notion—making sure that it didn't come to the attention of the teachers—that, in all things competitive, High Country was going to "Eft" its opponents. She and Gent created a student body cheer that addressed opposing teams, and ended with "Eft You." Among the student body, "Eft" had legs. Being *Fire Newts* helped considerably: *Fire. Fire Newt.* Student cars began showing up with flame decals. It also helped that Jo Mae and the other Junior Varsity cheerleaders had tongues of fire emblazoned on backside of their cheerleader shorts.

With his prize winnings, Council treated his four buddies to a movie and a fine meal at Makoto's restaurant—with much laughter. Gent named the place "Sling-Chows" because of the way the Japanese cooks tossed food and caught morsels of food with an expertise that never ceased to entertain.

Over dessert, talk drifted to the new football team, and to the junior varsity, which was considered a training ground for future varsity players.

"You ought to come out for the team, Lorne." Bryce urged. "With that leg of yours, you'd be a shoo-in."

"Thanks, but I'm going to join the cross-country team." Loren answered. "I'll have to take a pass on your offer."

"Don't need you to *pass*, we need you to *kick*. Come to the game this Friday. I think you'll change your mind."

Loren smiled at her friend, shaking her head. "I like to run. I'm going out for cross-country."

"Cross-country is not a man's sport. C'mon, we need that leg of yours on the team."

"No, I'm going to run while you 'real men' get your brains beat out."

"I like to run." Council said. "I run the forest trails a lot. Maybe you'd come with me someday?"

"Sure. Though I spect you'll be hard to follow, with those grasshopper legs of yours."

"If coach will let me, I'll do cross-country and football at the same time. But I doubt he will because of scheduling problems."

Gent raised his glass of tea, "Anyway guys—Jo Mae—here's to the future of the Fire Newts."

"Fire Newts!" The Group chorused.

CHAPTER 15

Everyone knew that the varsity was going to win. Everyone, that is, except the junior varsity team members who were to play them in a pre-season game. This first game of the High Country Red Efts was supposed to be a scrimmage, but many knew better. Erv Jaynes, an experienced veteran of many Friday nights, agreed to come out of retirement for one year to help start the athletic program at the new high school. The JVs mentor, Call Helder, third generation football coach, was just out of college, and didn't know his team could not possibly win. He did know that his front line outweighed the varsity line by some fifteen pounds each. He also knew that he had two excellent quarterbacks, and a 190 pound fullback who had been awarded the name "Train" by his teammates.

Loren sat with Bryce's father, Elden Trivette, who had quarterbacked his high school team some twenty years earlier.

"Bryce tells me that you're a good kicker," Mr. Trivette said as they waited for the game to start.

"We played set-back the other day. Bryce can throw the football a country mile," Loren said.

"He told me about it. He said you almost beat him."

"It wasn't very close, Mr. Trivette. Bryce is good."

"That's not the way he tells it. Hah, here they come." They stood up for the kick-off.

The varsity coach played his second string most of the first half, and didn't notice that Coach Helder did much the same thing. At halftime it was 6-0, varsity. Little attention was paid to the fact that both of the JV quarterbacks' uniforms remained spotless, and the Train had only been in on five plays, averaging over six yards a carry. Council Teague had not dropped a single pass. A great deal had gone unnoticed. The varsity taunted and postured during the first half, even after their point-after attempt was blocked. *Seniors Rule—and after all, we don't want to hurt the children.*

Coach Helder told his team that the first man who taunted or got in a fight would sit on the bench for the rest of the evening. He also told his men that when they crossed the goal line they should "act like they've been there before." At halftime, he asked them to say what they thought they could do better in the second half. After an awkward pause, the players pointed out the mistakes they had made, and how to correct them. The coach was satisfied. His last words were, "Remember, this is a *game*. We're supposed to be having *fun*. Now, let's go out there and show the varsity just how much fun we can have."

When they got to the bench, Coach Helder gathered his men. "Train, you start. Bryce, I want a touchdown in the first series. Go Big Red!"

Gent received the kickoff and spun, feinted, and sprinted his way to the opponent's twenty-yard line. Three plays later, Train took a tackle slant and went in standing. In less than one minute the score was JVs 7-6. There was stirring on the varsity bench.

The kick-off was lost by a varsity fumble, and the JVs scored two plays later. 14-6. The varsity didn't fumble the next kick-off and marched down the field to score. 14-13. The varsity bench settled back into jeering and taunting, knowing what was coming. They were going to cream the JVs.

The varsity kick-off was fielded by Gent who handed off in a cross-over with another small running back, Jamie Gragg, who followed "Student Body Right" down the field. Half the varsity was flat on the ground when Jamie crossed the goal line. He courteously handed the ball to a referee, and jogged back to the bench. 21-13. The varsity bench was a study of grim resolve as the players exchanged glances and nodded to each other. The war was joined.

This was no scrimmage. The blocking was solid and the tackling was vicious. More than once, Coach Helder had to admonish his men to "play clean."

But coach, they ain't.

We're not them. We're us, and we're proud. Play clean.

Loren and Mr. Trivette stood much of the second half as the tension mounted in the stands. They were watching a real football game.

"They could have used a good kicker here, Lorne." Mr. Trivette said to Loren when the JVs came within field goal range, and then lost the ball on downs because they didn't have a kicker.

Loren let her thoughts run. *He's right; I could have made that field goal.*

By the middle of the second half, several husbands had been cowed into going to their respective coach and asking that they ease off a bit—after all it's only a scrimmage. When assured that the coach would try, the men returned to their son's mother, who was wringing hands, wincing, and crying out in pain at the harsh reality of boys trying to murder their son. They had come to have fun.

Nearing the end of the fourth quarter it was 27-21varsity. Bryce was on the bench with a hurt shoulder, and Gent was getting his uniform dirty as back-up quarterback. The game had become three downs and punt, three downs and punt. Call Helder's father and grandfather had both been college linebackers before they went into coaching. Call was an all-conference high school and college linebacker. To him, defense *was* offense. If they can't score, they can't win, was the family mantra from Coach Helder's earliest memory. The JV front line was a wall. But the varsity had three years experience on them. Every play was a battle.

Forty seconds left and the varsity had to punt. The JVs received, and were stopped cold at their own twenty-five. Gent rolled out to the right and completed a short pass that was carried out of bounds. Second and four. Gent rolled to the right again completed a pass for two more yards before the receiver was pushed out of bounds. Gent's third pass was dropped, and they failed to call the time out that Coach Helder was frantically signaling for from the sidelines. Gent had a plan.

With seven seconds remaining on the clock, Gent received the snap from center, faked a hand-off to Train over right tackle, and spun to roll out to the left flat. It was then that the varsity discovered that Gentry Starr was ambidextrous. The pass sailed some thirty yards before floating into Jamie Gragg's waiting hands. He didn't even have to break stride to field the pass and make it to the goal line. The extra point was good. 28-27, Jayvees.

As soon as the ball split the uprights, Jo Mae streaked across the field carrying a banner sporting a Red Eft on a teal background. She threw herself onto a surprised and embarrassed Council Teague, as Gent walked to his coach to try to explain his failure to follow instructions.

In the locker room Coach Helder finally got his team's attention, waited for them to settle quietly for his comments.

"Well team, did you have fun?" He was deluged with a chorus of shouted responses.

"How do you like winning?" More raves.

"Remember this feeling. Fun is *Winning.*" The team roared in response.

"Gentry—a word, please." Coach Helder said softly as the team headed for the showers.

Loren and Bryce rode home with Bryce's dad after the game. Bryce and his father talked play-by-play on the way home.

When they dropped Loren off at her house, Mr. Elden said, "Lorne, the team really needs a good kicker. Field goals win games too. Think about it."

"I will, Mr. Trivette. Thank you." As she walked up the pathway to her porch she was smiling at what she would look like in shoulder pads, when she felt a wet nose touch her right hand.

CHAPTER 16

"Cider?"

"Yeah, apple cider. Do you like it?" Bryce asked.

"I like it a lot, but I've never made any."

"And here I thought you were a good country boy, Lorne. How come you not to know cider makin'."

"Where I come from, most of the apple trees are in orchards and sold off as fruit."

"Well, they're everywhere in yards hereabouts, most of them are old and in their last few years. This used to be one of the biggest apple growing regions in the country. There are still a few orchards around, but nothing, my pa says, like it used to be. Almost every yard had from one or two, to a half dozen trees. All different kinds— nothing like the junk you find all dyed and waxed in the grocery store. They's some sweet, some sour, some even bitter, but makes good butter. Most aren't pretty, but they have character—a lot like mountain people. They's Virginia Beauty, Northern Spy, Limbertwig, Black's Best. You won't find them in the store, but they're all over the county—and they make great cider if you know how to blend them."

Bryce Trivette had grown up with those apple trees as a part of his life. He climbed them, sampled their fruit and contemplated their uniqueness. Bryce was never one to take things for granted, nor to accept what appeared to be, without question.

"I'm glad you like cider 'cause we're going to have a lot of it," he said after being admitted to Lorne's living room. "I like real cider. I don't care for that junk they serve in the cafeteria."

"Good. 'Cause some of us are going to make cider this weekend. I was wondering if you want to help. We do it every year.

"Sure. I'd like to learn how to make cider."

"Nothing to it. All we have to do is pick the apples, wash em, crush em, and press em. The juice runs into pails, we strain it into jugs, and we got cider."

"I thought it had to ferment."

"That's *hard* cider. If you put the cider jug away in a cool dark place, with the caps loose on the jugs, for a couple weeks, you got hard cider; it's apple wine is all that is, and it doesn't taste nearly good as fresh apple juice. In fact, *nothing* tastes as good as fresh squeezed apple juice."

"When do we start?" Loren asked.

"Council's dad has the press and a pick-up. We're going to load the press tonight, and we'll start tomorrow morning at Widow Bellows' place. She's got really good trees. We're going to need jugs and pails, so bring what you can. If you have any cheese cloth bring it along—we need to strain the juice. We need funnels."

"What kind of apples make good cider?"

"I've heard tell there are cider apples, but I wouldn't know. What we do is blend different kinds of apples, some sweet, some spicy. It's the blend that makes good cider, not too sweet, not too sour. You get the hang of it after a while, you'll see."

Widow Bellows was one of those wizened mountain women whose bottomless strength and grit showed in the lines of her face and the brace of her frame. She and some neighbors worked alongside the boys and girls as the apples were picked, gathered, tub-washed, then crushed and pressed. The juice was blended in large tubs and sampled to determine the right balance of flavor. Widow Bellows was known to have uncanny skill in correcting the flavor until it was, in her words, *just raht*. When the blend was set, Miz' Bellows added what looked like an aspirin tablet to each jug. When Loren inquired, Miz' Bellows said, "Them's sulfur pills, the druggist calls em Camden tablets. They kill the yeast so's the juice won't ferment into hard. Hit's the yeast that makes a ferment. We're wantin' apple juice, not likker."

Bryce and Gent watched amazed at Loren's agility as she scaled the old apple trees. Others clung to ladders as though their lives depended on it. Loren used the ladder only to reach bottom branches to get into the trees, and the upper branches that would not hold her weight.

They picked and pressed all day Saturday, and Sunday afternoon. By mid-afternoon Sunday, it was apparent they were going to have a couple hundred gallons of juice. The tree owners took a share, and the boys had the rest.

"What are we going to do with all this juice? We can't drink it," Loren said.

"We'll keep some for ourselves and carry the rest to Wilson's Grocery. Mr. Wilson will let us store it in a cooler to help keep the flavor. That gives us more time to sell to the neighbors the money will go to Mountain Shade Baptist."

"Seems we're doing a lot of work for nothing," Gent quipped.

"Ain't for nothing. It's for the church." Gent fell silent to Bryce's logic.

By sundown Sunday, the press had been cleaned, thoroughly rinsed with fresh water and baking soda, and then stored in an outbuilding for the next squeezing, which would probably take place in a couple of weeks.

The young people had scattered to their respective homes, leaving Loren and Bryce on Loren's front porch. Loren made coffee and, in the cool of the evening, sat close to her friend on the porch deck, savoring the strong odor of coffee boiled with the grounds.

"We put in a weekend's work, didn't we?" Bryce said.

"Yeah, but I'm still not sure why we did it."

"We made cider for neighbors, some for ourselves, and a lot for the church. This winter, jars of preserves and sacks of vegetables will turn up on our porches. Some folks will give us a jar of honey, or a basket of eggs. It all works out. It's the way of neighbors. You won't even think about all the work we put in when your spreading that homemade blackberry preserve on your biscuit."

"It's like that in Pi... where I come from. People look out for each other."

"Thought you were from Blacksburg. Ain't that a big city?" Loren could see Bryce eyeing her in the soft evening light.

"I am. No, it's not a big city. It's a big town, and I lived on Pine Ridge Road, out in the country." Loren pointed at meadow across the road and said, "Man, look at the fireflies." She rose and turned to go into the house. "Let me show you something; I'll be right back."

Soon, music came from the living room, and Loren returned to her seat.

"Sounds like church music."

"It is. It's E. Power Biggs, a famous organist, playing Bach fugues. But just watch the fireflies and see what happens."

A minute passed, then another as the two friends sat and sipped coffee.

"Damn. The fireflies are keeping time with the music!" Bryce nearly shouted.

"I expect it only seems that way. I doubt they're really doing it."

"Whatever, it sure does look like they're flashing in time. That's really weird—where did you learn about that?"

"Momma and I discovered it one night some time ago. We were on the porch with hot chocolate and she put on this music—it was one of her favorites—and we saw how the fireflies looked like they were keepin' time with the music. I always liked it, and it makes me think of..." Loren stopped, fighting back sudden tears with clenched jaws.

Bryce draped a long arm around Loren's shoulder and pulled her close. "You must miss your folks at lot." He gave Loren a quick shake then dropped his arm.

"I miss my Momma. I never knew my father, and Momma never said much about him, except that he was nice, but they went their separate ways before I was born."

"I don't know what I'd do without my folks—and my brother and sisters. We tease and torture one another, but when it comes down to it, we're close."

Loren let herself rest close Bryce's warmth, it felt good. Safe. As they sat listening and watching, their breathing tuned to each other's rhythm.

Loren almost fell asleep with her head leaning against Bryce's shoulder when a car came down the road. Bryce abruptly righted himself and pulled away from Loren as the car went by.

"Damn, they probably think we're a couple of fairies," he said in disgust.

Loren laughed softly. "Who were they, d'you know?"

"I couldn't tell in the dark. I hope it's not the Clarens. Mrs. Clarens is the world's biggest gossip. She knows everybody's business."

As they sat in silence, Loren became aware of Bryce looking at her in the dark. His hand was rested on her knee. Before long he stood and said, "Reckon I better head on. See you on the bus."

"Right. Be careful riding that bike home in the dark."

"Okay—Mom."

Bryce activated the red flasher on the back of his bicycle, mounted the bike and coasted to the roadway, waving over his back to Loren. No Traffic. As he cranked up to road speed his thoughts centered on his friend and the worried feeling he had sitting close and warm.

In the last few waking moments before falling asleep in her bed, Loren's thoughts went to how good it felt to be in Bryce's close presence. She had interesting dreams that night. Dreams of being chased and dreams of being able to fly. She awoke after one arousing dream and rose to go to the bathroom. As she washed up she looked at herself in the mirror. This is not fair. I'm just a kid, and I shouldn't have to do this all by myself. Returning to bed she fell asleep immediately. She wakened at dawn, weeping from a dream of her momma.

CHAPTER 17

The following Friday afternoon, Loren answered her doorbell to find a grinning pair of girls, and Sugar, on her porch. Meredith and Tara carrying packages, burst into the house like a whirlwind.

"We come bearing gifts," Meredith said, grabbing Loren in a hug, and then touching a light kiss on her cheek.

"What's the occasion?" Loren asked, pulling away.

"The occasion, sweetheart, is the fact that you've been a boy too long, and it's time to come out of the closet. So my kid sister here—who would positively die from grief if I didn't let her come to visit every weekend—has decided that we should take matters in hand." Meredith opened up her package and withdrew a skirt.

"I've got the shoes, panty hose and…" Tara pulled out a transparent container of costume jewelry.

"What are you two up to?"

"Mischief and maidenly mayhem, my dear," Meredith said in a stiff formal voice. "We thought you'd like to take a short trip with us—as a girl."

"Trip? Where?"

"Have you ever been to Old Salem?" Tara asked.

"No, but I've heard tell of it. Momma talked about going there once, but we never were able to go."

"Good. We need to get you dressed, and we'll take off as three southern gals on the go. You need to try on these clothes and make sure they fit. We brought make-up, too."

"Make-up?"

"Yeah, you know," Tara said. "Stuff that girls put on their face when they want to look like girls."

"I hardly ever wore make-up. I don't even know how to put it on."

Meredith and Tara glanced at each other with looks that Loren knew could be interpreted as, 'we've got our work cut out for us.' "Well, it's time to learn, Gal," Meredith offered.

Loren stepped back from her friends and tipped her head to one side.

"What is it?" Meredith asked.

"I don't know. All of a sudden you two come in and sweep me off my feet with this trip to a place I've never been. It's just that you've caught me unawares and…"

"Well it's time to get aware." Meredith answered. "We're bound and determined to drag you kicking and screaming into girldom." She stood in front of Loren with her hands on her hips, and then leaned her head back in laughter. "Get with the program—Sis." She reached out and shook Loren by the shoulders.

"There's more." Tara chimed in as she dug into the shopping bag and came up a curly bond wig. "Ta-daah. Girl hair." The next ten minutes were spent in raucous laughter as the threesome tried on the wig

Meredith was the last to experiment with a curly look. When she was finished modeling it, she said to Loren, "Try this stuff on tonight, and we'll come by tomorrow morning around eight, and then we'll be on our way." She paused a moment in thought. "Better still, how about coming to my dorm room—you can sleep on the couch—and we'll have us a fashion show. Then tomorrow, first light, we'll head out for Winston-Salem—that's where Old Salem is."

"I'll have to ask Grandpa Gragg. He'll need to milk Alice tomorrow, and feed the chickens. I'm sure he won't mind. In fact, he enjoys it. Says it puts him in mind of his childhood. He's thanked me more than once for working it so's we could go fetch Alice, but I still want to clear it with him."

"Clear away, Loren. We'll go with you in case there's a need for feminine wiles."

"That would work. Grandpa really likes you two; he says you come from good stock."

Meredith laughed, "Mother would be proud. Yes, good stock. C'mon, Tara, let's take our stock over to see Mr. Gragg, and clear the way for a day of girl good times."

Old Salem, a faithfully restored seventeenth-century Moravian community in the middle of Winston-Salem, North Carolina, was only a two-hour drive from Boone. The girls arrived early enough to find a parking place on the main street after purchasing passes at the large ultra-modern facility that carries visitors on a remarkable trip some three hundred years back in time.

The three girls, smartly attired in fall skirts and sweaters, followed the recommended walking tour, lunched at the tavern, and sampled the delights of a bakery that traced its history back to the year 1800. Visitors found it nearly impossible to walk past the fragrances from the old-fashioned bakery oven. The girls purchased a variety of cookies and pastries.

"These Moravians were a lot like my neighbors," Loren said. "They either made what they needed or they made do."

"Made do?" Tara asked.

"Yes, they made do without it or used something else."

Meredith, looked over a display, "They made flax clothing, pottery, wooden tools, everything. They even smithied iron implements. I don't think I've ever seen anything like this."

"I love that bakery." Tara said with a smile as she dipped into the bag of cookies.

"Careful, Sis." Meredith mixed a frown with a smile. Tara broke her cookie in two and dropped a half back in the bag. "See what I mean, Loren. It's like having two mothers."

Loren broke off part of Tara's cookie, popped it in her mouth and said, "What I meant was the strength of their community and the way they practiced what they believed puts me in mind of my neighbors. I wish…" She fell silent and the girls walked with their own thoughts as they passed a couple of seventeenth century houses.

By midday Old Salem was crowded with visitors of all stripes, young and old, families, couples, bands of teens, elderly couples, and tour groups. As the three girls picked their way over the crowded stone walkways and sidewalks, Loren was aware of being watched. At first she noticed the boys who shot admiring glances her way, then she realized that men of every age gave the girls at least passing notice. Finally, she realized that ladies and older women cut their eyes at them as they walked by. Some stared, and sometimes the looks were sharp appraisals. For the first time in her life, Loren became aware of being a female that others found attractive. The revelation so stunned her that she stopped and stood quiet in thought. They were in the middle of the old cemetery, and Loren leaned against a tombstone.

"What is it Loren? You look worried and—and sort of lost," Meredith said.

"People are looking at us; some of them stare."

"Yes?"

"I've never had that happen to me before. I—I'm not used to it."

Meredith took her friend by the hand, "You're a pretty girl, Loren. Get used to it. Boys look at pretty girls—that's what they do."

"It would be weird if they didn't," Tara said, and danced into a twirl that lifted her pleated wool skirt.

"It's not just boys; it's everyone. Women look at us, old ladies. Old men."

"That's right." Meredith said. "Mom talked about this more than once over dinner. We have lots of dinner discussions. She told us about the staring thing. Boys look because boys are interested in pretty girls—it becomes a habit that men never get over, even old men. Women look to size up the competition and *they* never get over it. Mom told us two things. She said to get used to it—like I just told you—and she said it's okay to glance, but staring is rude and shows either bad manners or a lack of confidence."

"There's a third thing," Tara said. "Mom said to start worrying when people stop looking."

"Momma and I never talked about these things much," Loren said. "We talked mostly about keeping the farm up and paying the bills. I was such a tomboy that girl-boy things hardly ever came up. By the time I was twelve, Momma was so weak that we spent most of our time together just enjoying each other and trying to keep our spirits up. I read to her a lot. I learned a lot from reading. Momma talked mostly about trying hard and doing well at everything I tried. She wanted me to be independent, and mostly told me not to trust men. She said that men were interested in sex, and not much else. We didn't talk about the staring thing. I've always been more boy than girl. I even *think* like a boy, Momma says—said." The girls had moved away from the cemetery tombstones and took a seat on a large stone bench. Meredith and Tara sat in quiet anticipation. Meredith took Loren's hand and held it in her lap. "I know you miss your mother a lot."

Loren clasped Meredith's hands with both of hers, "we were all we had. Now she's gone. I wanted to talk with her about boys, but never really got to it. When

I started getting my period—she told me that it would happen—I wanted to talk with her more than ever because things started to change. I started feeling different, sort of separate—apart. I didn't have anyone to talk with. Momma was—really sick. Mattie Hooks was so much older—I didn't have anyone. Oh, I'm sorry, Tara, I didn't mean to make you cry."

"That's okay, I was just thinking how lucky I—we—are to have Mother. I was thinking about how hard she tries to balance everything—work, responsibilities, and us. Sometimes we act pretty selfish." Tara looked at Meredith for agreement.

"We're going to have to try harder, Sis," Meredith said, nodding.

"Anyway, now I've got you two. I've got sisters," Loren said in a burst of energy as she stood smiling at her friends. "And I wouldn't give anything for you." People walking by stared and smiled at three pretty girls sitting next to each other in a close embrace—somewhere between laughter and tears.

"C'mon," Meredith said. "Let's go look at the college."

Salem College was the last item on the girls' list. A private four-year school sharing the grounds with Old Salem, it had come about as an outgrowth of the church's need to educate its youth beyond high school. The girls made a brief tour of the main building, a Grecian structure dating from the 1800s, and then headed for their car and the trip home. During the ride, Loren smiled to herself. *So this is what it's like.* She settled into satisfaction as she thought of being an object of attention.

 Boone provided ample culture shock, bringing them back to the reality of their world. They had supper at Pepper's, long a favored restaurant in the region, then went to Meredith's dorm room where Loren metamorphosed into Lorne.

Loren looked at herself in the full-length mirror in Meredith's bedroom just before beginning the transformation. She ran her hands over her skirt and then reached up and caressed her curly wig.

Loren mused; I can manage a farm, run a tractor, and run long distances. I can mend, build, create, and I can figure out almost anything. I'm smart, a strong boy and a pretty girl. I'm independent. I want it all, I want everything, and I'm going to get it. Thanks Momma.

In ten minutes Loren stood before the mirror dressed in jeans as she wiped away the make-up with cold cream. The overhead lights highlighted her lean muscles, and she looked at her healthy body with pleasure. Being a boy is good, but being a girl is wonderful. I know this can't last long, but I love it.

CHAPTER 18

Bryce and Loren got off the bus that Monday and headed toward the cluster of students. They joined in bantering and horseplay, as the boys talked and laughed over the latest buzz around campus and class. Loren stood and watched her friends, responding only when addressed. Shortly, she drifted away from the group and climbed the stairs leading into the building. When she reached the landing, she turned to survey the throng of laughing students. She stood, a lone figure, book pack on her shoulder. Frowning, she reflected, do I belong here at all? She leaned against a support pillar and reflected on her situation. It was one thing to be at home, busy, and focused on any of a number of tasks, but it was quite another to stand in the midst of this swirling humanity where she was more alone than when she was alone.

As Loren turned to go into the building ahead of what would soon be a chattering mob in motion, she saw Bryce, standing apart from the others, looking at her.

The bell rang just as a gray Taurus, unseen by Loren, slowly wheeled into the parking lot.

CHAPTER 19

"Tell me again—why Cross-country and Track and why not football?" Bryce asked.

"I can run—I'm a good runner. Back home I used to run long distances through the forest trails near our house. Five or six miles was an easy run for me—in hills. I'm leggy and lean, I can run. Besides, I'd like to get a couple of school letters. I've watched you guys play football, and now basketball. Track season is open, and Grandpa told me it was okay with him. I'm not a good sprinter but I believe I can do well at the mile," Loren said. *Just a little prevarication won't hurt anyone.*

"Well, I'm going out for baseball this spring. I got long arms, Coach says I should make a good pitcher."

"Going to be a three-letter man, huh, Bryce?"

"I'm going to catch for him," Gent said. "Somebody needs to make decisions for him. He can't be trusted to think for himself."

Turning to Council, Loren asked, "You for baseball, too, Council?"

"Nope, my daddy says I'm for farmin'. He needs the help and we need the money. He says that football and basketball are enough play for me for one year. I'd like to run track, but there's too much to do around a farm in the spring, so I'll just stand back and watch you good-for-nothins' wallow in your empty pastimes."

"Empty pastimes?" Gent laughed. "Council, are you going preacher on us?"

"No, I'm just quoting my gramps. He don't take much to school sports. He says school should be about book-learnin', not throwin' balls."

"He *don't?*" Well, so much for preaching." Gent snorted.

"Don't make fun of the way I talk. You're not such a good friend that I wouldn't clean your clock. Second thought, you being such a runt, it wouldn't be seemly. I could get Lorne to do it, though. He's closer to your size."

Loren used the reference to make a suggestion. "Council, why don't you go out for track too? There's not such a tight schedule of practice like the other sports, and you and I could practice together. You bein' long-legged and all, you ought to be a good runner."

"Well, Gramps and Daddy both say how they used to run the woods when they were young. At times they ran all the way to town, and didn't think nothin' of it."

"Talk to Coach Lee, he'll probably let you and me have a flexible training schedule. We both got chores, but I believe we can work our farms and run too. I'll be glad to help you with your farm work."

Council proved to be a formidable running partner; his legs were indeed long, and he ran with a quiet lope that ate up the miles. Someone with less resolve than Loren would have fallen by the wayside, but she grimly matched Council stride for stride, and could, in fact, push him to fatigue on steep uphill climbs. Loren found herself enjoying their long runs at the end of the day, feeling more refreshed than before the run. Her greatest pleasure was to complete a hard run with an uphill climb, then cool down by jogging or walking the downhill trail side by side with Council.

One of their favorite runs was up what Council called "The Cone" because he said it reminded him of an ice cream cone, with many trails curving to the top. It was nearly a three-mile climb, and taxed them heavily if they pushed each other too hard, and they usually did. Walking back and enjoying the softness of the forest was a treat they liked and openly shared. Council seemed to know every plant and critter on the mountain. He had names for some of the trees and rock formations. Loren became accustomed to Council stopping to admire a particular plant or animal. He often ran with a light pack in which he carried a long trowel he would use to retrieve plants for his mother's wildflower garden. He was particularly pleased when he found a small stand of deep red trillium that was a harbinger of spring, hence its name—Wake Robin.

"Ma will purely love these. She's long said she wanted some, but didn't know where to find any."

Loren was both pleased and saddened by Council's mother's joyful acceptance of the plant from the forest. Loren remembered the gifts that she had brought her mother from forest walks. The Wake Robin were placed in damp shade where the mountain woman knew they would thrive. Then she set out some biscuits, preserves, and buttermilk on the porch for "her boys." Always made to feel part of the family, Loren reveled in being one of the boys, and responded with the spraddle-legged sprawl that teenage boys used to signal their budding manhood to each other.

CHAPTER 20

Sugar interrupted his supervising of Loren's repair of an outbuilding to announce visitors with a soft *woof*, looking in the direction of the house.

"We got visitors, Sugar? Let's check them out—you be nice now." Loren took the dog's head in her hands and said firmly, "Sugar, be good."

It was Jo Mae and fellow cheerleader, Audrey Wingate. The late spring weather encouraged shorts and light shirts, showing off the girls' healthy, youthful lines.

"Hey, Lorne," Jo Mae piped, then added softly, "Hello, Sugar, come here." The dog bounded to his friend and received pats, rubs, and a gentle fluffing of his ears. Loren's female friends and schoolmates adored the gentle bulldog. He was pronounced 'Sugar Sweet' by the girls, a title that caused Grandpa Gragg to chuckle in amusement while shaking his head. If they only knew.

Jo Mae and Audrey made their way towards Loren, who stood, hammer in hand, watching the approach of the comely girls.

"Hey. You're just in time. I need someone to hold some lumber while I nail it in place."

"Sure," Jo Mae said, always eager to show her practical skill in all things, in defiance of being labeled 'just a girl.' Following Jo Mae's lead, Audrey jumped to the task, always making sure that she was between Loren and Jo Mae—always closer to Loren.

"You sure do know how to handle tools," Audrey said to Loren.

"Here, you drive the rest of the nails on this board," Loren said, handing the hammer to the willowy brunette. She handed her a nail. "Set the nail where you want it to go—right there is good—and tap it easy to get it started, that's right, now you can hit it a little harder, just a little. You got it. Now you can drive it home." Audrey missed the nail. "Try again." This time she struck a glancing blow and bent the nail some. "That's okay," Loren said. "Tap it straight and try again."

After several efforts, Audrey had some nails in place. She returned the hammer to Loren, saying, "You sure are a good teacher."

"You're a better pupil. I'd have bent a lot more nails my first time."

The girl blushed and shook long brown hair out of her eyes. "Thanks," she said, placing a hand on Loren's forearm. Jo Mae stood, out of line-of-sight, smiling a pleased-with-herself smirk.

The work went quickly. Afterward, Loren and the girls gathered the remnants and discarded them on a pile pointed out by Loren. She collected the tools and returned them to the tool shed she'd been repairing, securing the door.

The carpenters settled to Cokes and iced tea on the front porch. Sugar rested his head in the lap of an adoring Jo Mae.

"I sure would like to have a dog like this," she said, softly stroking.

"They's plenty of his puppies about. Everyone wants one of his kind, and they've practically started a local breed in the valley. But Sugar's personality comes more from Grandpa Gragg than anything else. He's a good man with people and critters. If you want, I'll ask around."

"We've got a couple of poodles," Audrey added, "and they're almost like family. They are so smart."

Audrey took a swallow of Coke and looked at Jo Mae who furrowed her brow and gave her friend a quick nod. "I—uh. I watched your last race. You were great. I don't know how you run so fast," Audrey said, coloring slightly.

"Thanks, but I'm not as good as Council. All I can do is follow him. He comes in first, and I place way back. He's the most effortless runner I've ever seen. I bet he could get a college scholarship right now."

Jo Mae added, "You two are out-running a lot of other runners—and Council is out-running everyone. No telling what you'll do when you get to be seniors."

"The way things are going, by the time we're seniors, all I'll see of Council is his dust trail. He can go ten miles without getting winded. It just about kills me to keep up."

"He is *so* cute. I love that black curly hair of his," Jo Mae said.

Loren, blushing, had to stop herself from saying "yes." She felt a sense of jealousy, which caused her to flush even more. This did not escape the notice of the girls, who giggled at what they thought was embarrassment. Loren gathered herself and responded, "he's a good guy, one of my best buds," then added to Jo Mae, "He says you're one of the nicest girls he knows. I think he likes you a lot." Now it was Jo Mae's turn to color.

After they drained their glasses and refused seconds—Loren had taken to keeping Cokes on hand for her friends—Jo Mae said, "We gotta go. There are other tool sheds that need fixing up."

As they pulled away from a waving Loren, Audrey squealed ecstatically, "He is so hot. Oh-My-God. I want him."

"See, I told you he was nice."

"Nice? I'm going to marry him. We're going to spend a life together—forever. I'm going to have his baby. OhMyGod."

"Okay, but right now we've got to get this car home before the folks know I've been driving it around the county without an adult on board."

"Who you calling not-an-adult, Gal?" Audrey lilted.

CHAPTER 21

Summer in Appalachia. The county seat of Watauga County lies in a valley over three thousand feet in altitude. What this means to the Flatlanders is that they can sleep summer nights under snug quilts, and open windows. Evening fireplaces hold a utilitarian charm for children and adult alike, creating a full-bodied sensual experience of sight, smell, and sounds. It seemed that all of South Florida had discovered the charms of "The High Country" and made it their summer home away from home.

"Progress," Fields Gragg said, lowering the *High Country News* to his lap. "I call it the whore's argument." Not waiting for a request for clarification from his friends around the pot-belly stove of Wilson's Store, he continued: "S'pose your sister came to you with the notion to take up the world's oldest profession. You tell her she's takin' a wrong path. She says 'But look at how much money I can make.' You point out that she'll be running in rough company. She says, 'I'll be able to buy all the new shoes and clothes I want.' You argue, 'You'll lose your friends and some family, you'll become a laughing stock of your community.' She comes back with 'I'll be able to live wheresomever I want, and I'll get new friends.'"

Fields shook his head, opened the stove door and poked the burning wood aggressively. "That's their whole argument. Put everything aside—make money. It's the thinkin' of whores and drug dealers."

"Grew up here, man and boy," Fields said. "It was a fine place in the forties and fifties. I'd walk downtown Boone and I knew most every soul. Knew every car and truck. I miss that. It was a warm time in my heart. Our children came up here. They lived for Saturdays and would go into every store on King Street—knew every shopkeeper by name, and was knowed by 'em. Look at it now—when we go to town we don't know a soul." The assemblage nodded and grunted in agreement.

At home Fields made the same complaint, and Loren came to accept the way he felt, but she was caught up in being young, strong and filled with love of the social and natural world around her. That summer, she took long runs that carried her over mountain ridges and through rural valleys. It was nothing for her to run to town and back, a round trip of fifteen miles. She was struck with the ease of her runs. Fields called her a leggy colt, but in his mind thought of her as a filly.

In reward for good grades at the end of the school year, Fields gave Loren a gift certificate to the Boone Bike and Touring Shop, and an iPod. "If you're so bound to be mobile, you maught's well have good transportation and communication." Fields handed her a road safety pamphlet, saying. "Don't need to say be careful; you got more sense than most grown-ups I know—and every youngster. But, you get in trouble, call home."

The old gentleman didn't know how good call home sounded to his adopted "grandchild."

Loren's eyes widened when she saw the amount on the gift certificate. "I—I don't know what to say, Grandpa." They'd both grown fond of the grandpa-grandchild pretense.

"Just say thank you, and be on your way, child." It was a lesson in grace that Loren learned from Fields, and would ever carry with her. *Just say thank you.*

"Thank you, Grandpa." she said giving him a hug, and a light kiss on his cheek.

"You've been a boon to my old age. It's I that owes you. Let's go to town together one last time."

"One last time?" What does that mean?"

"I've raised two children, and watched dozens come up. Soon's they get transport, they're strangers to their family until they marry. I remember many empty places at the supper table."

"Well, I'm not that way, Grandpa. You're my best friend, and I not going to turn my back on you."

"Child, you got friends, and you got places to go, and now you got a way to go. Don't pass up your due to please an old man. It's hard enough on you pretending to be a boy—don't add to the strain."

Loren didn't answer this out loud, but made a vow to herself. "Let's go to Boone and do our shopping. You can help me pick out a bike."

That afternoon, Loren and Fields sat on "their" bench near Boone Drug on King Street. The sidewalk was crowded with well-fed tourists in tight shorts, college students studiously ignoring everyone around them, and the youths who spread out on the wide brick and concrete bench that bordered a parking lot on King Street. On pleasant days the bench was so crowded that some of the youths sprawled on the sidewalk. "Wonder why those young folks can't lay out in private," Fields said. "Seems they need to have folks see how much they don't want to be a part of things. 'Used to see that same thing in bars when I was soldjerin'. Every bar had one or two men who'd sit off by themselves, drinkin', smokin'—wantin' to be alone. Always wondered why they just didn't go buy a bottle and set out som'ers. That way they could drink and smoke in complete privacy, and it'd cost them a lot less; bar drinking is expensive. But, 'seems advertisement is the game." Fields sat, rocked, and gazed, then added, "Folks got too much time on their hands—a job would do'm good."

Loren looked and listened. She wasn't accustomed to people deliberately sprawled in sidewalk grime, and was confused about why they did it. The same people seemed to occupy the same places every Saturday. Fields mirrored some of her mother's attitudes. Her mother, had little tolerance for what she called the crime of sloth, and laid much of the world's ills to it.

Loren lived so much in fear of falling into the sin of sloth that Fields had to remind her from time to time that she was young and as such, should take time to enjoy herself. He so frequently expressed this frustration—"That boy don't know

76

rest, he's wearin' me down"—to his friends at Wilson's Store that they began to develop an uncommon respect for "that grandboy of Fields."

An unfortunate aspect of that fame was the good-natured ribbing Loren received at the hands of youths living nearby. It seems that their parents and grandparents would frequently hold "Field Gragg's grandson" up as example for them to consider.

"If I have to keep hearing Gramps go on about what a fine young man you are, I'm going to barf," Bryce said to Loren one day in the back of the bus on the way to school. "I made the mistake of not cleaning my room this week, and was told how you do everything to perfection. I'm about to lose my lunch. If you weren't such a friend, I'd purely hate you."

Loren grinned, "I'll save you, and try to be more of a slob. Maybe if I didn't bathe for a week, and wore the same clothes for three days, people would see me more like you."

"You sure you're a *boy*? I mean, I know some *girls* that act like you—but I don't know any boys."

Loren, stricken by the question, reddened and sat quietly with her lips pursed.

"Hey, hey, I was just kidding," Bryce said, seeing his friend's distress, which he mistook for anger. "You're a better man than most I know—'cept me, of course." He added smiling.

"Which reminds me," Bryce continued. "How about the team this year? We're short *numbers* and could use someone who can run like you. You're quick."

"If I go out for anything this fall, it'll be soccer," Loren said. "And I doubt I'll even do that. I like cross-country."

"Cross-country. There you go again. Hell, that's a wussy sport. C'mon. Football's a real man's game. Anyway, we really need a kicker, and you got that leg. Man, I've never seen anyone who can kick a football like you. I mean, between the uprights every time."

"I don't have much range."

"True, but we don't do much long field-goal kicking, and in you're range, you never miss—never. The team could really use you."

"You've got a kicker."

"Ollie? He's a lazy butter-butt. He's okay as a guard, but won't practice his kicking enough to be any good at it. We need you."

As they stepped down off the bus, Loren right behind, Bryce almost ran into Aldrich Herms who was standing in conversation with an assistant principal. She walked by the two men but had to stop because of a knot of students that had gathered before moving off.

"I believe she might be in the part of the county that's serviced by this bus and the one that comes right after it." She heard Herms say to the assistant principal. Loren walked around the group of students that was blocking her way. She didn't look back.

Later that day, Loren spied Herms in the office of the female coaches. He was holding out a photograph for them to see.

CHAPTER 22

In the summer before her sophomore year, Meredith re-claimed her old apartment. She said it was like coming home. She had Loren and Tara in for a housewarming and, as it turned out, style show.

"You look so *good* in that dress; I love that color on you." Tara exclaimed.

"Thanks. Meredith made me get it; I'd never have known to choose this one." Loren replied. "I don't have the sense that you two have about clothes, and I probably never will. I think I'm losing the clothing gene; all I ever wear is jeans and tees. I'm so used to pretending to be a boy that I'm starting to check out the girls as they pass by. Something else—I've never had my hair styled. I wouldn't even know what to ask for."

Meredith and Tara cut glances at each other, and then turned back to Loren. Meredith said, "You're lucky. Hair care can be a pain in the butt. You'll have plenty of time to catch up when you don't have to worry about the foster care people."

"Maybe," Loren said. "But right now I'm missing being a girl. I've never had a date, and everybody around me is pairing off. All the boys have girlfriends. All the girls have boyfriends. All I've got is buddies. The way things are, I'm not going to have any love life all during high school. That's just wrong, and it's wearin' on me." Loren walked over to Meredith's closet and held out a hanger on which hung some scruffy men's clothing. "Meredith, you've got Lance," she said, waving the clothing, "and Tara seems to have a new boyfriend every week. Me, all I've got are Grandpa and Sugar."

Meredith snorted in amusement. "Believe me, Sugar is a lot more desirable than most of the boys—they want to be called men—that I know. I told Lance to come get his clothes about two weeks ago, but he just won't let go. He's got to be in charge. Lance has got to have everything Lance's way. I can't believe that, in a campus with over five thousand males, I fell for such a jerk. Mother was right. Damn, it hurts to admit that."

"Your mother didn't care for Lance?" Loren asked.

"Didn't care for? She practically threw him out of the house the one time I brought him to visit."

"What didn't she like?"

"Well, it wasn't the dreadlocks, or the shabby chic clothes—although she did say later that it looked silly as hell to see someone driving a BMW sports car and dressing like a bum."

"What was it, then?"

"She said it was his manner. She said Lance was a typical narcissistic spoiled kid, just like the dozens she'd sentenced in court for traffic violations and for drinking and drugs. Lance does drive crazy, and drugs are what did it for Lance and me.

He does cocaine—he thinks it's smart. I've got no use for a doper. Relationships are hard enough as it is, but throw in drugs…"

Tara chimed in, "I thought he was kinda cute."

"Cute. That was probably his major problem. His whole family thought that being cute—and bright—is all that you need to make it. Lance has gotten by on looks and charm all his life. He is smart as hell, but he's lazy and undisciplined. To hell with him—and all the rest like him. They think they're doing girls a favor by dating them. What a prick."

Loren stood in open-mouthed astonishment. "I've never heard you talk like this. I'm sorry you got burned by this guy."

"Well, I did. I thought he was Mr. Right. A good guy. All he wanted was to get in my pants, and he was skilled at making the right moves. Why is it that jerks are so smart about things like that? Mom warned us. She's given us chapter and verse many times on how those creeps operate, and I fell for the first one that came along." Meredith turned to the picture window, and Loren knew it was because she didn't want them to see her face. Loren and Tara both went to Meredith and gathered her close and put their arms around her. Tara pulled the curtains shut, and they stood like three sisters, swaying and weeping together. Loren buried her face in Meredith's thick brown hair and felt her cheek wetted with warm tears.

"I—I feel like such an idiot," Meredith said. "After all the lectures and advice over the supper table…"

"Sis, you've learned. You got hurt and you learned from it."

Meredith turned to Loren. "I don't know what I'd have done without Tara— and now you. She listens better than anyone I know. We tease and squabble, but we truly love and look out for each other." Meredith gave Tara a hug.

"Me too, Sis," Tara answered.

Loren stepped back from her friends. "What did you learn?"

Meredith cocked her head and frowned over the question. "I learned that I want to become a lawyer, and eventually a judge—like Mom."

Loren was startled by Meredith's response. "How did you come by that?"

"Well, I remembered how long and hard Mom lectured to us on the ways of men, so I asked if I could come to court on days she had to deal with the kind of people she had warned us about. I'd never really had any interest in The Law before, but as I sat in court and watched the trials unfold I got fascinated with its workings. Everything would come to a head when Mom and I got together later and discuss the proceedings. I began to see the importance of law—and of order. I had always loved and admired Mom, but watching her in court made me so proud—I want to be like that some day."

"Sis, you never told me that," Tara almost shouted. "I'm surprised—and pleased."

"Your Mom and I have our differences, but I realize that she was doin' what she thought was best for me. Fields Gragg made me see that more than its comin' to me on its own. I think he really likes your Mom from what I've told him."

Meredith chuckled. "I can tell you now—from what I know of Mom and of Mr. Gragg—if there weren't such a big age difference, he could fill a really big hole in her life. If ever there was a perfect match…"

Loren and Tara burst out laughing at the pleasurable thought of Edythe Tilson and a younger Fields Gragg pairing off.

The following Sunday the three girls stretched out on piled up sofa cushions, surrounded by books and the debris of munchy snacking. Sunday afternoon get-togethers had become a near-tradition with the girls. Meredith would drive home Sunday mornings in time to attend church with her mother and sister. They would have lunch together—then the sisters would return to Boone to prepare for the next week's class work in their respective school. It was a system that worked especially well because Loren was there to make sure that the girls really did study. Meredith would drive Tara home late Sunday evening and spend the night, much to her mother's approval. Her daughters were doing well academically, and Judge Tilson was pleased that Meredith had apparently taken such an interest in her younger sister.

It was a week since Meredith's outburst over Lance, and the girls were settled in for a good four hours of study time when there was a firm knock at the door. The peephole revealed that it was Lance.

Tara and Loren were dispatched to the bedroom with instructions to leave the door ajar so they could overhear. Meredith opened the front door.

"Hello, Lance. Come for your stuff?"

"No. Well, yeah. But, mostly I just thought I'd drop by to see how you were doing. I mean, I was driving by and I thought I'd drop in to see you. To say hi."

"Well, hi. I've put your stuff in a trash bag. It's folded neat, though."

"I thought maybe we could spend some time together. You know, maybe go for a ride or something. I got the car back from the body shop yesterday and thought I'd take it for a trial run—sort of to see if they've done the job right. Thought you might want to go along. The job looks okay, but you never know—everybody's always out to do somebody else out of their money. Damn thing cost over eight thousand."

"What'd your daddy say about that?"

"He didn't say nothing. Never does. He just shakes his head and pays the bills."

"How are you going to pay him back? I mean, this is your third wreck, seems like he'd be a little put out."

"Well, the other two were sorta minor. They didn't cost more than a couple thousand each. I don't need to pay him back—he's my dad. He's doing what he's supposed to do; pay the bills."

"Does that seem fair to you?"

"Fair? Hell, fair. I'm his son. He raised me, I didn't ask to be here. I figure, being a lawyer and all, he'd know what he's getting into, raising a son and all. He's not stupid."

"You sure about that?"

"Hell, yes. He's the smartest man I know, and there's plenty of people in Miami who'll agree with me—he's got a lot of their money." Lance paused, looked around. "I've seen him pay more for a weekend fishing trip than this last wreck cost, and he

80

writes it off because he's entertaining clients. I saw one of the clients he was entertaining one time. She could entertain me anytime she wanted."

Meredith heard what sounded like a low growl coming from the bedroom. Luckily, it escaped Lance's notice.

"Well, how about it? I don't have all day—are you ready to go?"

"No. I'm not going with you. Not now, and not ever again. Here's your stuff." Meredith handed the black plastic bag to the boy, and started to close the door.

"Wait a second. I know we've had our differences, but you don't need to be such a bitch about it." He placed the bag in the doorway to block the door from closing. "I mean, we've had our share of fun. A few drinks, some laughs, a couple games and dances."

"Yeah, you got me drunk, and then tried to take advantage of me."

"Take advantage? Hell, you wanted it and you know it."

"Wanted it? What's that *it* you're talking about. Rape? Is that the *it* that you think girls want? I didn't want to be raped, and that's what you were going for, wasn't it? Count yourself lucky that you couldn't pull it off. If you hadn't had so much to drink that night you'd be in jail right now. Now move your bag so I can close the door."

"I thought we were friends, Mere. I thought we had something special. Guess I was wrong. I don't see anything wrong with a little affection. I spend a lot of time and money with you, hoping to prove I cared. I thought you might show you cared for me."

"Oh, I see. Payback—wait right here." Meredith went to her purse and returned with a fifty dollar bill. "Here. Here's your payback." She stuffed the bill into his shirt pocket. "It's probably a lot more than you spent on me or any other girl. Now take your attitude and bag of rags, and get out of my face—get out." Meredith shoved the boy and kicked his bag out of the door, then slammed it.

Meredith turned away from the door just in time to get a huge hug from Tara. "Wow! Way to go, Sis. You really put that sleaze-ball in his place. Darn, I'm proud of you. I'm going to be just like you when I'm in college. Are you going to tell Mom?"

"Are you crazy? After all those long talks and lectures we've endured since we were little girls, do you think for a minute that I would tell her that I totally ignored her advice the first chance I had? No way. Later maybe, but not now." Loren stood in the bedroom doorway. She had an amused but quizzical expression.

"Loren, you look like you're not sure I handled it right. Didn't I?"

"It's not for me to say, but I think he got what he deserved. I think if a few more girls treated him that way it might change things. But the situation you found yourself in could be seen two ways."

The sisters looked at Loren in amazement. Tara broke the silence. "That's crazy. The guy's a jerk."

Meredith was obviously angry. "If it had been your skirt his hand was groping under, I don't think you'd feel that way."

"You're probably right. I'd likely want to kill him." She paused, took a breath, then added. "But then I wouldn't have been drunk, either." The instant it came out, she regretted it.

81

After a long pause in which Meredith's face turned bright red, she said, "Get out. Pick up your belongings and get out."

"Meredith, I…"

"Get out. Get out! I don't ever want to see you again." Meredith was breathing heavily. "After all we've done for you, then you turn right around and put a knife in my back."

"That's not the way…"

"I've been your friend…"

"You guys are my best friends. I love you like sisters."

"You sure have a strange way of showing it—Sis. Please just leave."

Tara took her sister's hand. "Mere, don't do this. Loren is our friend. I don't want her to leave—I love her almost as much as I love you, and I know she loves us."

"I wasn't judging you, Meredith. I was just stating a fact. I don't drink. Someday I might, but right now I don't. I've got nothing against it, except that if you do it too much it's probably unhealthy. I wasn't judging you—I love you. I can't judge people I love."

Meredith's face color lightened and her breathing became gentle. "Well, tell me then—how can you feel sorry for such a creep?"

"Easy. Look at what he's like now. Then ask yourself, what kind of life do you think he's going to have? All I see in him is failure, disappointment, divorce, al-coholism and drug abuse. I see him in thirty years, a fat old man who has gone through his father's money, a couple of wives, and no real friends. Right now, he's young and full of life, but as his failures mount it's going to be a different story. I don't feel any joy in that. In fact I think we ought to pray for his loss."

"I didn't think you went to church," Meredith said.

"I don't, but you, your mom, and Tara do. Next Sunday when you're in church—you should pray for his lost soul. And while you're at it you might ask what could be done."

Meredith slid, back against the door, to the carpet. Her face turned deep red and she pursed her lips as her body convulsed with stifled sobs. Tara fell to her knees beside her sister saying, "Sis, I…" Meredith shook her head against what Tara was saying.

After a time Meredith said, "I'm sorry. I didn't mean to be such a bitch. You're right, of course. I sort of set myself up by drinking too much—something I'll never let happen again. I did like him, and I did want him for a friend, maybe even a lover eventually. I was already starting to plan things like the kind of house we would have, how many children… I guess the disappointment was the worst thing. It's just not fair. Life should be simpler than it is."

Loren joined her friends on the floor.

"You're also right about the prayer thing. I'll pray for his lost soul, and I'll pray for answers. But tell me this—how did you get so smart in so few years?"

Loren smiled. "I don't think I'm smart, but I *am* a good listener. My momma and I only had each other. I remember it like it was yesterday, the time she told me—A body's a carefree teenager for about six years—but an adult for sixty. Do the numbers. So, I don't think I'm smart at all. I just paid attention—and watched other people."

"Mom does the same thing with us. The only difference is that you listened."

Later that night, as the three girls left the dorm to take Loren home, they failed to notice the small red BMW parked in the shadows. As they pulled out of the parking lot, the BMW's engine came to life and it pulled out onto the street before turning on its lights. The girls were unaware of the red sports car following them a block back. In the dim evening light the car stopped a good distance away when Meredith pulled into Loren's driveway. It turned around and sped away unlighted as Meredith backed out of the driveway.

Bitch. She had her boyfriend hiding in her bedroom all the time. I'll bet he'd just finished doing her when I came to the door. Self-righteous, holier than thou tease.

Lance punished the BMW through the gears as he raced through the dark, the speedometer showed seventy, eighty, ninety as tree trunks and roadside shrubbery raced by in a gray-green blur.

I'll show her. When I can catch that candy-ass wimp with her I'll show him a thing or two about what a real man's like. That'll show her. No one talks to The Lanster like that. No one.

CHAPTER 23

The following morning, Bryce picked up Loren in his dad's pick-up. He had no reason to notice the little red car parked well up a side road, in sight of, Loren's cabin. It fell in behind them and kept about a quarter mile back all the way to town. Lance had to run two stop lights in town in order to keep them in sight. He parked near them in the school parking lot. It was obvious that he'd been jilted for a high school student. He followed the two friends to their group and was close enough to hear names being tossed along with the usual Monday morning jibes. He collared a student passing by and was able to learn Loren's name.

We'll see, Lorne Land. We'll see how bad a dude you are. On the way to his car he passed by Bryce's truck. He stooped and drove his pocketknife into a tire, then rose and walked away smiling in satisfaction. Looking back over his shoulder, he determined that he was unseen. He failed to see Gentry, who was late as usual.

Gent's attention was piqued by the body language of the stranger in the parking lot. At first he thought that the tall stranger had dropped something and stooped to retrieve it, but something didn't sit well with the man's movements. By the time Gent got to the row of cars where Bryce was parked, Lance had backed out and was moving away from his parking slot. He would have gotten away undetected had he gone in the right direction. As it was he had to move down one row and turn back to pass by the front of Bryce's truck just as Gent was reaching the rear of the truck. Gent saw Lance's profile and noted the make and model of the speeding car. The vanity plate read: BAAAD. He didn't notice Bryce's flat tire until he got to the next row and turned to look back. He watched as the red BMW left the parking lot and sped away. Gent returned to Bryce's truck and saw the slashed tire. He walked quickly to his friends who were waiting for the bell.

"Musta been a jealous husband," Ollie said over his school lunch tray.

"Naw, I think it was Bryce's gay lover, mad about all the attention he gets from the young boys on campus," Council said.

"Laugh, you jerks, but I've got a new tire to buy and I don't see any help coming from you."

Council slid a dollar bill across the table. A smiling Loren matched it. By the time lunch was finished, over ten dollars lay on the table. Bryce rose and turned, meaning to leave the money where it lay. Loren retrieved the cash, nodding to those at the table indicating that the money would go where it was intended.

Later that week, a smug Lance Van Riper rolled into the parking lot, keenly aware of coed stares and smiles. Leaving his top down, he peeled out of his car, gathered his books and headed to a morning lecture where he planned to catch up on lost sleep. He walked erect, chin held high, and hidden behind sunglasses. He appeared to have not the slightest regard for those passing by. Dripping cool.

Shortly after Lance left his car, a battered pick-up pulled up alongside the sleek convertible. There were two boys up front and two boys in the bed of the truck. All four were wearing large sunglasses and cowboy hats. A rag hung over the license plate. As soon as the truck stopped, the two boys in the bed jumped out, retrieved two large buckets of what the campus police would later identify as "barnyard mud," and dumped the contents of the buckets into the open convertible. They leapt back into the truck bed and were gone. It all took less than ten seconds. The dark ooze soaked into the buttery leather of the classy car, and then the sun had the rest of the day to bake it dry.

CHAPTER 24

On the first day of school as a sophomore, Loren was looking forward to meeting with her friends in the lunch room. "Where'd the summer go?" She said. "It seems like just a week ago we were having lunch together on the last day of classes"

"My pa kept me busy farmin' this summer," Ollie said. I got sores on my butt from our tractor. I call 'em Deere dents. We did good with cabbage and beans and taters, but, I'm here to tell you, I'm not goin' to go into farmin' when I get out of school."

Gent held up his hands saying, "These hands have seen more suds than my mom's clothes washer has seen the past ten years. I had a job at the car wash. I can't tell you how happy I'll be to get knocked down in a football uniform. Any change from the car wash is welcome."

Council leaned back in his chair, raised his hands over his head and stretched to the ceiling before tipping forward to his friends saying, "Sorry about the dish pan hands, Gent, and I'm sure there are plenty of linemen who'll be glad to help you get your jersey dirty. It's going to be a great year for us. Practically the entire varsity from last year has graduated—meaning that we are the varsity." This was followed by a chorus of affirmative comment.

Teenage warriors around the country suited up and buckled down. One-hundred-and-fifty-pound boys slammed themselves into believing they were men. Grown men with whistles and the deep voices that go with long vocal cords shouted order into the disarray of bodies as the sweat and sand of the gridiron was ground into memories that would last a lifetime. Autumn nights found old men, reflecting into the darkness on the feel, the sound, and even the taste of team play. Seventy-year-old men, in passing, would flicker the memory of teammates as one of their last conscious acts.

A short distance from the practice field, tossed pony tails and bouncing shorts of practicing cheerleaders ignited the fantasies of the gladiators who risked wistful glances between shouted instructions. Friday's brights beckoned the faithful to pigskin warfare.

First regular season game—Avery High lost by a single point to the "Mighty Efts." Then Wilkes High was another cliff-hanger victory. As the season passed, High Country High, better known as High-High, established itself as a defensive powerhouse. Its front line became known as the High Wall. The Efts' defensive backfield frustrated the plans of visiting coaches at every turn. Ashe County lost by a point. It was nearly impossible to score on High Country High, and almost as impossible for High-High to score. All of the offensive backfield had graduated the previous year, leaving the scoring responsibilities in the hands of sophomores. Their wins were by the barest margins.

Quickness, and doing the unexpected, would carry the Efts down to the red zone, but once inside the twenty, they stalled. The red zone was so named for good reason. It was where teams were bloodied, where masculine brute force rose against the wishes of opposing teams. Testosterone ruled. It was where the hearts of mothers stopped as they watched their children slammed to the dirt, and it was where the knee ligaments of Ollie Miles, strong guard, and the team's only kicker, were torn just enough to keep him out "for most of the rest of the season."

High Country suffered the loss of Ollie Miles in the next game. Two touchdowns and they could not make the extra point. The first TD they tried making the point by running. Five yards short. The next time they tried passing. The ball was in Council's steady hands, but slapped away almost immediately by a linebacker. 13-12, Spruce Pine.

The following Tuesday, team members and friends gathered around the lunchroom table to complain and eat the cafeteria offerings, sporting bandages and bruises aplenty.

"Lorne, we need you. The team needs you, and the school needs you," Gent said in a quiet voice, ever the picture of rational calm.

Bryce and Council nodded in agreement. "We need that leg of yours," Bryce said. "You've got to come out for the team now. We don't have a kicker, and you have that leg." He was almost pleading.

Council, nodded. "We need you, Lorne. Ollie wasn't a great kicker, but he generally got the job done—generally." Council shot Ollie an apologetic shrug.

It was Gent who pushed Loren near the edge. "Look, we're your friends. We like you a lot, and we respect your choice. But the simple fact is—you have something we want and need. Are you willing to give it? We'll accept your decision, 'cause you're our friend and good buddy. But I don't know how the rest of the school will feel. Everybody knows you're a good kicker—you've got that great soccer leg—and everybody expects you to step up to the plate. I've already had trouble avoiding two fights defending you. I don't want to force you to do something you don't want to do, but know this; your decision will pretty much determine whether we have a winning or losing season."

By this time, most of the football team had gathered around the table where Loren sat with her friends. Jo Mae and another cheerleader were in the crowd.

Loren leaned away from her food tray. "Look, here's my problem. I was raised in a strict religious family. We were modest about showing our bodies, and I'm uncomfortable with havin' to dress and undress in front of other people, and I don't want to see other people without clothes. Call it old fashioned if you want, but that's the way I am."

The group sat in silence.

"That's beyond silly, that's just dumb," Ollie blurted.

"No, it's not silly. It's what I believe. You believe what you want, and I'll believe what I want. But we can't tell each other what to believe. So don't call me *dumb*. I can't go out for the team because of the locker room."

"We can handle that at least a couple of ways." The group turned to look at Coach Call Helder, now head coach, who had come up carrying his tray. "Lorne, you can use the girls' locker room, or we can put up a partition in the boys' locker."

Coach Helder moved to sit at the table. The boys made room. "The fact is we need you, Lorne, and I want to encourage you to join the team. It's true that you might make the difference between a winning or losing season. I'm sorry to lay that much responsibility on your shoulders, but you probably know that I wouldn't say it if it wasn't so. Oh, I just thought of a third way we could handle the problem. You could suit up at home, except for your shoes and shoulder pads. When you get to the field you can put on the cleats and shoulder pads. What do you say?"

"Coach, I need two things before I join the team. I've got to have my grandpa's say-so, and I've got to make sure that the team doesn't resent my asking for special treatment. I hate asking for it—that's what it is—special treatment. I even hate the words, but I can't think of any other way." Loren's red face over the lie was mistaken for embarrassment, an error of judgment that served her well.

"Fair enough, you talk with your grandpa, and I'll talk with the team."

"I'll talk with Grandpa this evening. I'm not sure he'll favor my being on the football team." The class bell clanged the meeting to a close. As the group returned to their respective classes, Loren over-heard snippets of talk that let her know that her opinion of special treatment was shared.

"You beat all, girl. You want me to allow you—as your guardian—to let you get out on the football field and get killed by a bunch of wild notion teenage boys? You think I got tree moss for brains?" Sugar sat at Fields' feet watching their conversation as he always did. When Fields spoke, Sugar looked at him, when Loren spoke, the dog looked at her. They had frequently laughed at how the dog seemed to follow their conversation—in form and content. This time however, as Loren answered, Sugar's gaze remained on Fields. He rarely heard that tone of voice from the man.

"They need me."

"Hogwash! They want you—and they want to think they need you." The old man rocked in short quick cycles rather than the leisurely pace he normally used.

"You're wearin' out your daddy's rocker," Loren said evenly.

"If'n it goes, it's gone. I'll make me another. It ain't rocket surgery."

Loren smiled at the deliberately mixed metaphor.

"Well, rocket surgery or no, it's not worth getting so het up about."

The rocker slowed. "Don't tell me how I should feel, Gal. Fact is, I come to care for you like you was my own, and I won't see you busted up for no reason 'cept satisfyin' them who'd forget your name by year end if you's to get hurt."

"That ain't so. Those are…"

"Ain't! Ain't? Don't ain't me. What are you some kind of hilly billy hick?"

"You dang right—and proud to be what I am."

"Well don't say ain't. It ain't becoming."

"Dang it. You just…"

"I'm old. I can talk howsomever I please. You're young and just getting' habits. Get good ones." He paused while Sugar fixated on him. "And there you go—cussin' me now."

"No I wasn't." Loren choked as tears welled. "I just—it's just." She caught her breath. A deep breath. She said softly. "I'm not used to being told what to do."

"Well, child. I love you, and I'll say this. Get used to it. We all have to. Learn to deal with it with grace. When you love, you're entitled."

'Love' brought Loren up short. No one save her Momma and Mattie had ever used those words with her. No man had ever used those words with Loren. She felt her heart pound and her breath began to come short. Sugar rose and placed his head in her lap, and Loren's slender frame shook as she began to weep. Her tears fell on Sugar's forehead as she leaned forward over her canine friend. Loren, gazing through blurred tears at the green field between the roadway in front of the house and the river below, felt a movement at her elbow. Fields had come to stand beside her. His slender hand held a large slim volume. He propped the book open in her lap and returned to his chair. He had gone into the house and returned with characteristic panther quiet that let him go and come with no notice.

Loren wiped her eyes and picked up the book. Scanning the pages of the old high school annual her eyes lit on a skinny boy dressed in football pads and helmet, standing relaxed while holding a football against his right thigh. Below the picture she read, "Fields Gragg junior, quarterback. Team captain. All-state."

"You were handsome."

"Still am, some say."

"And humble."

"Coach said I was a sure thing for another all-state."

"Sounds like it didn't happen."

"It didn't."

"What happened?"

"A ten stone line backer name of Nelson Brave. He broke my leg. It was the third game of the season."

"That ended your football career?"

"Not just my football career, it ended my place in school, and it ended a college scholarship. I thought the students liked me because they liked me. I found out it was my passing arm and my running legs they liked. I could put the ball where I wanted—and no one could catch me in the open field; Nelson Brave hit me after the whistle. They said you could hear my leg break, even in the stands. I was in the hospital for a week. Except for the coach, my favorite teacher, Miss Beverly, and some of the team, nobody came to ask after me." Fields rocked and reflected before continuing. "Ceptin also Nelson Brave who came to visit me twice in the hospital and once here at home." He pointed to the house that Loren was renting. "So, don't tell me how much the team needs you when all it is's they want you."

Loren placed her hand over that of her Grandpa.

"That ain't all," Fields said. "That college scholarship was goin to make me an engineer—something I really wanted. It didn't happen. I lost my running legs and I lost the scholarship. There was no money for me to go to college. I wound up bein' this hilly billy hick you see here."

Loren reflected on the back and side walls of Fields' study. Door to door, floor to wall books. Not just books—Literature. Science. Philosophy. Grandpa Fields was a man of letters.

Later that evening, Loren was at her desk when she heard a car pull up in the driveway. It was Bryce, Gent, Council, and Jo Mae who jumped out and dropped to a crouch next to Sugar, assuring him that they were friends. Sugar knew Council and Bryce, but he wasn't sure about Gent—who reciprocated the apprehension.

"Sugar, come here," Loren called.

Once the group was settled on the porch, Sugar settled next to Gent, who was unsure as to whether he was being accepted or guarded. He placed a tentative hand on the dog's shoulders and was rewarded with a quick lick.

"I think he's accepted you." Loren said.

"You sure he's not just sampling me?"

"Just tell him that's your passing arm, and you seriously need it," Council said through a broad smile.

"I'd offer Cokes but I don't keep such around. I do have some good cold spring water if anybody wants a drink."

"Thanks," Bryce answered, "But we just came from Burger King."

"Yeah," Gent added. "We remembered your monk-like ways and decided to camel up before we came out here to the deep woods."

"Grandpa took a crusty-dish apple pie out of the oven about an hour ago. It's probably still warm. Anybody want a slice? Anybody except Gent that is."

"I withdraw my previous observation and offer sincere apologies." Gent offered in mock contrition.

Council shook his head, smiling. "Listen to him. He sounds like a blamed lawyer. I don't know why I keep him on as a friend. I guess it's just sympathy."

"Yeah, that and the fact that I put the ball exactly in your shaky hands so well that not even you would drop it."

"What are you saying? It's my long arms and legs that make you look good. There's no telling where the ball's going to go when you start flailing away in the backfield."

After the banter and chunks of warm, fragrant pie the teens settled with glasses of cool water or milk.

"We've got a reason for coming over this evening." Jo Mae said, while feeding the last of her pie crust to Sugar. She patted the dog's head into her lap then continued. "We put you in a bad place what with trying to get you to join the team."

"That's what Grandpa said this evening."

The group sat in silence for a time before Bryce spoke. "We wanted you to know that you're our friend, and, no matter what, you're going to stay our friend."

"Fact is," Council added, "We need you, but we don't want you to do nothing you're against."

Gent added. "We've talked it up with the team, and they want you to do what you want to do. If you join up we want you to be okay with it. As far as I'm concerned—and I think we all feel this way—your friendship is more important that your being on the team." Gent paused, then added with a grin. "We even managed to bring Ollie around."

The silence grew heavy with the sound of the last of the summer insects singing into the dark.

"Well," Council stood, "I said what I came to say." This brought the group to its feet.

"Yeah, we best be going," Bryce said. "Sleep on it, Lorne. Let us know what you decide tomorrow."

"No. I'll let you know now. Grandpa's not much in favor of my joining the team. We talked about it this evening. While he's not in favor, he says he'll accept my decision, and Grandpa doesn't say a thing unless he means it. When I tell him what you-all have said this evening he'll understand why I've decided to join the team." The relief of the group was immediate and palpable. "But, before you leave, I want to show you something and to explain why Grandpa feels the way he does." Loren went into the house and returned with Fields' high school annual.

Chapter 25

"That helmet and those shoulder pads make you look like a louse under a collar," Fields said, laughing out loud.

"C'mon Grandpa. I need your help, not your ridicule. I already feel awkward and clumsy in this get-up. Add the cleats, the pads, and the rest of the gear, and I feel like some kind of robot. I don't know why I have to wear all this paraphernalia; all I'm going to do is kick the ball. Even if we score four times I doubt if I'll be on the field more than one minute total."

Fields' voice and demeanor changed. "It takes one second to get crippled for life. Wear the gear and don't raise a fuss; all it will take is one hit to help you appreciate it." Fields went over Loren's equipment with his hands, checking for looseness and fit. He ended by slapping his hands down on her shoulder pads. "How does it feel now? Is it comfortable enough to wear for the next three hours?"

"It's okay, but I'm going to take off these shoulder pads until just before the game. I'm going to meet with the team in the locker room. Everyone will be suited up and ready to go, Then I'll put the shoulder pads back on and Coach will check me out. So, I'll carry the shoulder pads until then, and I'll keep them on until the game is over. Will you drive me home after the game?"

"Ain't you going to the dance after?"

"No. If I went, I'd wind up having to dance with Jo Mae or some of the other cheerleaders, while the only people I'd care to dance with are Bryce or Council, and I don't think that would go over very well."

"You've laid a tough row to hoe with this charade of your'n. Is it worth it?" Fields' lean face softened, and he reached out to place a gentle touch on Loren's cheek. "You got to know, Gal—I care for you like you was one of mine. Our children were good people, and strong, but you do beat all. If you was my daughter I couldn't ask for you to be more than you are."

Loren stood speechless in the face of a torrent of emotions—coming from Fields. Her eyes welled, and she gathered into an embrace of the man who was dearest in her life. She had hoped to hide her tears, but, standing in his arms with her head on his chest, she began to sob—at first softly, finally uncontrollably. The old man said nothing, being content to stand, holding the weeping girl with shoulder pads.

High Country scored first under the bug-bombed lamps of the home stadium. They received the opening kick-off and proceeded to march down to the red zone in a handful of simple plays. Danny Miller lived up to the nickname "Train" by moving the whole right side of the line for the five yards to cross the goal line. Loren was swept onto the field with the defensive team members for the extra point try.

Council was the holder. The ball was snapped, grabbed, and placed. Step, step, step, kick. The ball sailed through the uprights as though it were afraid not to. Loren and the team leapt with ecstasy as they tumbled raucously from the playing field, slapping backs and shoulders, and helmets pounded and banged together.

The Sparta bench and bleachers stood silent. High Country had scored in five plays in the opening quarter. A grim resolve was evident when the Sparta team returned to the field for the kick-off. The air was electric on the High-High side. They were going to win!

Sparta took the kick-off, burst through the middle of the High Country defense and quieted the jubilation as their star backfield runner crossed the goal line untouched. A grim resolve set in on both benches.

Neither team got past their opponent's thirty-yard line for the rest of the first half—a long and fierce half. Every player was muddied and bloodied. By the end of the first quarter the players stopped leaping up from pile-ups and were beginning to move like old men. Midway through the second quarter, most players were running on auto-pilot, eyes glazed.

In the half-time locker room Coach Helder spoke with his hallmark quiet decisiveness. "Get your heads off your knees and listen up." The players shifted to positions of attentiveness. "You're up against an equal who has come to win. Hear me: An equal come to win. They're as good as you, as strong, as fast, and as well-trained. On any given night they could beat you, and on any given night you could beat them. Gentlemen, for the rest of your lives this game will stay with you, win or lose, you will remember this game. You'll remember it when you wake up tomorrow morning, for sure." He paused and smiled at the acknowledging groans. "You'll remember it next week, next year, and long after you've graduated. When you are grandparents you will talk about this game. Why is that so, gentlemen? Why this game, and not others?" The team realized that he expected an answer. As the silence lengthened, the tension in the room became a palpable presence.

"Because it's hard. And the harder it is the more important it is. If it wasn't hard everybody'd be doin it." No one could recall Ollie having made a statement that long in his life.

"I couldn't have said it better, Ollie. The difficulty of standing out in that field of battle, trading blow for blow, makes each of you a better man because you know there aren't many who can do what you are doing tonight. Many in the stands, young and old, would like to be in your pads tonight. They can't be and you can. They aren't and you are. Tonight, as much as any night in your life you are aware of being alive. Tonight, you are you more than any time in your life."

The team, to a man, was sitting on the edge of their seats or standing at attention. They appeared to hardly breathe at all. They were as one—a single beast crouched and ready to spring. Their coach continued. "I said on any given night." He left his position at the front of the group and moved in among his charges. "But we're here, now. We've got to deal with this night, and this night you are going to win. There would be no dishonor in losing a game like this, but tonight you are going to win. You're going to win because of what you—as individuals and as a team—decide right this instant. You're on a field of struggle with an opponent who is your equal. Your resolve will win the night, and that resolve will come from what you decide, right now. I want each of you to think about the position you play. I want you to think about what you can do in this last half to play your position the best it can be played. Not just the best you can play it, but the best it can be played—period. I want you to focus on your thoughts." His voice rose, "I call to mind a saying from India that goes—'There is no force on earth superior to the focused human mind'." He stopped and looked out over the players. "I believe that saying and I believe in it. It is an idea that you can live by—in this game, and in your life. Your focus is going to win the game. Now go out there and prove me right! Go! Go!"

Whatever the Sparta coach said to his team must have been just as stirring. The battle resumed in mid-field and stayed there all through the third quarter. Runners were stopped cold, quarterbacks were sacked, and passes knocked to the ground. No longer bouncing to their feet after a play, linemen struggled to rise from the muck of battle. Midway through the fourth quarter both coaches had played their entire benches to keep the first-string players from falling out from sheer exhaustion. As the grim specter of a tie loomed large, Loren sat alone in a spotless uniform at the far end of her bench. For the first time in her life she felt impotent and useless.

Six minutes left. Coach Helder called Loren and a second string back, Ben Stiles, to his side. He spoke his instructions softly. Loren and Ben returned to the bench. Few in the stands noticed when Ben sidled away from the team and moved out of sight. He was shortly followed by Loren. In less than a minute they were in the locker room practicing field goals. Loren was stretching and kicking while Ben gathered the balls from the net set up for that purpose.

With one minute left the Sparta quarterback had the ball knocked from his hands as he tried a bootleg end-around fake. High Country recovered on their own forty-yard line with fifty-four seconds remaining in the game. Coach Helder sent a player to the locker to get Loren and Ben.

A short pass right and out, short pass left and out, end-around right and out. First down. No huddles, just plays. High Country had one time-out left. Sparta, none.

Bryce took a risk that stopped Coach Helder's breathing; he threw a short pass over the line to Council, who was moving right to left at the top of his speed. Council grabbed the ball, tucked it and raced for the left sideline. He just barely made it out of bounds, but he also just barely made a first down. The ball was on Sparta's thirty-three. Four seconds remaining.

"Let me try the field goal, Coach. I'm warmed up."

Coach Helder looked down impassively. "It's too far. We weren't able to get the yardage I thought we would."

"Two things, Coach. No, three. Maybe it's not too far. What have we got to lose? And, you've got to let me play at least once in this game."

Coach Helder looked into the nearly frantic face of his charge.

"Go for it Lorne. Prove me wrong."

"No, coach. I'll prove you *right*. *Focus*; remember?"

Helder laughed. "Do it." He signaled to the quarterback as Loren jogged onto the field.

Everyone on the team knew it was too far, but no one said so. In the huddle Loren looked into the silent faces of her fellow team members. She saw, fatigue, muddy faces—and resolve. She knew then that she would always remember those faces at that instant. Most of all she remembered the unblinking determination. She knew that, if she failed, it would be because of what she did. She knew that each man would do his job.

Just as the team lined up, Bryce looked over at the bench. He signaled "time out," and led the team over to a waiting Coach Helder. As the team approached, Helder dropped to his knees and signaled that he expected the same of the team. Hands were grasped. Coach Helder turned and nodded at Jo Mae who, along with the rest of the cheerleaders urged quiet in the home stands.

In their kneeling huddle, Coach Helder said. "Once more: No force on Earth superior to the human mind. Now, I want each of you to focus on what you must do to make this field goal work. Elden," Coach Helder said to his fast halfback, "Line up behind the left tackle, about halfway between the center and the holder. I want Sparta to think that this just might be a run. Bryce I want you behind the right tackle, be ready to defend a guard or tackle breaking through. Elden as soon as the ball is snapped I want you to run to the right. That giant left end of theirs is almost sure to break through. I want you to take out his legs. When the ball is in the air, he should be falling to the ground. Got it? The team looked at Elden, who may have weighed in at one hundred forty-five pounds, wet. However, Elden was also a wrestler. It was one hundred forty-five pounds of muscle.

"Got it, Coach." The team knew that Elden would complete the assignment.

"And Elden, when you line up I want you to make sure that you glance over at the right flat twice. Don't make it too obvious though."

"Got it."

"Everyone: No force on earth... Now is the time to test it."

"Bryce; long count. If we can draw them off-sides it'll help a lot."

Bryce nodded.

Coach Helder rose and the team rose with him. "Folks in the stands think we have just had a prayer. Truth is—we did. Go do it."

"Amen," Council shouted.

"Amen," the team responded.

Jo Mae signaled the stands, which broke into loud cheering.

The players broke from the huddle, each locking to his position. Loren dropped back with measured steps. She looked up once at the twin posts, then at Council who was kneeling to accept the snap from center. Loren nodded. The ball sailed into Council's hands where it was turned and set in place as Loren was moving into her kick. She didn't feel the kick, she didn't hear her foot come in contact with the ball. The only awareness she had was the sight of the football and the roar of the crowd. Loren fell to the ground from the force of her effort. For a few brief moments she lay on her back looking at the dark sky. She could see stars. Council snatched her from the ground and threw her into the air like she was a doll. "Home: 10. Visitor: 7" flashed on the light board.

Loren kicked the ball to Sparta, a deliberately short stumbling kick to prevent the repeat of the only other High Country kick-off. Sparta had time for one play—a desperate Hail Mary, as High Country fans held their breath. Then, pandemonium. The war was won.

Coach Helder was mobbed by the team, the cheerleaders, and a few fans who rushed onto the field. Euphoria. Ecstasy. Blind joy. There are no words to exactly capture and communicate the feelings that were rampant in those few moments following the victory. Slowly, the chaos lessened, and then the players, one by one saw their coach walking out to midfield toward their opponents. The opposing coach walked to meet him. Council was the first player behind his coach, then Ollie and Gent. The rest of the team followed.

Loren found the Sparta quarterback and extended her hand. "Great game. You were great."

The boy looked at her, nodded, and took her hand.

"This is the best game I've ever played in my life," he said. "You guys were awesome."

By then the rest of the High Country team had caught up with their coach and was passing among the Sparta players. Each man was looking for the one he had played against. The exhausted players shook hands, nodded, and exchanged very brief acknowledgements. One or two players were heard to say softly through a smile, "Next year." The fans roared their approval.

The coaches stood, shook hands, and spoke briefly. Each was heard to reveal that this was the most memorable high school game they had ever witnessed. The coaches agreed to meet over a meal soon and discuss the events of the evening.

As Loren walked back to her side of the field she felt the pressure of hands from behind. Suddenly she found herself riding the shoulders of team members. No fan had turned to leave. They were standing at their seats shouting and clapping praise and approval. Loren learned what it felt like to be a member of a team.

CHAPTER 26

Fields shifted the old pickup through the post-game traffic. Loren, still in uniform, sat with her shoulder pads in her lap and her helmet on the floor. Sugar sat between the two, supervising the driving.

"Well, Gal, how'd you like your first football game?"

Loren didn't respond until they cleared the parking lot and were a good mile away from the stadium.

"It wasn't my game."

"How do you figure that?"

"I sat for two hours and watched my friends get beat to a pulp and couldn't lift a finger to help. I just sat there in my squeaky-clean uniform. I never felt more useless in my entire life. The people in the bleachers did more than I did. Them cheering the team made all the difference."

In five minutes they were out of the town following the high beams through the dark, pastured hills. It was only then that Fields replied.

"So you don't think you gave to the team effort?"

"Not much."

"You kickin the winning field goal don't count for much then?"

"I went into the game for less than a minute. I kicked the ball once. I didn't even get to kick the two times we kicked off before I kicked the field goal. Council kicked off—he's got good range. I asked Coach Helder to at least let me kick off and he said that he didn't want risk my getting hurt because I don't have the size or experience that Council and the rest have."

"You won the game for the team. Council couldn't have done that—nor could Ollie or anyone else on the team. Gal, I think you're being too pride-filled and I can't hold with that. You're a part of the team and what you do you do well. I got no place in my heart for your self-pity."

Fields' hard manner took Loren by surprise. They were silent the remainder of the trip home. When they pulled into the driveway Loren quickly opened her door, gathered her gear and jumped down; she was stopped by Fields' soft voice.

"Loren." It was almost a question.

She stopped and turned to face the old man whose kindly face was outlined in the shadows cast by the headlights. "Yes?"

"I'm proud of you."

Sleep didn't come until sometime after two a.m. as High Country's place kicker tossed and turned, re-living the game and her frustration from the bench. Loren slept until 8:30—a first. As the cobwebs cleared she became aware of the bird song coming from the maple outside her window. She listened to the woodland tenor singing his heart out, and she tried to place the variety of bird. A large head appeared and loomed over hers as paws were placed next to her shoulder.

"Sugar, what are you doing in the house?" Loren then became aware of soft sounds coming from the kitchen. There was the unmistakable aroma of Neese's sausage. Rising, she pulled on her jeans and a tee shirt. She found her grandpa fixing breakfast.

"This room come with meals now?" Loren jibbed.

"Only for the victor. One called Hammer."

"What?"

"The Hammer. That's what the boys around the pot-belly at the store were calling you this morning. They got it from the radio announcer who covered the game. I basked in the glory of grandfather fame for some ten or fifteen minutes this morning. It was a sight. Thought I'd come home and honor myself by fixing your breakfast. How come you sleep so late this morning? It ain't like you."

"I had a hard time going to sleep. Ain't? There's that ain't again. How'm I ever going to grow up to be somebody important with you setting such a poor example?"

"Like I said before—I'm old, ignorant, and set in my ways. I come up from the dirt and mud of this farmland. I guess it's just too much to ask for me to speak the King's English."

Loren laughed. "In the first place, I've seen that wall of books you have in your study. Wall-to-wall, floor-to-ceiling classics, and your study light's on all hours of the night. You're probably better read than most of the professors over at the college. Second place—King's English? Knowing about such gives you away as a closet intellectual."

"Gal, you're the one that sounds like a college professor. Where did you get such a manner of speaking—you barely old enough to drive? And what's this about having a hard time going to sleep?"

"Momma insisted on clear accurate language—it's second nature to me now." Loren held her plate out as Fields slipped two over-easy eggs onto it from the skillet. She added a dollop of grits while he forked up some sausage.

"That answers my first question." Fields said as he placed two patties on Loren's plate. "There's biscuits."

"I think I'll over-sleep every morning—could you serve this in bed next time?"

"What's keeping you awake all hours?"

"All I could think about was sitting helplessly on the sidelines watching my friends fight a war."

"You won the game."

"I kicked a field goal."

"A field goal that won the game."

"Are we going to have this argument again?"

"Not over breakfast—it ain't civil. But I want you to remember one thing: Your teammates carried you off the field on their shoulders. That counts for something. What are your plans for the weekend—Hammer?"

"Ain't, ain't, ain't," Loren said with a grin.

Chapter 27

"Good morning, Dead Eye," Bryce said as Loren jumped into his truck. "Ready for another Monday at High-High?"

"I'm ready. Seems like I worked most of the weekend catching up my schoolwork."

"Yeah, Pa had some plans for me to work around the farm this weekend, but he was at the game and decided that I wouldn't be worth much for a day or two. He was right. I tried to help out some yesterday but it was like moving through molasses."

"Well, I didn't have that problem. As you know, I spent most of Friday night on the bench. The only sore part I got was my butt."

"Yeah, but when you got off the bench, we won the game."

"Anybody could have done what I did. You guys won the game. You were great."

"I was on the phone a lot this weekend, and I can tell you that most folks don't see it the way you do. Those I talked with were talking about that unbelievable kick you made."

"I wish I could have done more."

"Why? So you could be limping around like the rest of us? Some of the linemen didn't get out of bed until Sunday afternoon. Get real."

Walking from the school parking lot Bryce and Loren saw a white paper banner that had been hastily painted and strung over the building entryway. It read, "HAMMER RULES!!"

"Seems that you're a local hero hereabouts," Gent said, as they approached the group of friends who hung out in front of the school waiting for the bell. It went from bad to worse for Loren. Everyone was talking about "the kick." Loren was greeted, congratulated, hand-shaken, patted, and generally admired the entire day. In all, it was a long day for her. Possibly, the worst moment came up when a pair of freshman girls asked for an autograph; hero worship was written all over their scrubbed faces. Unfortunately, the two girls did this in front of some of the team members. It wasn't until the next game that Loren lived it down. All week it was "Great game, Hammer," or "Go, Hammer" and, "Put it to em, Hammer." Team members were relentless with their teasing. All but a few walked up to Loren, pencil in hand and requested an autograph in simpering tones.

Council finally got the team to stop the tease. But Loren became The Hammer.

Loren kicked off in the game following the Sparta game. Coach Helder let her do it only if she agreed not to risk an injury trying to stop the receiving runner. The discussion began the Monday following the Sparta game.

"What if the receiver breaks through and comes my way."

"Then you have to help stop him." Coach Helder replied.

"I don't know how to tackle."

"We'll work on that."

By week's end Loren was sore and bruised from tackling and blocking exercises. By Friday she had the rudiments of tackling but was barely able to kick extra points.

At the game, she missed two field goal attempts, either of which would have prevented the tie score at the end. Both attempts were inside the thirty-yard line. Loren, still in uniform, sat alone in the back of the bus during the two-hour ride home. The next morning she called Coach Helder at his home.

"Coach, I'm sorry but I think it's best if I quit the team."

After a lengthy silence, Loren said, "Coach?"

"I'm here. But I just couldn't believe what I heard. You want to drop out of the team?"

"Yes."

"Would this have to do with the two field goals you missed last night?"

"Yes, mostly"

"Mostly?"

"Yeah, there's some other stuff, but it's personal."

"I see. Personal."

"Yes."

"Have you discussed this with anyone?"

"No. It's my decision."

"Of course it is. Let me suggest that you talk it over with Bryce. You two are good friends. A lot of times we need to talk over important decisions with others who care for us."

"The team deserves more than a player that does nothing but sit on the bench the whole game. I'm taking up a place that a real football player could occupy. It's not that hard to teach somebody to kick field goals. The team deserves a real player, one that doesn't have to have a private dressing room I don't need to talk it over with anybody I know my own mind, and..."

"I'm sure you do. But what you're about to do is going to affect those you hold in high regard. In fact, it's going to hurt a lot of people."

Loren held her tongue while she sifted the notion that her decision would hurt others.

"I missed both field goals last night. I just don't have the ability to do what you expect me to."

"I don't feel that way. I think you're learning. You're an excellent athlete with a lot of promise. It's a decided mistake to judge yourself on the basis of a single bad night. Frankly, if I didn't know you so well I'd be tempted to think of you as a quitter, and I know that's not the case—isn't that true?"

"No. No, I'm not a quitter. I've never quit anything in my life."

"Then why start now?"

"I don't want to let my friends down."

"Well, you made all three extra points last night. I hardly think that's letting anyone down."

"I missed both field goals."

"I've thought about that a lot. You're pretty sore from this week's practice, aren't you?"

"Yeah, I'm kindly sore, but that's not..."

"If anyone let down the team, it'd be me."

"How is that so?"

"I'm the coach. I'm the one who set up a practice program that caused you to be less than your physical best. I think a lot less block-and-tackle practice this past week would have enabled you to make those two field goals. It's not only your failure, it's mine too. But I'm not going to quit. I'm going to change my strategy. When I saw your level of block-and-tackle skill, I was determined to bring you up to speed—if for no reason than to keep you from getting hurt."

"I was the one who missed the field goals."

"Tell you what. I want you to stay on the team. We need you. I still want to bring you up to speed, but we'll go at a slower pace. This should keep you in good shape and at the same time give you the kicking practice time you need. I think we can design a practice strategy that will cover all the bases: It'll keep you in shape, maintain a high level of kicking skill, and at the same time let you acquire the blocking and tackling skill. Don't go dropping out right now. We need you. Let me put it this way: Why don't we give both of us another chance?"

"I don't..."

"Don't answer me right now. Think on it, and we will talk about it this coming week. Okay?"

"Fair enough, Coach."

"Great. See you Monday then?"

"Monday it is."

After hanging up, Coach Helder placed calls to Bryce, Council, Gent, and Jo Mae. Most of his morning was taken up with phone calls. His last call of the day was to Fields.

That evening Loren took Sugar down to the stream that ran through the meadow below the house. She settled on a flat rock that jutted out over the water. Sugar flopped with a soft *pfht* next to Loren, who pulled his head onto her lap. The dog closed his eyes and went limp as Loren gently stroked his side.

The clear stream ran with autumnal confetti: Yellows, Reds, Orange, and many shades of brown. The water even *looked* cold. Loren studied the leaves as though she could somehow read a solution from their patterns or color.

Just as the last fireflies of the summer began to light up, Fields hallooed from his porch. He had fixed supper. Loren stood and waved in acknowledgment, then headed, dog in tow, up to the house.

After supper, Loren and Fields took coffee and pie on the porch.

"Coach Helder called me today," the old man began. Loren was quiet over her pie. "He said you wanted to quit the team."

"Yes. That's true."

"He said you were disappointed in your showing Friday night, and that's why you wanted to quit. He says you think you let the team down."

Loren finished her last bite of pie and handed a piece of the crust to Sugar.

"You goin to kill my dog with all your treats."

"I figure he needs to know someone cares for him."

"Oh, so that's it. Early death by love then."

"There's more than just my missed field goals Friday night."

Fields reached up and patted his left shirt pocket. "Dang it, I miss smokin'. Right about now is when I'd be lightin' up a Lucky." He let out a deep breath. "What more is it then?"

"I just couldn't abide the hero worship thing. The other day a couple of freshman girls asked for my autograph. The afternoon of this Friday's game, a girl came up to me with a pair of scissors and wanted to know if she could have a lock of my hair. That kind of thing is foolish and insulting."

"So you're quitting because you succeeded, and because you failed, is that right?"

"That's one way to see it I suppose. I don't like being worshipped, and I hate to fail. I don't see anything wrong with those values. I don't need other people's approval to know who I am."

"Gal, I swear, you talk like a lawyer."

"That's just the way I think, I can't help it."

Fields rose from his rocker and began gathering plates and cups. "I'll clean up."

CHAPTER 28

Loren and Fields had long since found that it was to their mutual advantage to take meals together. This worked particularly well, because each of the two tried to give more than the other; more cooking, time, more effort toward cleaning up after. The following morning was no exception.

After the utensils were cleaned and stacked to dry, Loren and Fields rocked on the porch with their coffee and morning air.

"I do like the way you have with an egg, Gal."

"Thank you. They were good this morning. Good hens I reckon."

"Can't hurt."

The two rocked and savored the last of their coffee.

"I see you found that big flat rock down on the river bank." Fields' gaze went to the rock where Loren and Sugar had sat the previous evening. Loren saw his eyes glaze and his features soften.

"It's one of my favorite places."

"The missus and I used to enjoy that rock. Some nights we'd pile quilts and such on it and sleep all night to the sound of the water music. We'd wake covered with dew, and then we'd hang the bedding out to dry in the sun. When the children came, we'd picnic on the rock. Both our children learned to swim at that spot. They were like a pair of waterdogs," Fields smiled as he referred to the fat foot-long salamanders found in the river.

Fields had never mentioned his wife and children in such a personal way. Loren knew him to be a private soul.

"Last night you said you disliked the nickname your friends gave you. Hammer, I believe it was."

"Yes, that's what they all call me now; Hammer. I really don't like it, but there's not much I can do about it. I like my given name."

Fields rocked a while before answering. "I reckon you know that my given name is Warren, not Fields."

"Yes. I've seen paperwork with your full name on it. How did you get to be called Fields?"

"It happened when I was sixteen. There was this young girl teacher, name of Beverly James. We all called her Miss Beverly; it seemed the natural thing to do. Miss Beverly was my first love. I took my first science course from her. Science became my second love. I had two years of science under Miss Beverly. She's the one responsible for my goal to become an engineer."

"She must have made quite an impression on you."

"Impression? The word falls far short of what Miss Beverly meant to me. There are no words to clarify the feelings I had toward her. Even after I was married with two children, my mind had many ways to find her."

"What did she look like?"

"Beautiful, in every way. Her face was the most comely I've ever seen. Her figure had - - - let's just say that when she walked down the street, all heads turned to her. I've seen grown men stand and gape the first time they saw her walk. She had a pile of sandy brown hair thicker than any." Fields paused, thought a moment, then said, "You're the first soul I've told this, Gal."

"I respect that."

"I know you do. She had that beautiful pile of hair, but the thing that stays most in my head was the way she smelled. She had a perfume that must have been made for her in Paris. I've smelled that perfume on other women and it just wasn't the same."

Loren knew that Fields was about to go where he had never gone before with another. She leaned back in her rocker and gazed at the blue of the October sky.

"It was a fall day like this one, and I was as at a harvest festival with my folks. I was standing between my mother and Miss Beverly, when she told my mother she thought I was so much in love with the outdoors that my name should be something like Forrest or Fields. Mother agreed, and said that I was forever out in the fields. Miss Beverly laughed and gathered me to her breast, placing a kiss on my forehead. She and mother laughed and moved away to where some musicians were playing, leaving me with some classmates who had overheard them. They teased and started calling me *Fields,* and the name stuck. Funny thing is, by Thanksgiving all my school chums knew me as Fields, but the two women I loved, Mother and Miss Beverly, were the only ones who still called me Warren. At the end of the school year, Miss Beverly moved away to marry a man she had known in college. I never saw her again—except every day in my memory. I still do now. Some mornings I wake up thinking of that beautiful girl with the piles of red-like brown hair. I guess I never fell out of love. I've not spoke this to a soul because it sounds faithless to the woman I married and love like the air I breathe. I guess a body can hold two loves in his heart at once't. The one who took my last name, and the one who gave me my first."

Loren puzzled over the story and was wondering why Fields was telling it.

He continued. "When I'm laid out in that black suit hanging in my closet, there'll be wrinkled old gray-hairs standing over me and thinking of me only as Fields. None but a few even know my given name. My name, my nickname, was given me in fun by a woman I adored, and was taken up by my classmates. I woke this morning with that fine lady on my mind—I'll ever puzzle on her outcome."

"There's one thing you got to know, Gal. To be given a nickname by your school friends is a badge of high honor and is not to be taken lightly or to be cast off easy. Sixty years from now there will be old men and women who, when they think of you, they'll think of you as Hammer, and they'll likely remember the game that gave you that name."

"Well, I don't..."

Fields waved her silent.

"It's because I care so much for you I have to tell you I got no patience with your sorry meanness when things didn't go the way you expect. This is a good time to give it up and go back to being the outstanding lady you've demonstrated dozens of times."

"It's not that."

"Seems to me—reading the papers and such—that over half the children of the world are suffering from lack of attention or affection—not to mention food. I'd think that a body being admired as you are, a body would be pleased with all that attention. Others starve for just a drop of what you're gettin' like rain."

Loren's eyes flashed in anger. "Are you through?"

"No, I'm not. Seems you'd want to use all that mindless adoration to reach out and help those in need." Fields was breathing hard. "Now I'm through." He rose and left Loren to Sugar, her rocker, and her thoughts.

The big dog rose and placed his head on the lap of his pensive friend.

CHAPTER 29

The following Monday afternoon, Coach Call Elder answered a knock on his door. It was Loren, who entered wordlessly and was signaled to a chair beside the coach's desk.

"What's up, Lorne?"

"I came to apologize, Coach."

"And that would be for. . ?"

"For bein' selfish. It took Grandpa to bring me to that notion. I'm sorry."

The coach laid a giant hand on his kicker's shoulder. "It takes a big man to realize when he's wrong, and an even bigger one to apologize."

Loren sat quietly looking into her coach's eyes.

He dropped his hand from her shoulder and motioned her to sit closer to the note pad he'd slid to the corner of the desk. "I have a plan in mind that should let you keep your kicking skill sharp, and at the same time bring you up to speed on blocking and tackling."

Loren leaned close over the list on the coach's note pad as he ticked off the items.

"It'll take a little longer to get your blocking and tackling up to speed, but it'll be worth it to keep your kicking skills at the level needed to prevent a recurrence of Friday's performance."

"You're goin' to let me back on the team then?"

"You were never off the team, Lorne, except in your head. You're as much a part of the team as I am."

"Thanks, Coach. I don't deserve it."

"You do. But I won't argue the point."

Loren hesitated, looked down at her shoes, and then into the eyes of her mentor. "Coach, Grandpa got me to thinking, and I've got an idea I'd like to ask you about."

That Thursday, a select group of faculty, coaches, and students met during lunch hour in the school auditorium. Coach Helder had asked for the meeting and saw to it that sandwiches, beverages, and fruit were available.

Coach Helder took the mike on the stage and addressed the small gathering. "Thank you for taking your lunch time to answer my invitation. I'll come quickly to the point and be brief." This was met with mutterings of approval. "This weekend I was given an idea by a member of our football team. I was so impressed with the young man's suggestion that I wanted to pass it on to members of the faculty and staff. I also asked that select students be included in the discussion." Coach Helder gestured to a small knot of students seated at the rear of the assemblage.

"As you know there is no small amount of hero worship of our athletes by the younger students. This can be a distraction from our job of teaching, or it can be put to use in productive ways." This was met with nods and sounds of agreement.

"My Team members saw how much influence our athletes have on young students, and that those students were often in need of emotional support and guidance. I propose that the school develop a plan using some of the more mature students as mentors. I think it would be smart to pair selected scholars and athletes with those who could benefit from the association. The faculty, staff, and coaches are in the best position to determine who might be helped by such a plan. The student who proposed the idea calls it the "Good Buddy Plan," and I feel that name clearly describes what it is about. I'm in favor of his idea and want to hear your thoughts about exploring it, but first I want you to listen to the student, Lorne Land, who brought the idea to me."

Loren rose from her chair as Coach Helder returned to his. Her heart was pounding and her palms sweaty. It was her first experience with an audience.

"Thanks for coming to the meeting"—Coach Helder had told her to start with that—"I'm scared to death in front of you-all because I've never done this before so I don't know where to start. But I want to tell you about what happened to me that gave me the 'Good Buddy' idea."

Loren realized that her audience was sympathetic and attentive.

"About a month ago when I was going to the cafeteria, a freshman girl came up to me and told me how swell she thought I was. She was as embarrassed as I am now." The audience laughed. "I thanked her and asked her if she would join me for lunch. We sat with my usual crowd and I introduced her to them. She was shy and quiet, but I got Gentry and Jo Mae to talk some to her, and it sort of brought her out. On the way back to class I asked her if she would join us the next day, and she said she would. Later, I talked with Jo Mae and asked if she could sort of give me a hand. The girl—Coach told me not to say her name—was overweight, scared, and didn't seem to know much about how to dress.

Next lunch period I noticed what she ate and compared it with what I ate. There was a big difference, but I didn't say anything. Well, she ate with us from then on, and her food choices began to change. Jo Mae helped her some with make-up, hair, and stuff, and she began to look better and act more relaxed around us. In a couple weeks she'd lost a few pounds and was starting to look better. Jo Mae and some of the other cheerleaders were a big help. Jo Mae told me that one of the teachers told her that he was glad that she was helping the girl with her schoolwork because she was turning around completely. Jo Mae thought that was funny because she hadn't helped at all with her schoolwork." Loren left the mike and returned to her chair beside Coach Helder, who was caught in surprise by the abrupt ending. He regained the mike.

"Well, there you have it. I want to thank Lorne for sharing his experiences with us. I couldn't help but compare his first experience in front of an audience with mine, and I don't mind saying that he put me to shame." The grinning audience members took up a light applause.

"I want to bring this idea to the next staff meeting and will be interested to hear your ideas. Your students are invited to come to that meeting if you want. I'll see to it that Lorne's idea is first on the agenda so you can get away quickly. So, before we adjourn I'll take any questions, thoughts, ideas and so on."

Loren listened as the teachers, ever practical, began discussing the difficulties of making the plan work. She felt a strong sense of having done something good. What do you think, Mom; did I do all right? She hoped that no one saw the tears she was fighting back. Wish you were here.

Once again, Loren tossed herself to sleep that night. She dreamed of her Momma all night long. She and her mother were trapeze artists in her barn. They were able to fly, and did so from rafter to rafter, laughing and giggling.

CHAPTER 30

Each week Loren looked forward to her Sunday afternoon with Meredith and Tara. They ordered pizza, and Loren brought a plate of veggies, fruit, and dip. The gathering proved to be the highlight of the week for the three friends. The events of the past week were, in Tara's words, "cussed and discussed." It was usually about boys, school, parental demands, and peers—and boys. Personal problems were hauled out for public display and mediation. Loren often found herself surprised at the girls' candor and willingness to talk about their most personal experiences. At first, she was unable to explore her own life with much openness, but over the weeks she came to follow the lead of her friends, finding relief and solace in the exchanges with her vivacious "sisters." More than once, she confided that they and Fields Gragg were her only family, and how much she had come to care for them.

"I don't know what I would do without you two to talk with. It's like I'm livin' in a bubble all week long, and on Sundays I'm free to be who I really am. Fields and I have a really great relationship, but we come from such different worlds in time. I love him to pieces, but I can't open up with him like I do y'all. Please, don't ever give up on me. Don't abandon me. I've never had friends like you."

"Don't worry, darlin'. You're stuck with us—we've adopted you, and you ain't getting away," Meredith answered in the semi-tough manner she liked to take on in moments of levity.

Tara added, "I feel like I need these Sundays as much as you, Loren. All week long I think about what we talked about the past Sunday, and I think of things I want to talk about the next Sunday. We've got a great thing going, and I don't want to give it up. I could see us doing this when we're forty. One thing, you guys have really helped me with how to handle boys. I've learned so much from you. But you know, it's a funny thing—I keep on coming back to the fact that Mom is right. So much of what she's tried to teach us about boys is true. Almost everything she's said to watch out for has come up, and almost everything she said to expect was right on. I know I sound like a goody-good, but Mom is worth listening to. Between you two and Mom, I feel like I could handle almost anything, even dating."

"I have to ask this." Loren said. So I'll apologize before I say it." The girls grew still and waited.

"Most sisters I know try to avoid each other when they can, but you two don't do that. I don't know many college girls who want to spend their Sundays with their sister. I really admire you two for doing this, but I can't help but wonder..."

"Pity." Meredith broke in. "I feel sorry for the poor thing, being deprived of my fine character all week, so I cut her a break on the weekends and give her the opportunity to enjoy herself. Besides, it's good for a child to have outstanding positive role models."

Tara rolled her eyes. "The truth is, Loren, I'm worried for Sis. I mean, all week long all she is surrounded by real college men and women who have their stuff together. So she takes an emotional beating six days of the week. On Sundays I come along and pump her back up. It's not easy, but what's a sister to do? There it is." Tara popped a grape in her mouth and pretended to look away with the smug satisfaction of someone who just completed a difficult task that needed doing.

Loren looked from one sister to another, and then said in mock seriousness, "Thanks, I needed to know."

Just then Meredith blapped her sister with a cushion. Tara returned in kind, and a pillow fight ensued among the three.

The laughing and giggling ended with the three girls stretched out on the backs looking up at the ceiling while they caught their breath. Finally, the girls righted themselves and returned to the business of pizza. Loren was the first to speak.

"I need a girlfriend."

In mid-pizza, Meredith and Tara looked at each other then back at Loren.

"Homecoming dance is in two weeks and I need a date. Most everyone is lined up already, but several girls have hinted that they are open and willing. One or two have outright asked me to take them. A cheerleader named Audrey Wingate has all but proposed to me. Everybody has tried to fix me up with double dates that I keep sayin' "no" to. Gent told me word is out that I'm gay. He said everybody would be sure I'm gay except that several people have seen me ridin' around with you two. Seems that one of you is my mystery lover."

"Me," Tara pulled herself over to Loren and leaned against her while placing her head on Loren's shoulder. "I can be your mystery lover."

Loren smiled, shaking her head.

"Why not?" Tara asked feigning a miff. "I thought we were friends—in fact, you're just about my best friend."

"Thanks, Tara, but it won't work. You live an hour away and neither of us has a car. I need someone who is visible. But I didn't mean for you two…"

"I'll do it." Meredith said with a finality that sounded as though she had been agonizing over a decision for some time. "I'm here, in Boone, I have wheels, and I'm certainly available—what with the man-is-taken situation on campus."

"Now, I wadn't tryin'…"

"I didn't think you were," Meredith said. "But one of us two would be your best—in fact, only—choice for this."

"What 'man-is-taken situation?'" Loren asked, diverting the subject. "The university has thousands of men. I mean, it's like they're everywhere."

"Boys, not men. I'm sure there are a lot of good men on campus, but they get snatched up pretty quick. Mostly what's left are what can be called boys. There's a huge difference between the two. The one good thing that came out of the Lance experience is that it really opened my eyes. I mean, the guys are cute, don't get me wrong, but some are such outrageous children. And when they're running in a group, it almost makes you gag to watch what they go through to prove themselves to each other and to the girls. Graduate students are more mature, but all they want is to have sex and get gone. Every grad I've dated has wanted to get me to his apartment to pour a couple drinks down me. It didn't take but once or twice to make me a skeptic."

The three girls were sprawled comfortably on the floor around a coffee table as they finished the last of the pizza.

"I'd make a better girlfriend, being the prettiest and all," Tara chimed with a mischievous grin. "And smartest," she added.

"I don't know that Loren's taste goes to baby fat," Meredith chided.

"See what I have to put up with. You ought to choose me, out of sympathy if nothing else."

Loren said, "I wasn't serious, I was just commenting about problems I have—what with everybody else paired off or dating, while here I am, living like a monk."

"Well, I am serious," Meredith said. "We could pretend to be an item, and that would get everybody off your back. Looks like you've got a date for the dance, my adopted sister—and now hot boyfriend."

"I can't dance."

Meredith and Tara exchanged glances again. "What was that thing you showed us in the barn when we first met you?" Tara asked.

"Freestyle dance. It's totally different from dancing with a partner. Mom never taught me partners dancing, and I've never once done it. I don't know how."

Meredith rose and went to her CD player. "No time like the present," she said, motioning for Loren to rise and join her to the gentle sounds of a female vocalist.

Loren held back.

"C'mon, this'll be easy. Mom taught both Tara and me to dance—we're old hands at it. In fact, we all still dance together once in awhile. C'mon."

Loren rose and placed herself in front of Meredith, who proceeded to show her where to hold and how to be held.

"First thing, relax. You're stiff as a board. We'll just stand here a minute and get the feel of the rhythm of the music. Just sway with me, don't move yet. That's right; just sway." Meredith pulled herself closer. Loren could feel soft hair brushing her cheek. "That's good, relax and enjoy the music," Meredith said.

As the music rose and fell the two dancers pulled closer together until Meredith was pressed full against Loren. Both girls were wearing lightweight shirts and no bras. Loren became aware of Meredith's full firm breasts pressed warmly against her chest and blushed furiously. She grew warm and felt perspiration rising. Soon her heart was pounding. Meredith, aware of her distress, pulled away.

"Oh, I didn't mean to embarrass you."

"I'm sorry, it's just, just—I've never held anybody in my arms like that before and it's new to me, and I don't know how to. I've fantasized about holding Bryce or Council in my arms, and it only frustrates me."

"My turn," Tara sang out as though to ease the tension.

"No, I think we ought to give Loren a second to catch her breath, she's embarrassed by all this contact."

Loren noticed Meredith was flushed and there was a line of perspiration on her brow.

Tara, seeing the stimulated state of her companions, said. "Wow, maybe you *should* be Loren's girlfriend, Sis; the way you turn each other on."

The remainder of the afternoon was spent in study, snacking, and an occasional stab at dance lessons with the two sisters. Loren sensed a new shade of relationship with Meredith who she found staring at her from time to time. Both girls avoided the close contact they experienced during the first dance. Just before releasing Loren after the last dance of the evening, Meredith reached up a placed a light kiss on Loren's lips, bringing a bright crimson to Loren's face.

Meredith and Tara drove Loren home on their way back to Tennessee. She pulled her car into Loren's driveway as Loren began unbuckling her seat belt and gathering her belongs, Meredith turned around to face her in the back seat, "Tara and I love each other, and have always enjoyed each other's company. We share everything, and have no time for petty competition. Also, She is a touch of the home life I miss. That's why we want to spend most Sundays together—and now you're a member of that circle. The circle of Family."

Loren reached forward from the back seat and hugged the sisters, giving each a light kiss before getting out. "Thank you." She waved them goodbye just as Sugar placed his head under the other hand, which hung by her side.

That night, Loren tossed and dreamed tumultuous dreams, unaware of the red sport car parked a short distance from the house. The next morning, Fields followed Sugar's curiosity over a small pile of cigarette butts in the driveway down the road from his. He noted the tire pattern and emitted a small grunt before scooping up the pile of spent filters. An empty pint vodka bottle lay a few feet away in the grass. The hair on Sugar's back and shoulder stiffened as he sniffed the area. When Fields rose from his litter clean-up his face was grim and his eyes narrowed to small slits as he glanced from the tire tracks to the small home of the girl he loved. He reached down and stroked his friend. "Sugar, looks like you and me needs to start us up a neighborhood watch." The dog seemed to nod agreement with his panting. "Son, I'm going to cut us a dog door in the wall, so's you can come and go at will." Sugar cocked his head at the man he adored.

CHAPTER 31

The game with Yancy High School—in a cold drizzle—was a tedious 13-13 tie played to exhaustion in a mud swamp. It was the last game before the homecoming game. The team trooped quietly to the respective locker room. Loren went to the school bus where she changed into her street clothes, alone and in the dark. She claimed a seat in the back of the bus where she could sit in silent remorse over the missed extra point she should have made and that would have won the game. Loren was the only one on the bus who felt that she was personally responsible for the loss. She saw it as "her" loss. As the team members got on the bus there was none of the usual horseplay or banter. Players threw themselves wordlessly into the respective seats, buddies paired off and shared seats. Loren had never known such sullen silence from the normally boisterous team. Some of the linemen were asleep before the bus started to move on its lumbering trip home. Normally, Loren would have paired off with Council or Bryce, but tonight she wanted to be alone in the dark corner of her misgiving as she mentally replayed the missed kick.

During the fifth review of the kick that hit the field goal and bounced back rather than through, Loren's bubble of self-recrimination was burst by Audrey Wingate who slid into the seat next to Loren.

"Mind if I join you?" The cheerleader van was out of commission, and the girls were allowed to ride home with the team—after a stern lecture from Coach Helder regarding boy-girl interaction.

Loren, wanting to be alone, chose not to answer.

"I know you feel bad about missing that second kick, but you shouldn't."

Loren remained silent as Audrey sat down.

"I mean, everyone makes mistakes, and you can't blame yourself. The field was all mud, and no one could be expected to make every kick like that. I think you were great, you made the first kick. If you hadn't done that we would have lost instead of tying the game. You kept us from losing—is the way I see it." She waited in the dark for a response.

"Don't beat yourself up, Lorne. No one is blaming you. I think you're great." Saying this, Audrey pulled herself next to Loren and planted a kiss on her cheek.

"Look," She said firmly, "I know you feel bad, but I want to make that go away and I know just how to make that happen." Moving quickly she swung her leg over Loren and sat straddling the astonished girl.

"Let me show you how to feel good again." She put her hands on Loren's shoulders and leaned face to face with the object of her affection. Pressing her lips to Loren's she thrust her tongue into Loren's mouth, causing Loren to turn away in shock.

"I love you." Audrey whispered into Loren's ear, just as the lights came on in the bus.

"Everything all right back there?" Coach Helder's voice boomed against the silence in the bus, waking some of the exhausted players. Audrey dropped away from Loren's lap and sat erect beside her blushing seatmate. She waved *okay* at Coach Helder who rose from his seat and swayed his way toward the back of the bus, where several couples were leaned together.

"Let's keep our private lives private. I have parents to answer to, and some of you might not want to hear what I say." There was a nodding of heads as couples pulled apart. After Coach Helder returned to his seat, Audrey rose and started back to hers, and then she turned and flashed a smile just before the lights went out. "Feel better now?" She whirled away and flounced into her seat.

Alone, in the back of the darkened bus, the taste of Audrey's fruity gum mixed with the salt of Loren's tears.

Homecoming dance. Loren and Meredith were the center of focus at the dance. Everyone wanted to meet Loren's date and their history.

"How did you two meet, anyway?" Jo Mae queried.

'I was looking for a book in the ASU library when he came up and pulled the one I was looking for off the shelf and began thumbing through it. I told him that was the book I was looking for and asked if I could have it when he was finished. Being the gentleman he is, he handed it over right then. I thanked him and asked him if he was interested in dance—it was a book about the history of dance—and, well, he said he was, but didn't much know how to dance. I was so taken by those eyes of his that I up and asked him if I could teach him. We had a cup of coffee together—one thing led to another—and here we are. Like I said he is such a gentleman. He even insisted that Tara come with us to the dance."

Joe Mae's curiosity satisfied, Meredith asked Loren for a dance. By evening end, all the girls and many boys knew the story.

It wasn't difficult for Loren to sit out as many dances as she could—a strategy that was aided by the fact that Meredith was asked to dance nearly every number. She danced with almost every member of the football team at least once. Even Coach Helder gave her a turn around the floor. Council managed to dance with her three times. Meredith found him to be an excellent dancer and a courteous, almost courtly, gentleman.

"Sis, you and Council look great on the dance floor," Tara said with a grin. It was one of those inquiries that sisters learn to pass between each other without having to ask a question.

"We fit perfectly." Meredith said to Tara just before her younger sister was whisked away by another dance request. Both sisters were busy most of the evening.

Just after eleven that night, a slightly inebriated and very angry Lance Van Riper slipped into a side door of the gym as a couple 'headed out for air." He made his way to the snack table, breaking in ahead of several students in line. He piled his plate with some wings, and a couple large doughnuts, and then walked over to a shadowed corner where he stood eating while smiling smugly at the celebrants on the dance floor.

After he'd worked his way through half the pile of wings he laid his plate on the nearest table and walked over to the line of tables set end-to-end for the team members and their dates. He stopped in front of Meredith, who was talking with Jo Mae about college campus life.

"S'up, Mere?"

"Lance. I haven't seen you this evening. You have a date here?"

"Naw, I don't rob the cradle like you. I'm only interested in grown-up action. Apparently you're not." Lance swayed and caught himself on the table's edge.

"Scuse me," Jo Mae said as she rose to leave.

"Looks like your high school chums are deserting you, Meredith."

Loren came up behind Meredith with a dessert plate.

"Try this cake, Meredith, it's really good." Loren placed the cake before his date without looking up at Lance.

"Don't mind if I do, schoolboy." Lance said as he reached across the table and picked up the piece of cake and stuffed half of it into his mouth. Loren recognized Lance's voice from Meredith's room.

"You'd be Lance, then."

"I am that, schoolboy, and you'd be?" Lance answered, mocking Loren's manner of speech.

"My friends here call me Lorne, but you can call me Mr. Land."

Meredith rose and quickly came to stand before Lance; Loren behind her.

"This is between me and Lance, Lor—Lorne. You stay out of this."

"Afraid I'll hurt your pet, Meredith?" Lance didn't notice that Jo Mae had come up behind him, leading Council and Bryce. Gent, from across the room, sensed something wrong and moved to join his teammates.

"I don't know what you're doing here, Lance, but this school dance is open only to students and their dates. I'd like you to leave."

"I imagine you'd like a lot things, but don't expect to get them. I don't know though—do you always get what you want? I expect you do, being a mama's girl and all."

"Lance, please leave."

"I'll leave when I'm ready, and I'll be ready when you're ready to walk out of here on my arm." Lance's voice rose.

"Lance, that's not going to happen, now leave." Meredith found it difficult to disguise her anger.

"Still got that temper, huh, Meredith?"

Loren moved between the two, and faced Lance who stood several inches taller. "Lance, Meredith's asked you politely to leave. Now, I'm asking you."

Lance made a huffing noise of contempt. "Well, I know when I'm not wanted." He turned as though to walk away, and then quickly pivoted and hit Loren a hard backhand, knocking her to her knees. He grabbed for Meredith, but was stopped by Council who spun him around and hit him twice before he hit the floor.

Council stepped over the prone figure, and hoisted Loren to her feet.

"You okay?"

"I'm okay."

"Good, let's get away from here. We don't want to get caught fighting. Bryce, get Coach Helder, he'll get this guy out of here—him smelling so strong of booze and all."

Council led his friends away from the gathering crowd as Lance got himself to his feet. Bryce returned with Coach Helder, explaining that this drunk boy had crashed the dance and was making trouble when he tripped over his own feet and fell, hitting his head on the table. A tight-lipped Call Helder took Lance by the arm, and led him to the door, where Lance broke free from him and ran into the night.

Council and his friends watched from the team table as Lance was led away by the coach.

"I'll bet we've not heard the last of him." Jo Mae said. "Did you see his eyes? He's crazy."

"I bet he hopes it's the last we hear of him," Ollie answered. "You really nailed him, Council. Man, I never want to mix it up with you."

Council stood like stone as he looked to the doorway where Lance had broken free. He was barely breathing and his eyes narrowed to slits. Blood was rising on his skinned knuckles.

Before the dance was over, a cold wind rose and blew in from the north. By 2 a.m. the temperature had dropped ten degrees and the clouds disappeared from the harvest moon as the wind became an animal force, both quieting and masking the night sounds. Not even Sugar heard the idling car back slowly into the abandoned driveway north of Fields' house. Nor could the sleeping dog hear the footfalls of a black-clad figure as it passed downwind from his house and into the side yard of Loren's house.

After a last glance in the vanity mirror, Loren turned off the bathroom light and returned to her bedroom in preparation for going to bed. She neither saw nor heard the dark figure watching through the open curtains of her bedroom window. Loren slipped out of her things and into her flannel pajamas. She slid under the covers, enjoying the sensation of the cool sheets, knowing that she would quickly warm under the down comforter Fields let her use. She reached up to turn out her bedside lamp. The wind masked Lance van Riper's muttered expletive as he clearly saw that Meredith's homecoming date was a girl. He caught himself to keep from falling off a wooden box he'd pulled out from under the porch so he could see above the window sill. He stumbled from his perch, and nearly ran to his car, muttering curses. He coasted down the drive and turned toward town. A quarter mile down the moonlit blacktop, Lance turned on his headlights, accelerated to high speed, and only then took a long pull of vodka. "Damn!"

CHAPTER 32

"Come in." Coach Helder answered the knock at his door, and looked up to see the team kicker. "Hello, Lorne."

"Hi, Coach. How are you doing?"

"I'm fine, Lorne. Pull up a chair. What's up? Not planning on dropping from the team, are you?"

"No, Coach. I think you'll have to put up with me, at least until the end of the season."

"Well, it's only two more games. I think I can make it—if you can. That leg of yours has helped us win nearly every game. Our opponents will do almost anything to keep us from getting inside the thirty-yard line. I think next year we're going to be a contender for state championship, and your kicking is going to go a long way toward making that happen. Anyway, is this a social call, or did you have a specific reason for the visit?"

"Coach, I need a favor."

"Sure, Lorne. If I can help you I will."

Loren sat in the chair next to Coach Helder's desk. "Your wife works for the school administration, doesn't she?"

"Yes, she works with records."

"Could I go talk to her sometime? I think she can help me with a problem I'm working on."

"I don't see why not. I'll call her right now if you'd like, and you two can work out the day and time."

"Thanks, Coach. I owe you a game win."

"I'll hold you to it—Hammer," he said as he punched in his wife's number.

High Country High won the last game of the season over Mitchell High; 3-0 in the last twenty seconds of the game. After a grinning Loren Creek was grabbed and hugged by the coach, she pushed him back to arms length and said, "I pay my debts."

Meredith and Tara watched the game and arranged to attend the after-game dance with Loren. The two sisters and Fields met Loren at the sideline as the team members made their way to the lockers.

"You were great, Loren—Lorne!" Tara corrected herself.

Fields gave his "grandson" a long hug, and then stepped back to look at her. A gentle nod told the girl all that was needed.

Meredith, in the role of Loren's girlfriend, planted a long kiss on the blushing field-goal kicker. Loren didn't know if it was out of affection or if Meredith just had fun embarrassing her in front of friends.

The three girls went to Meredith's apartment where Loren changed into a man's suit as Tara experimented with the football pads and uniform. The energetic teen was nearly bouncing off the walls with enthusiasm for Loren's achievement and with the anticipation of going to a dance where she would be surrounded with members of the football team. The team members were quite taken with the two beautiful sisters who were often seen with their field goal kicker.

Loren came out of the bedroom in her suit. Her shirt was open at the collar and she held a tie in her hand. "I don't know how to tie one of these."

"I do! I do! Tara exclaimed. "Come here." She beckoned Loren to the full-length mirror on the back of a door.

As she stood before the mirror, Tara removed Loren's coat, threaded the tie through her collar and, standing behind her, reached around and expertly tied a Windsor knot. "There. You are one handsome feller now. Remember, I want you to treat my sister right. I don't expect you to try to take advantage of her, and I want you to get her home before midnight. I guess I just better go along with you and make sure you two don't get in trouble." Tara spun away laughing. "Let's go dancing, Sis." She handed Loren's coat back to her and fled to the bedroom to take off the pads and uniform.

The team had pooled their resources, sponsored a couple of barbecues, and raised enough money to get the same band they had for the Homecoming dance. Once again, Meredith was whirled around the floor by several members of the team. It was Homecoming all over. Council wisely divided his time between Meredith and Jo Mae. Audrey Wingate, resigned that Loren was spoken for, nevertheless scored two dances with Loren. Gent discovered Tara, and the two of them spent much of the evening in each other's arms on the dance floor. Toward the end of the evening, Tara and Gent appeared to find the dance hall too warm, and frequently discovered the need to step outside for some fresh air. At midnight they clung together like the last song was the last dance of their lives.

Tara didn't say a word all the way to Loren's. Meredith and Loren exchanged meaningful looks when they arrived at Loren's, and Tara announced she really had "the best time ever." She thanked Loren three times for inviting her, and waved all the way out of the drive.

At home, Loren rinsed her face, slipped into pajamas and then into bed. Normally, she would drop off in a few minutes, but memory of the lingering kisses Meredith placed on her lips kept returning and puzzling her. As the evening passed the kisses had become more and more lush. Loren was both aroused and repulsed. She rose restless and got a glass of cold water and returned to her covers. After half an hour she fell asleep and was soon in a disturbing dream involving Meredith. Once she awoke briefly, but soon went back to sleep, returning to the same dream.

Around three a.m. Loren came full awake with the sensation of choking. She immediately became aware of a man astride her, her throat in the tight grip of his left hand. The hallway night light revealed a large hunting knife, its blade pressed against her cheek. The man was wearing a woolen ski mask that covered his head and face.

"Wake up, bitch, I want you awake. You need to feel what it's like to be with a real man." The man's voice was low and muffled by the mask. "We got something to do, you and me, little Miss *Loren Creek*, and you're not going to make a sound unless you want me to pet your face with my friend here." Light from the hallway nightlight reflected the blade gleaming over her eyes. Loren could smell the heavy scent of alcohol.

"What do you want?" Loren choked.

"I think you know what I want. Now, are you gonna give it to me nice and polite, or are we gonna have to negotiate for it? Believe me, you don't want to negotiate with my friend."

"Please don't do this."

"Believe me, you're gonna like what I have planned. Before the nights over, you'll probably be begging for more."

"Please."

"See? You're already starting to beg. That's good. Now I'm going to tell you how to get started."

Loren's sleep fog cleared and her mind raced. She knew what she needed to do. "Wait, don't hurt me. Please."

"You're showing good sense. Let's take off those pajamas."

"Please don't do this. Please don't hurt me."

"Take 'em off."

"Why are you doing this? I'm just a girl. You don't want to hurt a girl do you?" Loren reached up with her left hand to take a firm hold of his collar.

"Like I said, you're gonna love it. He grabbed her pajama top and ripped it open."

Under the sheets, Loren spread her legs and raised her knees, planting her feet flat on the mattress.

The heavily breathing figure leaned back from her face as he fumbled with his clothing. The bright blade moved to his side.

"Okay honey, now you..."

In one swift move, Loren pulled him to her and brought the heel of her right hand sharply against her attacker's nose. He screamed in pain and rocked back, easing the weight on Loren's body. As she slid out from under him, Loren drew an object from under her mattress, rose and raced from the room. As she passed the hallway nightlight she slapped it from its socket, eliminating the light. The intruder came behind her, cursing in the dark. He caught her by the hair and slammed her head against a doorjamb. Dazed, Loren collapsed to the floor as her attacker stood over her.

"You're gonna get it good now, missy. I was gonna be nice, but that's over." He bent to pull her to him.

The dark clad intruder didn't hear the low growl at the other end of the hallway.

Several things happened almost at once. As the intruder turned to the sound of running claws on wood, Loren swung a ruler-size length of iron pipe, catching the man on his left cheek; it connected with a definitive *slap*. Once again, the man

119

screamed in pain. His scream was cut short as Sugar's jaws clamped on his throat, ripping at tendons and flesh. In a purely defensive movement, the man buried his blade in the side of the furious bulldog, who, crying in pain, continued attacking the man's upper body and arms. The hallway overhead light came on as the man yanked out his knife and, fending the dog with his left arm made a second wild swing with his knife; it never found its target as Fields Gragg whipped his shotgun stock against the man's temple. The intruder slumped to the floor.

Loren rose to her feet, pipe in hand and saw Fields, in his underwear, standing with his shotgun ready. She quickly took in the sight of the prone man bleeding through his woolen mask and from throat wounds. Sugar was struggling to rise in attack.

"Put a tight hand over Sugar's cut while I go call 911," Fields ordered. "Are you okay?"

"I'm okay." Loren answered.

"Do it then."

Loren knelt to the dog, and pressed her hand over the wound in his side. Fields laid his double barrel next to her. "Safety's off. If he gives you trouble, shoot him." he said, gesturing at the prone figure. "I'll be right back."

Loren nodded as Fields turned away. She pressed her palm against the wound and spoke softly to her friend. Sugar's breath was coming rapid and ragged. For the first time since her mother's sickness, Loren sent a silent prayer for help. Her eyes clouded and her nose began to run. She wiped it with the back of her free hand as she began sobbing.

Fields soon returned, clothed, and carrying a handful of towels and a first aid kit.

Help'll come quick, the station's only two miles away, and the dispatcher said there's a deputy car in the area. "Get your clothes on. I placed an emergency call to the vet, and to the sheriff. Go, boy, go."

The "boy" registered clearly with Loren. They were to continue the façade. Fields took her place on the floor and she scrambled to her feet, then raced to her room. Pants, shirt, sneakers and she returned to find Fields sitting next to Sugar.

"We're supposed to meet the vet at his office. He said he'd be there in ten minutes. As soon as the deputy and the emergency people get here we're going to the vet. We'll answer questions later. Take off that feller's headsock, I want to see his face." Loren gasped as she removed the ski mask.

"You know him?"

"Yes, he's the boy I told you about who was so mad at Meredith. He's a student at ASU. His name is Lance van Riper."

"Well, he's in deep trouble now. How's he to come after you?"

"He thought that Meredith and I were dating, and he was jealous. Somehow he discovered I'm a girl—he called me by my real name—and I guess that made him mad. I think he's either drunk or high—or both."

"The law doesn't need to know the whole story then—until they need to know it." Fields said.

"He called me Miss Loren Creek. He knows."

Fields was silent, his lips pulled tight into a taut line. He slowly fingered the trigger guard on his shotgun. Loren, reading his thoughts, said softly. "No, Grandpa. No."

After a brief exchange, the deputy, a friend of Fields, agreed to escort him to the vet. While Loren held her palm against Sugar's wound, Fields and the deputy carefully moved him onto a blanket that served as a litter. Following the deputy's car, Fields and Loren laid out their story and plan of action.

The vet's office was fully lit, and the front door stood open as they pulled into his parking lot. Doctor Hiram Jackson, known as HiJack among his admiring clients, was waiting at the door. Fields and the deputy carried Sugar directly into the operating area.

"Lay him there," the vet said, pointing to a stainless table. Loren laid the hunting knife beside the dog, and the doctor's eyes widened when he saw the size of the blade. "Bowie knife," he said. "Good to know what I'm dealing with. Thanks."

"That was smart, son, thinking to bring that knife," The deputy added.

"I held it with my handkerchief by the blade in case you wanted to look for prints.

"Smart work, Lorne," Fields said, maintaining the grandson façade.

As the veterinarian worked his magic, the two stood off to the side while the deputy took a seat and started his written report.

"Doc, I need to use your toilet," Fields said.

HiJack pointed a direction. At the same time a sleepy-eyed veterinarian assistant appeared at the door and, without a word, put on rubber gloves and came to stand next to her boss. HiJack spoke soft instructions to her as the two worked quickly and efficiently to stop the flow of blood and to start an IV. Sugar's breathing became slow and regular.

After twenty minutes or so, Loren went to look for Fields. She found him standing in the parking lot smoking a cigarette.

"The Seven Eleven across the street was open. It's the first cigarette I've had in over ten years. I forgot how good they feel," Fields said. He fought the convulsive body movements of a man refusing to let his sobs come out. Loren put an arm around him.

"I fair love that bulldog like a child." Fields lit a second cigarette off the first.

Deputy Grimes came out to the parking lot. "We need to go to the station. I have to take your depositions."

"I'll go right now. Grandpa needs to stay here."

"Good enough, as long as you come soon, Fields."

"I'll do that, Billy. But I need to stay with my dog—you understand."

"I do. Let's go Lorne."

"Just a minute I want to see the vet."

In the operating room, Loren approached the two figures bent over Sugar.

"I've got to go to the Sheriff's office and give a deposition to the deputy. How's he doing, Doc?"

"It's close. Another five minutes and he'd have been gone. But he's young and strong."

"Please, Doc. Do what you can. Money's no object."

HiJack stood erect and looked down at the young teen. "You said that right, money is not the object here."

"I don't mean insult, Doc. Please save him. If we lose Sugar, I'll have Grandpa to bury."

HiJack handed Loren a box of tissues. "Wipe your face. We'll do everything we can to save him—and your grandpa." Another veterinary assistant entered the room, put on gloves, and came to stand over the operating table.

"Thanks, Doc." Loren turned and went to the waiting sheriff's vehicle, placing a kiss on Fields' cheek before she got in the car.

CHAPTER 33

On the fourth morning after the home attack, Fields received word from HiJack that Sugar would be okay to come home in a couple of days, but he would have to wear what he called an Elizabethan collar for a month to keep him from pulling out the staples that held the wound together. Fields hung up the phone, got in his truck and drove to the Watauga Medical Center.

The left side of Lance's entire face was purple and swollen. His throat was covered with thick bandages. Both upper arms had extensive suturing. Painkillers kept him sedated.

Seated at Lance's bedside was a large, fleshy man working at a laptop. A small desk had been pulled in beside his chair, and was piled with papers.

"What?" he said as he looked up and saw Fields standing in his cover-alls in the doorway. A deputy sheriff was standing behind him.

"I'm Fields Gragg. I own the house the boy broke into."

"Then you'd be the man for whom I'm drawing up this lawsuit. I'm Willard Van Riper, his father."

"How's he doing?"

"Not that it's any of your goddamn business, Gragg, but he's going to live—despite everything they did or didn't do here at Podunk County Clinic."

"Good. I'm glad he's going to make it."

"That's an odd sentiment coming from someone who brutally attacked and almost killed my only son."

Fields stood silently in the doorway.

"Well, Gragg, what do you have to say for yourself?"

"Mr. Van Riper, you can all me Mr. Gragg, or you can call me Fields. You can't call me 'Gragg,' and I don't like hearing the Lord's name taken in vain."

"You seem to have a lot of demands, fellah," Van Riper said as he rose from his workplace and approached Fields.

"There's more. I'd hope you'd show more appreciation for the hospital staff that saved your son's life, and probably prevented his wounds from turning out worse than they could have." He raised his hand to cut off van Riper's retort. "I'm not finished. Evidence shows that your boy broke into our home and threatened my grandchild with his knife. The fingerprints will confirm this. Our dog came to Lorne's rescue, and was almost killed by that knife. I came along in time to prevent your boy from doing serious harm to my grandchild. That's it in a nutshell."

"We'll see what the courts have to say about this—Mr. Gragg. I've got some high-class attorneys working on this case. I'm going to wind up owning that property you say my son broke into. Mr. Gragg, I've got the know-how, and I've got deep pockets."

"I probably shouldn't be doing this, but I'm going to go ahead and tell you that the sheriff's people have found illegal drugs in your son's car, and they've also found false identification papers—that allowed him to get his liquor from the ABC. There's more. Do you want me to go on, or have you heard enough?"

Van Riper's face was nearly purple and his fists were clenched at his side.

"Why did you come here, Mr. Gragg? To gloat?"

"Nossir. I came to see how your boy was doing."

"Fearful of a homicide charge then?"

"No, I wanted to see to him. I've done a lot of thinking these past three days—and no small amount of praying. I've searched my grand daddy's Bible for answers, and I've not found any yet. I need to know your boy better before I can find answers. I come a hair trigger from putting a load of shot through your son's brain, Mister Van Riper, and that doesn't set well with me. Sometimes what a body does in the heat of anger can bring shame and regret later. I did what was needed—I almost done what wasn't. I been wakin' of a morning in a cold sweat. Praying for forgiveness helps some. I sought out our preacher—it was he that put me on the path that brings me here. This hasn't been an easy choice, Mr. Van Riper."

"You've come to pray over my son, old man?"

Fields thought a moment. "If it comes to that."

Van Riper was breathing heavily. "I could throttle you with my bare hands, you hypocrite. If you weren't so old, I would. Now get out of my sight."

The deputy seated outside the room heard the exchange and rose to meet whatever was called for.

"Mr. Gragg," he said softly, "It's best you go."

As Fields walked away, Willard Van Riper shouted down the hall, "I'll see you in court, you damn hillbilly."

After Fields left and Van Riper was once again at his laptop, the deputy turned off his pocket tape recorder.

The following day, Fields showed up at Lance's room again. Lance was sitting up sipping ice water through a hospital straw. His father, still clicking away on the laptop, turned red when he saw Fields at the doorway.

"What do you want—to gloat some more?"

"I didn't come to gloat. I came to see your boy."

"Who is this, Dad?" Lance croaked.

"This is the man whose dog almost ripped your throat out, and who nearly decapitated you with that gun butt of his. This is Mr. Fields Gragg."

Lance said nothing. He merely stared at Fields as though trying to determine what species he was.

"Son, I came to see how you were doing, and to talk with you. I didn't come to make trouble—or to gloat as your father said. I came to see if there was anything I could do for you."

"Do?" Van Riper shouted. "Haven't you done enough, old man? You've damned near killed my boy, and you're no doubt going to be a material witness in his trial. Don't you think you've done enough? My boy has lost his golf scholarship, and he's been kicked out of this hick school you people call a 'university,' and finally, his reputation has nearly..." Van Riper was cut off by a choking sound his son was making. The two men moved to the bedside. Lance was trying to cry, but trying not to because the pain in his face was so fierce. Van Riper turned away from the awful struggle. He walked to the window and stood with his back to the room—rocking on his heels.

"The charges." Lance choked out.

"Yes?" Fields asked.

"Charges true."

"Don't try to talk, son. There'll be plenty of time to hash this out later. Right now, you work on getting well." Fields said.

Lance nodded, almost relieved that he didn't have to speak. Beads of sweat came to his brow from the exertion and from the pain. Fields pulled tissues from a bedside box, and wiped the boy's brow.

"What do you want here, Mr. Gragg? Absolution? Sympathy?"

"None of those, Mr. Van Riper. I came to see how your son was doing."

"You can't convince me that you don't hold a great deal of anger toward him, not if you believe the charges that are leveled against him."

"Yes, I do have a great anger in me—and that troubles some. All I see right now is a hurt, scared teenager facing some serious charges that might make a long jail sentence. You think I rejoice in that? What sort do you think I am? What kind of man are you who would think such a thing as my wanting absolution?"

"Then why are you here?"

"I've told you more than once why I've come. I'll not say it again because it makes out that I might be some kind of a liar who has to insist on the honesty of what he says."

Van Riper slumped into a chair. "My boy is hurt, Mr. Gragg," he said in a soft voice. "He doesn't need condemnation or judgment right now." Van Riper breathed in a long shuddering breath. His hands were shaking slightly.

Fields walked to the window overlooking the valley below and stood in thought.

"Mr. Van Riper, let's you and me go get us a cup of coffee."

The hospital cafeteria was glass on two sides. It overlooked a broad vista of mountains and valley in which the community and college nestled side-by-side. Take away some three-story buildings and it would be a picture post card.

The two men settled beside a floor-to-ceiling plate glass wall. Fields took a drink of coffee and settled back to take in the scenery. "Some view for a hospital, wouldn't you agree?" Lance's father grunted in acknowledgement.

"Mr. Van Riper, I wanted us to set and talk about your boy. I don't want to see him in court, or having to go to jail. I couldn't abide being a part of that. Nor could my grandchild. We talked it out—we talked it in and out and sideways. There's got to be some other way than bringin' the full force of the law down on your boy. I'm ripped apart with this, Mr. Van Riper: On the one hand he tried to harm that which is dearest to me in this world. Other hand, he's a boy. He'd been drinkin'.

I think on the fool things I done when I was in love with alcohol—and I ponder the time a judge kept me out of long jail. I've never know'd why he did so, but his suspended sentence and probation turned around my life in the doin' of it. Like I said, I came near to killin' that boy of yours—and I'd of got off scot-free. But now, my head is clearer and my heart less hard. As tryin' as it is, I've set aside my need for revenge, and want only to seek justice as the court sees fit."

"What are you saying, Mr. Gragg?"

"I don't blame your boy for being what he is, Mr. Van Riper. I'm only sad for him." Fields searched for the words to express powerful emotions, suitable for one stranger to another. "My missus and me, we had two wonderful children who grew into young people that would make any parent proud. The Army took my boy in one of their wars, and a drunk driver took my daughter. The losses coming nearly together like they did, was more than my wife could bear. She went to join them within the year. I'm left here to live out my days, knowing that when I go—it's all gone. My line ends with me. Then one day this near desperate girl showed up at my door, looking for a place to live."

When the story of Loren was finished Van Riper rose and got two glasses of water. Setting them on the table he asked, "Why are you telling me this? Don't you know that I could turn you in, and you could be tried for any number of crimes?"

"I 'spect that's so, but here's the way I see things. You and I were blessed with children. God lent me and my missus two, then took them back in their prime. I don't know why, and I can't say that I didn't question God's doings. If I claimed not to be angry about it, I'd be lying."

"I'm sorry for your loss. It must hurt." Van Riper's expression softened.

"It does that. Now going on—God gave you one son, a handsome, intelligent boy who should be able to make his way in any man's world. God graced you with this wonderful gift. But for some reason you chose not to respect that trust He gave you, and by things you did or failed to do, you've tarnished that gift, and we've wound up with that beat-up boy upstairs. I don't blame your boy for what he did. I blame you."

Van Riper stiffened and turned bright red.

Fields raised a staying hand. "I'm truly sorry to say such a thing, and I don't blame your anger. But I believe that, if you think it through, you'll agree with what I said. I'll ask you to accept my apology for saying such a hurtful thing, but it's honest and I can't take it back."

"Mr. Gragg, Lance's mother is in a near-by motel room most likely crying quietly, to herself. Every couple of hours she puts on a happy face and comes to Lance's room to sit until she can't hold it together. She then returns to her room and her tears. You don't know how glad I am that she was not here to listen to what you just said to me." He rose from the table they were sharing, "We're through with this conversation, Mr. Gragg." He stalked out of the room.

Fields Gragg turned his gaze to a far mountain. His work-worn hands were folded together on the table. *Help me through this, Lord. Tell me what to do.*

The following day, Willard Van Riper looked up to a knock at his son's door, and saw a slender dark-haired boy dressed in jeans and polo shirt.

"Mr. Van Riper?"

"Yes."

"Mr. Van Riper, my name is Lorne Land. Fields Gragg is my grandfather. Can I come in?"

"Yes."

"I've come to see how Lance was doing. Grandpa said he was hurt bad."

"He's sleeping right now, but he's getting better every day."

"When will he be able to leave here?"

"Three days, the doctors say."

"Is he going to have to go from here to jail?"

"There will be a bond hearing. I'll make bond."

Loren nodded, and then stood in silence.

"Is there anything else you want to know? I've got work to do."

Loren took a deep breath and exhaled sharply.

"I'm really very busy, young man."

"I'm sorry about Lance getting hurt like this." Loren approached the bed. When she got close enough to see Lance's black and blue face and the extent of his injuries she made a sharp intake of breath, and then turned away with a hand over her mouth. "I'm sorry," she said backing to the doorway. "I never seen a body hurt so bad."

Van Riper could see she was fighting back tears.

"I'm sorry too—young lady. I've seen injuries like this before, but not to someone I love."

Loren rushed to the man, and grabbed him by the arm. "We've got to stop this. Lance is goin' to have to go to court. He could serve jail time. We got to stop it now. It's—it's not right. You're a lawyer—Is there nothing we can do to end this mess?"

A startled Van Riper looked into the fervid face of the youth holding his arm. "Young La—Lorne, what is it with you mountain people? First it was your grandfather, and now you. You two almost killed my son—and now you say you want to save him. That doesn't ring true."

"We fought Lance as an intruder in our house. He'd been drinkin' and was angry about losing his girlfriend, and him blamin' me. Now, I'm not excusing Lance for what he did. But I'm hopin' that the court will find ways to deal with him other than a long term in jail. I'm hopin' he can be turned to the good. Grandpa and I have talked this out til we're blue in the face, and the more we talked, the more we come to see that there's no worth to sending him off to a long jail sentence. I guess it's a matter of simple mercy. That's all the words I know to explain why we stand where we do. Now, if you can't see what I been sayin' then I'll have to ask Grandpa to come and explain it. He's better with words than me." She let go of Van Riper's arm and stepped back. "Why don't you tell me what you think we should do?" Then she added in finality. "We are a Christian people." As Loren said this she rose to her full height and raised her chin slightly.

Van Riper walked to the picture window, and with his back to Loren said, "It'll have to go to court; we can't stop that. Now, what happens in court is going to be up to the judge and the lawyers. All I—we—can do," he turned to face her, "is damage control."

"Damage control?"

"Yes, that's when you try to see to it that as little harm as possible comes as a result of a situation."

"Sounds like something you'd do during a flood. Like in Noah's time; I guess Noah's ark was about damage control."

"Yes. An ark, that's good." Van Riper smiled. "We need an ark."

"Is that what lawyers do? Are you an ark, Mr. Van Riper?"

"I have been." Van Riper paused. "But then, sometimes I've been the flood."

Loren thought a moment. "I understand—sort of."

Van Riper moved toward his chair. "Thank you for coming by Miss, now I've got…"

"Could we go for a drive Mr. Van Riper?" Loren cut in sharply.

"What?"

"It'd only take a couple of hours. I'd like to show you something—a place—a house—that belongs to me. Grandpa said that he told you all about him and me. I know that if it comes up in court he won't, no—he *cain't* lie. It could put him in jail, and I'd be to fault. I think you and I need each other, Mr. Van Riper. If we go for a drive, we can talk in private, I can show you our beautiful mountains, and I can tell you my story. Maybe you can tell me Lance's and yours."

"Young lady—young man, whichever, you're wise beyond your years. I'd be glad to get away from this place for a while. It's almost time for lunch—my treat."

"Let's keep me as 'Lorne' Mr. Van Riper, it'll be easier in the long run. But, it's not *my* wisdom, it's Grandpa's. He's more upset than me, and he wants to see right done."

Van Riper set aside his work. "I need to talk with him again. I owe an apology, for some foolish things I said. I don't let my obligations hang."

"He wants to talk more with you—he says that, under your anger, you're a good and decent man."

Van Riper took a deep breath, stepped back, and then regained his composure. "I—You don't know how long it's been since I've heard someone say that of me. I'll be happy to go to lunch with you. We have differences to work out—big ones."

"Good. Do you like barbecue?"

"It's one of my favorite foods. I gather you have a place in mind."

"There's a place about five miles north of Elizabethton—out in the country. It's called Ridgewood Barbecue. The Proffitt's been makin' converts there since 1947. The first Mr. and Mrs. Proffitt were friends of my grandparents, and later my Momma. Ridgewood Barbecue was about the only restaurant meat my Momma would let me have. I've not had any Ridgewood in nigh on two years, and I feel deprived. Some travel magazines have named it the best barbecue in the country. I'd not call them mistaken. But, you can judge for yourself."

It took horrendous effort and a lot of background negotiation to get the judge to agree to a suspended sentence and closely supervised parole. The judge would not permit Lance to leave the state for rehab or treatment, so Van Riper had to agree to turn his affairs in Florida over to his staff for a year in order to obey the judge's ruling regarding rehabilitating his son. Van Riper's wealth secured the best legal help available, and expensive therapists to work with him and his son. In the end, Lance's mother agreed to come live near the father and son in their mountain condo in an effort to start anew. She saw it as the last opportunity to save their son—and her family. Weekly, then monthly, reports to the court were required. Through it all, Loren's true identity hung like a guillotine. It was Lance who constructed a tale that the court accepted.

"I broke into his house because I wanted to scare him away from my girlfriend, Your Honor. I didn't intend to hurt him, but he had no way of knowing that. I just wanted to scare him." Fields was able to persuade the sheriff to set aside the evidence against Lance uncovered in the investigation, but he was told that—given the slightest cause—the evidence would be "discovered." Powerful favors were called in and political gain was no small consideration.

The court accepted Lance's motives and moved on to determine what to do with him. Negotiations were long, complex and clearly drawn out in paper. A misstep would put Lance behind bars for a considerable time. There was much to gain, much to risk, and very much to lose.

CHAPTER 34

That winter, Loren and Council resumed their cross-country runs, weather permitting. There was rarely a week when they were not able to run their minimum of three days. Fields frequently commented on the recent mildness of the winters. The ski resorts suffered, but the weather kept Loren outdoors and happily running.

In the mountains, late March and early April are the cruelest time of the year. A week of warm weather and budding plants could be followed by a week of bitter cold accompanied by sleet, snow, and rain. Bryce told Loren about the year they had over two feet of snow in mid-April. Freeze and thaw were the order of the day. Finally, Mrs. Teague's Wake Robin bloomed, and spring came as though on call.

Sundays went the same as usual with Meredith and Tara. However, in the winter months, the three girls studied road maps of southeastern United States and most especially, Florida. Careful planning was needed for the coming event. Spring Break. Loren let her hair grow longer—a shaggy mountain boy look for Lorne that could turn into a tousled, short bob when Loren made an appearance.

Loren's place as a member—and sometimes a leader—of The Group became firmer and finally entrenched. She was one of the boys.

"Let's meet back at the shoe store in the mall," Bryce said rising from the school entryway steps where he and his friends had met after classes. "I need some new running shoes."

"Okay, Council answered. "I've got to pick up some layin' mash for ma's chickens at Southern States, then I've got to drop off some metalwork at Clemmons on Niley Cook Road. After that, I'm free."

"My old shoes are about worn out," Loren said. "I'm ready for new."

"I'm good for shoes," Gent said, "But I'll go along just to keep you guys from buying anything too girly looking."

Council grinned at his friend, "Well, if anybody would know 'girly', you would." This brought some low laughter and guffaws from the group.

"That's true," Gent answered. "Hanging with this crowd has helped me understand how girls dress and act."

"I know the girls hereabouts won't have nothing to do with you, so I'm glad we could help you out," Council quipped.

Loren always enjoyed the friendly give and take among her friends. She added. "I can meet y'all at the mall but I've got to get together with Meredith later. She and Tara and I are planning a surprise for Grandpa. A surprise he'll never forget." Loren said with a grin.

The group moved slowly down the steps and toward the parking lot as the boys tried unsuccessfully to pry the nature of Loren's "surprise" out of her. Loren picked up her bicycle from the bike rack along the way.

"Five o'clock at the shoe store then?" Bryce asked his friends. There were nods all around.

Loren picked up some Astyptodyne for her 'grandpa' at Boone Drugs on Deerfield Road, and then peddled over to Black Bear Books where she browsed the book shelves and perused a couple of books that she thought might be of interest to Fields. Later, she peddled to the Goodwill Thrift store where she found a nice pair of used jeans, and then she made her way on to the mall, where she chained her bike near the front entry of Belks. She cut through the women's department on her way to the shoe store. The perfume displays caught her eye, and she stopped to smell the aroma of one in particular. She sprayed some on a swatch of paper provided. It was a disappointingly cloying aroma. She dropped the aromatic square of paper into the receptacle provided. The varied array of bottles, boxes, and paraphernalia associated with female charm arrested her attention, and she stood and scanned first up close, then further away. Counters topped with carousel displays, glass tiers of shelves, all accented with appropriate color and lighting—it was a marvel of well-designed marketing. "This should be my world." Loren mused as she put a hand to her mouth and furrowed her brow.

"Who is she?" The query snapped Loren out of her reverie. A matronly sales clerk stood off to Loren's side with a want-to-understand smile on her face.

"Um. Oh. I was just—just. I was just looking."

"Something for anyone in particular? Your mother maybe?"

"No. I was—no, nothing in particular."

The kindly lady moved closer. "A girlfriend then. A handsome young man like you must have a string of young ladies interested."

"Not really." Loren was recovering her composure. "I don't have any girlfriends." She looked for an escape route.

"Then I have something for you that will help attract the young ladies, come with me." The saleslady, her name tag read *Eva*, led a charge to the men's counter where Loren was greeted with a well-planned lay-out of "masculine" products. The colors featured browns and deep golds and reds.

"Here's one I think you'll like," Eva spritzed a paper square. "Try this."

Loren sniffed the paper and turned away from the musky odor. "No, I don't think so."

"Now here's one that we used to carry years ago and is making a comeback. It's called "French Leather." Another spritzed paper presented to Loren's nose. It was a handsome scent. She thought of Council, then blushed furiously.

"Why, I believe you like it." Eva said with a broad smile.

"Not for me. But I think it would make a great gift for someone I know."

"You're dad?"

"No—no. My—grandpa." She laughed out loud at the thought of Fields wearing 'perfume' that masked the over-powering turpentine scent of the Astyptodyne that he applied liberally to cuts, abrasions, bruises, and chapped hands. He once

131

persuaded Loren to try it for her stuffy nose. She applied a drop under each nostril, and in ten minutes her nasal passages cleared, but she smelled like a fresh cut on a pine branch the rest of the day.

'I'm surprised you don't drink that stuff.' Loren once chided Fields as he rubbed it into his hands following some outside chore done in the dry mountain air.

'Tastes awful.' Fields replied shaking his head as he replaced the cap on the small brown bottle, and returned it to a bib pocket of his overalls.

"I'll think about this one. My—grandpa has a birthday in a month."

"Okay then. I'll look forward to seeing you again before too long."

Loren nodded to the lady then walked toward the entryway that opened into the mall passing back through women's perfume. A familiar label caught her eye; *Jasmine*. It was the scent her mother had used. Eva, ever the saleswoman, quickly proffered a sample on paper. Loren felt herself go dizzy as she began to sway. She caught herself on the glass counter and took in a deep breath, then another.

"Child. Are you alright? You're pale as a ghost." She took Loren by the arm and led her to one of the tall metal chairs that beauty seekers sat on in their quest at the counter. "You sit here. I'll be right back."

When Eva returned with a paper cup of water, she saw that Loren had been unable to control her tears.

"Oh my. What's the matter? Was it something I said?"

"No. No. It wasn't you." Loren said, drinking down most of the glass. "Jasmine was my Momma's perfume."

"*Was?* Oh, my Dear." Eva produced tissues for both herself and Loren.

"I am so sorry." She moved next to Loren, put an arm around her, and pulled their heads together. Loren choked back sobs in an attempt to stop.

"Tears are nothing to be ashamed of, my dear. More than anything, they're a sign of your love. It would be a terrible thing to not grieve the loss of your mother."

Loren nodded in silent agreement as she tried to regain her composure.

"What's wrong?" came a familiar voice. Loren looked up to see Council standing beside her. She took a deep breath, fighting back her feelings.

"Are you okay?" Council asked.

Loren nodded.

"He smelled the perfume that his mother used and it—it sort of overwhelmed him."

"Are you okay, Lorne?" Council said softly. "I can take you home if you want."

"No. I'm okay." Loren downed the remainder of the water and returned the cup to Eva. "Thank you." She slipped from the chair and stood erect, gulping air.

"I've got to go," she said to Eva.

"You come back and see me real soon. We'll have a cup of tea on my break."

"I'd like that," Loren said.

"Good. Now, you take care of yourself; you're such a fine young man." Eva turned and walked away before her tears showed too plainly.

"She reminds me of my grandma," Loren said.

"She seemed nice," Council answered, still with a look of concern.

Loren brought herself to an erect posture, "let's go get shod," she said brusquely.

CHAPTER 35

"Florida? What have you lost in Florida?" Fields snorted.

"Nothing. It's spring break and I wanted to go with Meredith and Tara. They're going to Orlando to see Disney World."

"You gals goin' to go to those wild beach parties where the girls show the boys everything they have, and then law the boys when they get molested?"

"We'll probably stop at one of the beaches for a night, but I'll try to refrain from stripping down to my birthday suit. It'll be hard for sure."

Fields grinned his best mischievous grin. "I reckon if I's the age of those boys in this day and time I'd be down at Lauderdale with my antenna up too."

"I reckon you would, you evil old man."

"Is that a way to talk to your grandpa? I tell the boys down at the store how you disrespect me at every chance."

"Well, somebody's got to keep you honest, lest you get biggety."

Fields chuckled. "You'll send a postcard?"

"Every day."

"Well, go then."

"Thanks, Grandpa."

"I'm meeting with the Van Ripers again today for lunch. Anything you want me to say?"

Loren paused in reflection. "How's Lance doing?"

"He's recovering pretty good. His wounds are healing, but they's a lot of inside work left for that boy. I'll tell 'em you asked after him."

"I just as soon you didn't, Grandpa."

"Okay then."

Interstate 95 was a ribbon of moving steel, bumper to bumper, side by side traffic cruise-controlled at 80 miles an hour, and then choked with stalled traffic crawling at walking speed until whatever mess that had occurred was cleaned up. The three girls laughed, squealed, pointed and laughed some more as they checked out the boys in nearby cars, and got checked out by them. It was a totally new role for Loren, one she took to, quickly.

They were in Orlando the next day. Disney World! By day's end they realized that Disney World was definitely not where they wanted to be, and they returned to the beaches for a couple of days before turning west to attend to the real reason for the Florida trip.

Interstate 4 took the girls across one of the Tampa Bay bridges to Saint Petersburg and on west to the community of Seminole, Florida. They found the mailbox of the person they were seeking on a side street called Pineapple Lane.

Leaving the sisters in the car, Loren went to the front door and rang the bell. She was answered by high-pitched barking. The door was opened by a handsome slender woman who appeared to be of social security age.

"Yes?" The lady asked in a pleasant well-modulated voice.

The first thing Loren noticed was her vivid smile. The next thing noted was the lady's pile of thick auburn hair.

Fields was awakened by a banging on his door, and Sugar barking. He pulled on his jeans and a shirt, and then went to the door. The porch light showed a beaming Loren Land holding a white puppy in her arms. Fields opened the door and joined her on the porch. Only then did he see Meredith and Tara, also holding puppies. There was a white bulldog with them—evidently nursing.

"What did you...? How..."

"Not 'Welcome back, Loren,' or 'I've really missed you, Loren,' or even, 'Did you have a good time?'"

Fields laughed. "This one here looks exactly like Sugar"—who was investigating the strange female dog on his porch—"when he was a pup. Where did you get these critters?"

"We stopped by Steinhatchee on the way back. It took some searching but we found someone who had a female with pups and was willing to part with her. I met people who remembered you. They said you left town just ahead of the sheriff." Loren chided with a broad grin.

"It's good to have you back. I've missed being ragged by you every working moment of the day."

"Good to be back. I thought we could plan on raising a couple more like Sugar. Tara says she wants one, but I expect her mother will have something to say on that. I know Bryce will want one."

"I declare, Gal. I'm fully surprised."

"Like they say, Grandpa. You ain't seen nothing yet."

Several days later over breakfast coffee, Fields sensed that Loren had something on her mind, so he asked her.

"I have a surprise for you," Loren said. "I was going to surprise you, but after springing Bess and her puppies on you, I've had second thoughts. Just think of it as a small gift from someone who loves you."

Fields rocked and waited.

"I went to Florida to try to find an old friend of yours. We found her and asked if she would come and meet with you and renew acquaintance."

"Her?"

"Yes. I don't know how to say this except that she's someone out of your long past. She remembers you and is looking forward to seeing you again."

"What have you done, Gal?"

"Coach Helder's wife works in school records and she was able to help me locate the lady you knew as Miss Beverly James. It took a while because she's been married and has her husband's name."

Fields' rocking stopped for several beats then resumed slightly faster than before.

"Her widowed name is Mrs. Cash Winters. She lives alone with her little dog in Seminole, Florida—it's like a suburb of St Petersburg. She remembers you, she says, 'with fondness'. She also remembers 'with fondness' her short stay in Watauga County, and is pleased to come back for a brief visit."

"Seeing as how you've got my entire life planned out, you could likely tell me when this 'brief visit' is goin' to happen."

"Mrs. Winters drove up from Florida three days ago and has been renewing her memory of the mountains for the past three days. She's staying at the Holiday Inn and taking her meals at the restaurants around town. Claims she'd forgotten how beautiful these mountains are."

The rocker stopped again missing four beats, then resumed at a rapid pace.

"She's here." Fields said softly.

"Yes, and she wants to see you."

The rocker stopped as Fields rose and went to lean against a porch post, his back to Loren. She noted his rapid breathing. After a deep breath and exhale, he turned to face Loren.

"She'd always claimed that I was her prize student. She said I had a future— now she'll come here and see me as the failure I am. I've done nothing with my life. Nothing. I'm a hick farmer with a high school education. I know you think you've done me a favor but, Gal, all you've done is embarrass me to someone I've held dear all my life." Loren had never seen anger in Fields, it was a terrible thing to behold. "I'll not see her. I'm not much, but I have pride. Tell her to go back to Florida."

Loren fell into a rocker, mouth agape at Fields' bitter response to the plan she had worked to bring about. She thought of the months of planning and anticipation, the long trip to Florida, and the enormous delight she felt in carrying out her plan. She rose from her rocker, walked past Fields down the steps and to her house. Sugar followed her, but returned shortly to Fields when he was excluded from Loren's doorway. Fields went into his house and dug out the remainder of the pack of cigarettes from the night Sugar almost died. He smoked for nearly an hour before walking over to Loren's.

She had nearly finished packing when he found her in the bedroom.

"Going off somewhere?"

"Yes. I'm going to take a room somewhere, but for right now I'm sure that Meredith will put me up until I can find something; a place where I don't have to worry about insulting someone with my loving intentions. I'll come back later to get my belongings."

"Is that how you see it then?"

"That's how I see it."

As Loren rode away in Bryce's pick-up, she saw the glow of Fields' cigarette from the winter cold of his darkened porch.

CHAPTER 36

At eight in the morning, Fields was sleeping in his clothes when Sugar's barking wakened him. He rose awkwardly from the couch, noting the crumpled cigarette pack on the coffee table as he hobbled to confront the figure outlined in the glass of his front door. He opened the door to find Willard Van Riper on the other side of the screen. Sugar was not happy.

"Yes?" Fields asked stepping out onto the porch and leaving Sugar inside.

"Mr. Gragg, I need to talk with you."

"What has that boy of yours done now?"

"No, no. Lance is doing okay. Clara and I are delighted with his progress. It's Loren."

"Is she okay?"

"She's not physically injured if that's what you mean. But she's certainly not 'okay'. She's utterly miserable, and it's your concern."

"How did…"

"Last night after she crashed at Meredith's, she went to a late supper at Ruby Tuesday's. She was off in the corner quietly crying into her salad when I saw her. Clara was quite distressed and insisted that I inquire. When I went over to her, the dam broke and she told me about her attempt to reunite you with an old acquaintance from your youth. She told me about your angry response and described why you felt so intensely about what she worked so hard to achieve—to please you. And frankly, Mr. Gragg, I was truly disappointed in you. That girl loves you like she was yours, and now she's certain she's lost you."

Fields took a leash from its hanger on the doorframe to secure Sugar.

"Have you had coffee?"

"No. Clara was pounding on my door at dawn this morning, demanding that I go immediately to talk with you. Hell, I've still got sleep in my eyes."

"Come in."

When Van Riper entered, Fields leashed Sugar and handed Van Riper the leash. "Here, take hold of Sugar and get acquainted while I get coffee started. He'll accept you while you're holding the leash, you'll see."

Van Riper took the leash and followed Fields into the kitchen. He saw the full ash tray.

"I didn't know you smoked."

"I don't. I used to—like everbody—but I quit about ten year ago. Last night got me started back up. I'm quittin again, and reckon I'll go for another ten before I buy my next pack."

Fields fired up a gas burner under his antique enamel coffee pot, and then scooped up some coffee in a small tin cup while waiting for the water to boil.

"Hobo coffee." Van Riper said.

"What's that?"

"Hobo coffee is what my mom called it. It's what the hobos used to make in #10 tin cans. You boil the water and drop in the coffee, stir it and wait for the grounds to settle. It helps if you have some egg shells to throw in. The coffee stays good all day. You can even add more water as the day goes on and you've still got excellent coffee. We used to make it in the Boy Scouts and later on hunting and fishing trips. It remains my favorite to this day."

"Well, it's all you'll get here, so that works out good."

The two men were silent as the coffee ritual was completed. Van Riper took the opportunity to pet and get acquainted with Sugar, who apparently was taking a liking to the man.

"This is a fine animal."

"He was, til that girl of mine ruined him. Now he's gotten to where he'll take up with anyone who speaks kind to him. I reckon I'll keep him though. I've got four more just like him in a pen out back, a bitch and three pups. The pups are spoke for and I'm keeping the female."

The coffee was poured. Fields was pleased to see that Van Riper took no sugar or cream.

"That girl of yours— is why I've come to talk with you. I was angry with you when she told me about how you responded to her gift of love. I wanted to come here and tell you to go to hell, but I don't see how any good could come of that. I admire you too much to do that and besides, I owe you a debt I'll never be able to repay. Our son seems on the way to becoming a decent sort, and I think I am as well. My Clara is seriously considering taking me back and, all in all, our lives are turning around. I figure I owe it all to you and Loren. So it seems I've got to step up to the plate and take a turn at trying to reconcile you two, Mr. Gragg."

"*Fields* will do."

"Good, my friends know me as *Will*."

"Fair enough. I don't think you need to do any reconciling—Will. I was up until three or so this morning, smoking and cussin' my mule-headedness. I was wrong and I want to set things right, if Loren will let me—though I couldn't blame her if she didn't. She's got a strong-will, that girl. Too strong at times, but there's none finer anywhere."

"I agree, Mr.—*Fields*. I know that she'll hear you out. She wants to make amends as much as you—even though she was the wronged party, I might add. That girl has character." The two men nodded in agreement. "I'll take some more of that brew."

Van Riper frowned over his second cup of coffee, slowly and repetitively turning it between his hands.

"Is there something else?" Fields asked.

"Yes. Yes, there is." Van Riper pursed his lips, his jaw clenched.

"Best to say it then, Will."

"Clara and I have had a lot of time to talk, and it's just that, I've never owed anyone as much as I've owed that girl of yours." He smiled through his growing discomfort. "Clara has really taken a shine to Loren. They met at Lance's first hearing and fell into an immediate friendship."

"She is something special." Fields said hoarsely, blinking back his feeling.

"Yes, she is. I can't tell you how moved Clara was last night when she heard of your falling out."

Fields nodded. "There was no fallin' out. If you hadn't come here this morning, I'd be on the road tryin' to find her."

"I've never asked a body to do this, Will, but I'll swallow my foolish pride and ask you and your Missus to run interference for me. Tell her I'm sorry. Tell her I hope she'll come back. And tell her that if she doesn't come back I'll have to go get her. And—tell here I love her."

"I'll—we'll do that, Fields." Van Riper took a long pull from his mug. "That's fine coffee." He said clearing his throat.

Fields tipped the old pot over Van Ripers cup again. "How do you like your eggs?"

That afternoon Loren showed up on Fields' porch with an attractive lady on one side and her suitcase on another. Sugar was ecstatic. Fields didn't wait for a knock before opening the door and stepping onto the porch.

The lady was attired in a modest blouse and pleated skirt that showed a trim athletic figure.

Fields stood silently, his lips slightly parted.

"Warren. It's me. Beverly—*Winters* now—but you knew me as *Beverly James*."

Field regained his composure, "I knew you as *Miss Beverly,* and I always will." He gestured to the rockers, and then silently took Loren in his arms, knowing that words were useless.

The handsome lady gracefully took a seat. She waited as Loren and Fields disengaged, each nodding to the other. Their eyes said it all.

"And you, Warren—I've held you in my memory as Warren for these many years. I can't count the times my mind flew to you. I've often wondered what had become of you. I assumed that you had married, had children, and now grandchildren. I found myself envying your wife and family. Our marriage proved childless, and I took solace in my work with school children and with teaching them the wonders of books and reading."

Fields sat in silent astonishment at the disclosure. He responded. "We had children and lost both to tragedy within six months of each other. They were both in their early twenties. My Ellie couldn't stand the loss. She went to join our children."

"I see. I'm so sorry, Warren. I know you must love them, and now the memory of them, dearly."

"That is so. But now I have this—grand child—here who has brought such joy to my remaining years that I no longer dwell on the losses of the past. I can only look forward to her future." Fields looked directly into Loren's eyes. "She is all that really matters to me now."

Loren moved again to Fields' embrace. They held onto each other in brief silence as Sugar wagged his stub and danced merrily near them. Beverly Winters sat by in smiling approval.

"You smell like an ashtray, Old Man."

"It's good to have you back, Gal," Fields said, grinning widely. Why don't you take your suitcase to your house while Miss Beverly and I renew our acquaintance?"

Loren rose and placed a quick kiss on Field's cheek. "I won't be long."

Fields pulled his rocker close.

"You've changed so little since I was your student. How did you do that?"

Beverly blushed slightly and laughed away the compliment. "You always were the courtly gentleman, Warren."

"If courtly is seeing and saying the truth, then I plead guilty. I'm courtly."

"Thank you, Warren. You're too kind. But look at you. I've traveled the world with my husband who was a military man, and if I had seen you on the streets of Germany or Japan I would have said, 'There's Warren Gragg.' You are the boy that I recall—grown handsome."

Field flushed slightly as he sped his rocking.

"Do you still read, Warren? I remember how you devoured books when I knew you. I couldn't keep you in books—you were forever finishing them off in a single day or weekend."

"I still enjoy the reading."

"The reading. That's what you always called it. Warren, I'd forgotten that phrase. I have to admit, it makes my heart race to hear it from your lips."

"My grandfather named it. He encouraged the reading even more than my ma—mother and father. He gave me that turn of word."

"I'll have to confess, Warren; one thing that has bothered me all these years is the fear that you'd given up the reading. But I had an even greater fear, one that nagged and tore at me so that I nearly called here a half dozen times after I left these mountains. Once, I even had your family's phone ringing, but I hung up before they answered."

"I can't imagine what would worry you so about me."

"I knew that you had plans for college, and I had a fear of you going off to be corrupted by the ways of the world. I saw you going to a major university, fitting into the social stream, joining a fraternity, and becoming one of the boys. I knew you as a kind and decent boy on the way to manhood, and I feared for that goodness in you. I never wanted to see you become one of those quasi-sophisticates I've watched today's college's churn out by the carload. So many universities manufacture half-men who have forgotten their roots. You were on the way to becoming a full man, and from the conversations I've had these past three days with those familiar with you, I see that you have attained that stature in the eyes of the community. You are what I'd hoped you would be."

"I'm a farmer with a high school education."

"Nonsense. Loren has told me about the wall of books in your study. She says you can match wits with anyone, but more important than that, she says you are the most honest man she has ever met. I've heard that repeated by at least two other people in the county."

Fields fixed his gaze on the large flat rock by the river as he spoke. "I'll say this. Our meeting has gone on as though we are old friends who have never been apart. We've jumped in with both feet. Right into a close way I've had only with my wife, and I don't know how to take all this by the handle. You've come here, Miss Beverly, and taken me by storm."

"Is that a bad thing, Warren?"

"As good as it feels, I'd say not. But I wasn't finished."

"Oh. I'm sorry."

"That's okay, we're so full of ourselves for each other that we're tumbling all over ourselves to get out what we've held for these many years."

"What was it I interrupted, Warren?"

"I believe that we are both good judges of character, do you?"

"Yes. I believe that to be true. I would call it good instincts."

"Good, that's important for what I have to say. I want you to consider marriage."

Beverly Winters didn't flinch at the thought but merely sat wide-eyed. In fact, it was at that moment that Fields realized how truly beautiful her eyes were.

"Now understand, I'm not proposing to you. I'm asking you to consider my intention to propose at a later time. As we get to know one another, I may change my mind, and—if you acknowledge and accept my intent—you might change yours. This leaves our choices open as we explore the possibility. It also lets us fall in—or out—of love. You don't have to answer me right now, in fact you might choose to walk away and never return and I would neither blame nor fault you."

Then came the silence of two people stunned: One by what was said, and the other by the fact that he said it. Neither rocker rocked.

"Warren Gragg. We have met and talked for twenty minutes. You are a case."

"I've heard that said."

"Well, Warren, I will punish your intentions by accepting them. I do believe that, if you had not made such an offer to me by this day's end, I would have made it to you. We're both old enough to say, "Damn the torpedos!" Fields nodded and resumed rocking. "Straight ahead."

Loren and Sugar trotted back from her house. Sugar went immediately to Beverly, placed his head on her lap and peered up with wise brown eyes. Beverly looked at Fields and gently shook her head in wonder, then she slightly tipped a head signal toward Loren for Fields' benefit.

"Gal." Fields said softly, "We have something we need to tell you."

CHAPTER 37

By mid-May, Fields' 'intention' became a 'proposal' and an engagement ring was produced and accepted. Beverly was to become a June bride in a simple ceremony with a small attendance. The day after Beverly accepted and put on her engagement ring, Fields announced that he had something he wanted to show his friends, and that he needed their help with an idea.

A few days later, Fields, Beverly, and Loren—Sugar was added at the last moment—were picked up by Will and Clara Van Riper and, under Fields' direction, were driven in their large SUV to a spot in the south part of the county about ten miles from Fields' home.

Will was instructed to park on the roadside next to a large open field that showed signs of having once been an apple orchard. Most of the trees had been cut down and the stumps removed.

Fields said, "Clara, you're a realtor, and now that you've got your license to practice in North Carolina you can probably give me your opinion of this tract of land that lay here."

"What piece are you talking about, Fields?"

"Well, everything you see here, from the hills to the left to the highway to the right, then on to that ridge line in the distance."

"That's over three hundred acres, I can't tell you anything about it from here. I'd have to walk it, look at the survey of it and do the research work in the court house."

"It's closer to five hundred. Would you do the research for me?"

"Of course, but it will take a few days. Are you considering purchasing it?"

"No. It's my land, I have an idea about how to use it, and I need your realty skill to help me out. I'll need Will's lawyerin' too."

"You own five hundred acres of cleared, undeveloped land in Watauga County?" Clara asked incredulously.

"Yes, but that—and where I live, is all I own."

"Fields, this land is probably worth several million dollars in today's market."

"I don't doubt that. I just need to determine what to do with it. I have an idea or two, and I thought that you and Will could help me out."

They spent the day walking the property, which had two ponds, a lake and a protected trout stream running through it. When they had walked themselves to fatigue and returned to the car, Clara said, "I was wrong, Fields. That property is worth tens of millions. All the while you've been telling everybody that you're just a poor dirt farmer.

Beverly, give the man back his ring—he's been lying to you all this time."

"I just might do that, Clara. A man that will lie about being a millionaire will lie about anything."

"Right, give him back his ring. I want him." Clara said, laughing.

Fields said, "I am a dirt farmer, and I am made poor paying those ever-rising taxes on such a sizeable piece of land. Like I've already said, it was bought by my grand-uncle who planted the apple orchard. When he passed, it went to my father, and then to me. You wouldn't believe what the taxes were back in the 1930s and 40s."

Back in Fields' kitchen the small group settled around the coffee pot and reflected on Fields' recent disclosure.

"What I had in mind was something like a housing development for working folks. There's no such thing—except trailer parks—nowadays, and I thought it would be a good thing to help young and middle couples with children or plans for children to have a nice home with a little land in a decent neighborhood."

Will observed, "Fields, it sounds like you're talking about building a town."

"Yes, I am that."

"That's quite an undertaking. It will take a team of people to work it out."

"I know. I was hoping that you and Clara and Lance would help out."

"Lance?"

"Yes, he's smart, people like him, and I reckon he's a quick learner. A while back, you said you wished that he and I could spend some time together because you thought that it would do him some good. I told you that I wouldn't do such a thing because it insulted him and me. It was a contrivance, and like all contrivances, false and doomed to fail. Well, here's an opportunity for Lance to work with you and Clara, and me. I believe he might learn from us. But you ought to insist on his finishing his college while he's working with us. If we work on it I think we could bring your boy around."

Clara began tearing up. "Fields, it's just not possible for one man to be as good as you. If we could save our son I'll go to my grave a happy woman."

"Well, don't go dying on us, Clara. You and Will have a long life to live and, with luck, a lot of grand-parenting to do."

"I think I'll keep the diamond." Beverly said. There was laughter all around.

Within a week it was evident that the "simple ceremony" with a "small number of friends" in attendance was a ridiculous dream. Loren could only gape in wonder as she watched the wedding plans spiral out of control. It was as though the wedding had a mind of its own—much like a spoiled, churlish child. To Loren, it was turning into the wedding of the decade.

The third Saturday morning in May, Loren rose from sleep and found a note and a brochure on the kitchen table.

The note was scripted in Beverly's smooth flowing hand.

Dearest Loren,

We've eloped. We will return in a week. We can be reached at the motel on the brochure. Take care of things. Love,

Grandma and Grandpa

Loren laughed out loud in pleasure. She went to Fields' house and was greeted by Sugar. After the coffee pot was set up, Loren began making phone calls. She found an envelope on Field's kitchen table addressed to her.

Gal,

I can't thank you enough for bringing Miss Beverly and me together. You've turned my life around and hers too. We both owe you a debt that cannot be paid, but we will make every effort to do so. I've grown to love you as much as I remember loving my own children. As far as we are concerned you are our child and will be our child for the rest of our lives and yours as well.

Fields

Loren smiled to herself. Fields had penned a perfect note in excellent English.

She had noticed that since Beverly came on the scene, Fields' vernacular underwent significant changes. He now spoke the Queen's English. When she chided him about it, he responded with a slight miff, saying that he could speak in any manner of his liking.

Loren dropped it.

CHAPTER 38

Loren, Meredith, and Tara sat quietly waiting in front of the snacks and drinks that sat untouched on the coffee table of Meredith's living room. The TV was on but the sound was muted and the only sound was the soft murmur of the air conditioner. Loren studied the faint pattern of the carpet.

The girls jumped at the knock on the door. They exchanged looks, and then Meredith rose and answered the knock.

"Good evening, Lance."

He stood in the doorway, his hands down at his sides. "Meredith. Hi Tara, Loren." Tara and Loren responded with a quick head bob in his direction.

"Come in, we've been waiting for you."

"When I got your call I didn't know what to think—or what to say for that matter. What did you want to talk about?"

"As I said in my call, Loren wanted to talk with you. She didn't want to do it alone, and that's why we're all here. Have a seat over by the window, and I'll get you a drink. Coke okay?"

"Yeah, Coke's fine."

"We've got some cheese and crackers. Make a plate if you want."

"No thanks, I'm not hungry. Just Coke." Meredith poured Coke into a tall glass of cubes and brought it to Lance.

Lance took a sip of his Coke, sat it on a coaster, and then looked directly at Loren. He looked pale and gaunt. "What did you want to talk about?"

Loren had not taken her eyes off Lance since he entered. It was as though there was a viper in the room. "I felt the need to talk because of the business deal that Grandpa and Beverly are entering with your folks. This arrangement is going to throw you and me together a lot, and I wanted to do what I could to avoid friction. I don't want problems."

"That's it?"

"That's it."

"Okay, I don't see where we'll have any problems. What's past is past, and I want to get it behind me as soon and as much as I can." Lance said with obvious conviction in his tone.

"Good. I feel somewhat the same."

"Somewhat?"

Loren took a sip of her drink. "Yes."

"I've never apologized to you in private. Oh, I know what I said in court—and I meant it. But I feel the need to say to you face-to-face how truly sorry I am for what I did. I don't expect your forgiveness, but it's important that I tell you what I feel."

Loren thought for a moment. "And just what is that?"

144

"Regret, sadness, disgust with myself. And worst of all, shame. Over these past months I've come to know about you from my folks and others who know you. Everyone likes you and talks about what a good and kind person you are, and this makes my—what I did—even more mean and low-down. Knowing what a decent person you are has helped make me see how sorry I am. It also makes me see how I've messed up my life. The therapists and members of my therapy group are helping me search my life and my background in the hope that it will bring about some sense to what I am."

"Which is?"

"The psychologist says that I'm a moderate narcissistic personality. She says that I lack the ability to empathize with other people's needs, and that I only care about my own needs. That pretty well describes me. Dr. Hawkins—that's her name—says that there's not a lot of hope for a cure. She says that I'll have to fight this condition the rest of my life."

"No cure?" Tara asked.

"That's right. There's no drug or therapy, that'll change me. But she says it's not hopeless, that sometimes, personality-disordered people like me mellow out when they reach their thirties—sometimes earlier, sometimes later. She said strong support at home can make a difference. One of the other therapists said that because I had such a loving early childhood, and because my—my condition is only moderate, that there is a possibility—with therapy and a lot of effort by me—I can turn myself around."

"What are you going to do?" Meredith asked.

"Do? What I'm doing right now: See the therapist, go to group therapy, monitor my behavior, thoughts and feelings, and report them to the therapist. I'm going to start back to school this fall, but the thought of it scares me."

"Why's that?" Meredith asked.

"Well, there's so much temptation. I don't know if I can stand up to it."

"What kind of temptation?"

"It's everywhere. Pretty coeds, drugs, booze, parties. It's everywhere and it's constant. I don't know if I can stand the temptation—the constant pull to give in to my impulses."

Tara leaned toward him, "Can't you just shrug it off and go your own way?"

"No Tara, I can't. You don't know what I'm like. When I see something I want I take it. When I see a pretty girl, I want to have sex with her, and I generally won't take "no" for an answer. These coeds are so easy to con, it's laughable. They'll believe anything if it touches their heart. I lie, cheat, or steal at the drop of a hat. I don't have a conscience like normal people. Basically, if I like something, it's okay. Society's rules are for other people, not for me."

"That's awful." Tara said.

"That's me." Lance answered. "I'm sorry. I wish it wasn't true, but it is."

"How can we help?" Tara asked.

"I don't know how you can help me, but I know how you can not help me. I've already said that you shouldn't excuse or allow any misbehavior by me. Don't overlook or shrug off my faults. Be a friend—that would help. I'd like to be able to confide in you three, and no one else—outside of my therapy group. I don't know anyone else I can, or care to, trust. It would help me a lot if I could use you as sounding boards. But I don't expect you to help me for nothing. If we can make some kind of friendship, I can help you understand men—the wrong kind and the right kind. It might make your lives easier down the road."

"No." Loren leaned forward in her chair. "No. I don't want to participate in what you're asking, and I don't think you can help us understand men. Boys, yes, but not men. The only thing you understand is how to be a boy. Maybe someday you'll reach manhood, but you're going to have to do it without my help. It's going to be a long time before I see you without thinking of your Bowie knife pressed against my cheek. So, I wish you the best of luck in your therapy. Meredith and Tara can, and probably should, give you the support you need, but don't ask me to."

"I understand," Lance nodded.

"I don't care if you do or don't understand. That's the way it's got to be with us. I'll work with you and right next to you, and I will cooperate in every way I know how to help you make Grandpa's development a success. Just don't ask for my friendship or to concern myself with your personal life."

Meredith and Tara looked at Loren in astonishment. Tara said, "You're not even considering giving him the benefit of doubt?"

"That's right. I don't care what Lance says. The only thing that means anything is what he does."

"That's fair." Lance responded.

"I don't care about fair. I do care about protecting myself—and my friends—from the likes of you. That's all I have to say to you. But I have something to add for Meredith and Tara." Loren paused, and then turned to her friends, speaking in softer tone. "Since the attack, I've been reading a lot about people like Lance. I've come to learn that they are sociopathic, and I believe I'm startin' to understand them. They're people without a conscience. Oh, they may know ethics backwards and forwards, but they lack morals. I read *The Sociopath Next Door*, or *The Mask of Sanity*. Those are some books that identify the likes of Lance. Books like *The Wendy Dilemma* will help you learn how to protect yourself from them. There's lots of men and boys like Lance out there, their numbers are growing, and they're getting smarter. One last thing, Lance. If I'd known then what I know now, I'd never have gone to the hospital to try and help you. Before I started reading on the subject I saw you as just a party boy—someone just interested in having a good time, with no cares for other people. Now that I've had time to read about narcissistic people I have a better understanding—and dislike—of where you're coming from."

Lance spoke up. "She's right. Everything she says is worth listening to. I don't like being talked about like I'm not here, Loren, but you're right in what you say and what you're trying to do for Meredith and Tara."

"I don't need your approval, Lance. But I apologize for talking about you the way I have. I won't do that any more. I've asked Grandpa and Beverly that I not have to be around you less'n it's necessary, and if it is, then don't worry about it. We'll make do."

"There is one more thing," Lance said.

The three girls sat waiting. "It's about my mom and dad. This mess I've got myself into. Well, it's brought them back together. They'd already started divorce papers when I came to school here, but when they had to come help me out of my troubles, it—it changed everything. They've been going to therapy with me, and it looks like they're going to get together again. I guess that's one good thing that's come out of what I did. I owe you, Loren. I think I owe you more than I'll ever be able to repay."

Loren nodded in acceptance.

"I owe Mr. Gragg too. I want to go see him and tell him how I feel. He and Mrs. Gragg have been really great with my folks. They do a lot of stuff together, and I think that your grandparents have had as much effect on my folks as the therapist—maybe more. Mom really likes Mrs. Gragg."

"I'll tell him," Loren said. "But don't come by unless you call first. I don't think Sugar will let you on the property—no matter what."

"Good enough. I'm not here to convince anybody of anything. But I am going to try to prove myself to me—and to my folks." Lance rose and walked to the door. He stopped and turned. "Thanks for listening to me." He left, closing the door quietly.

Chapter 39

Beverly answered Loren's soft knock on the door. "Come on in, Loren. Why are you knocking at the door?"

"I wanted to talk to Grandpa for a second."

"Loren, this is your home—even more than mine right now. You never have to knock on the door. As far as Warren and I are concerned you are our only grandchild, and we hope you will accept us as grandparents. We love you, Loren. You don't have to knock on the door of those who love you."

"I should have known that. I'm sorry."

"No apology necessary, Loren. I've just made coffee, would you care for a cup?"

"Yes. I'll tell you something if you promise not to tell Grandpa."

Beverly nodded approval.

"Your coffee is better than his."

"Now that hurts to the quick," a smiling Fields said from behind Loren.

"Oh. You are such a sneaky old gentleman," the embarrassed girl said smiling.

"I don't sneak. I just don't racket about like some teenage girls I know. And her coffee *is* better than mine."

"Well, as long as I'm off the hook."

"Oh, I didn't say that, young lady. I've still got you dangling, you talking about me behind my back and all."

"Tell you what. I'll try to make it up to you by teaching Beverly how to milk Alice. That way you'll never have to depend on my services again for the delivery of milk."

"I grew up on a farm, Loren. But I haven't milked since I was a teenager. I'd love to try my hand at it again."

"Alice is peculiar in her old age, but with a little gentleness we'll be able to let you milk her. I was fixin' to go right now—if you'd like to give it a try."

Alice proved to be a little anxious at first, but Beverly's gentle hands and Loren's quiet voice and manner calmed her, and the milk flowed, albeit a little slow.

"This brings back wonderful memories—the smell of a milk cow, the warmth of her against my forehead. This is wonderful."

"You sure have a different grip from any I've seen—the way you bury your thumb in your fist and all."

"That was the way I learned to do it. I was the only one in the family that gripped that way, and no one seemed to mind, least of all the cows. This milk smells so good."

"It's the timothy and alfalfa that makes it smell such, and gives it a good flavor. We have good pasture here. Fields has kept up his land even though he stopped farming long ago."

"He would do that, wouldn't he?" Beverly said as she shot streams of milk into the pail.

After the milk had been strained, funneled into jugs, and put up to chill, Beverly and Loren strolled down to the flat rock over the river. Fields watched from the porch rocker as the two women in his life chatted amicably. He could not hear a word of what they said, but he knew it was a pleasure to both. There was laughter, soft female laughter, and gentle touching. Fields rocked slowly in his contentment.

Over supper that evening, Beverly told Fields that they were planning a trip to Beverly's house in Seminole, Florida.

"I was just getting used to being a husband, and now you're going to leave me to my own resources. How do you know I won't just go out and find another woman to do my cooking and cleaning?"

"Warren, we thought we'd just give you an opportunity to enjoy your bachelor life once again. It should let you see just how sweet a woman's presence is. But joking aside; it's time for Loren to experience being a young woman for a while. It's getting close to time for her to go back to school, and she needs a break from being a boy. In Florida she can wear dresses, experiment with make-up, and see what it feels like to associate with young men as a young lady rather than as one of the boys. I believe that we two girls need to get to know each other better, and I cherish the opportunity to be a grandmother to this beautiful young lady." Saying this, Beverly took Loren's hand in hers. Fields knew that the ladies were right.

"Well, Sugar and I were doing okay before you two came along, and we'll probably not starve—or choke in our own grime."

"Grandpa, I'll write every day."

"When were you two planning on abandoning me?"

"We thought we'd leave next Wednesday. That will give us plenty of time to plan the trip and to see to your care and feeding." Beverly said with a mirthful lilt.

CHAPTER 40

Beverly and Loren had been in Florida for nearly three weeks and, true to her word, Loren wrote every day—as did Beverly. The coffee table was covered with a growing pile of letters and correspondence. The mailman, who generally arrived around two in the afternoon, had grown accustomed to Fields waiting on his front porch, eager for the mail. This day was no exception. Just before the mailman was due, a gray Taurus pulled into Fields' driveway and Fields watched as a man who appeared to be in his forties approached the porch. The gray-haired man was wearing a gray suit. Fields recognized him from his visit to Wilson's Store. He put Sugar in the house.

"Howdy."

"Hello." Fields answered.

"Would you be Fields Gragg?"

"I am."

"Can I have a word with you, sir?"

"Are you selling something?"

"No, sir."

"Come on up then, and take a rocker."

The man climbed the steps and offered his hand. "Aldrich Herms. Please to make your acquaintance, Mr. Gragg." He sat in the rocker signaled by Fields.

"What brings you here, Mr. Herms?"

"I'm looking for somebody."

"You a bounty hunter, or some such thing?"

"No sir, I work for the state of Tennessee—foster care office."

"What can I do for you, sir?"

"I'm looking for this young girl." Herms handed a poster to Fields.

"She wanted by the law?"

"Not as a criminal, but as a ward of the state who escaped from state care."

"How does that concern me?"

"I'm pretty sure that she's in this county. In fact, I have reason to believe that she is somewhere near Boone—most likely in this part of the county."

"How so?"

"I've placed posters of her all over the region within two hours of her home in Piney Flat. The posters I placed in Wilson's Store keep on disappearing. Nowhere else, just Wilson's Store. I believe that someone who doesn't want her recognized keeps taking them down."

Fields cupped his hand over his mouth and lower jaw, and then pulled away as though stroking a beard. "She looks right young."

"She was fourteen when she fled. It's been two years now."

"You've been looking for her for two years?"

"She's one of my cases. I have several, but she's the only one I haven't been able to clear up."

"Clear up?"

"Find her. I always get my man—or girl in this case."

"What has she done?"

"She fled foster care."

"Does that make her a lawbreaker?"

"Technically, yes."

"Technically?"

"You seem very interested in this case, Mr. Gragg."

"Well, yes, I am from what I heard you say. I can't help but wonder that State of Tennessee employees could better spend taxpayer money than by chasing after someone who hasn't broken any laws."

"Mr. Gragg, I've been spending my own time, before and after working hours on this case. I'm on vacation time today."

"That's commendable dedication, Mr. Herms."

"I feel that I owe the state of Tennessee the best I can give them, even if I have to use my own resources to do it."

"Why are you here?"

"I'm checking with all of the people who have teenagers in school. I'm told you have such."

"Indeed I do."

"Is she about?"

"No, he and his grandma are traveling about the country."

"Oh, your grandchild is a boy then?"

"Wait here, Mr. Herms."

Fields went into the house and returned with a high school annual. He opened it to the pages containing the football team. "Here is my grandchild, Mr. Herms." It was a photograph of Loren. She was standing in her football uniform and pads. Her helmet hung in her left hand. Hers was the only picture in which the subject was smiling—other members of the team were trying to look as bad as they could muster. Under her picture it read: Lorne Land, place kicker. Sophomore. (Hammer).

"That's a fine looking young man, Mr. Fields. You must be proud of him."

"There's none better. Yes, I'm very proud."

The postman pulled up to Fields' mailbox and passed a wave after putting up the mail. Fields rose to get his mail, signaling to Herms that the conversation was over.

"Thank you for your time, Mr. Gragg."

"Have a good day, Mr. Herms, and good luck to you."

"One more thing, Mr. Gragg."

"Yes."

"Could I use your restroom? I've been drinking coffee since five this morning, and it's catching up with me."

"Of course, but let me tie up my dog first, he doesn't take kindly to strangers." Fields went into the house and called Sugar to follow him. On the way to his bedroom he walked by the coffee table and scooped up the cards and letters from Florida. After Sugar was secured he returned to the door. "The coast is clear."

When Fields returned to the porch with his mail, Herms was descending the steps.

"Thank you for your time, Mr. Gragg."

"Hope I've been some help." Fields said as he lowered himself into his rocker.

"You've helped with my process of elimination."

Herms folded into his Taurus, started it, and began to back out of the driveway. He noticed that, while Fields appeared to be reading his mail, his eyes were on his departing guest—a contradiction that Herms studied as he drove to Boone, and to appointments with certain members of High Country High teaching staff.

CHAPTER 41

The three weeks in Florida extended to four, allowing Loren to return just in time for football practice.

Loren wore the pads, shoes, and helmet of a football player, but her head was elsewhere. There was the closet in Seminole Florida, hung with summer dresses, blouses, and lightweight clothing suitable for Florida's blazing summer. The dresser in her Florida bedroom held shorts, tees, and clothing that allowed her to be an attractive teenage girl who turned heads. There were perfumes, powders, make-up, and an expensive curly wig that she and her 'grandmother' picked out of a line-up of mannequin heads.

"Land!" The command crackled across the green of the practice field.

"Yes, Coach."

"Get your head out of your back pocket. Summer is over. This is football practice, and we would very much like to have you with us. Would you care to grace us with your attention as well as your presence?"

"Sorry, Coach."

"This is Friday. Next Friday we will be playing the first game of the season. We would like to win that game. Don't be sorry, Land—be here—now!"

"Okay, Coach."

"You've been back two weeks now, and should be able to show some kind of ability. Get your mind off your summer vacation and back on football."

"Right, Coach." She missed the next three field goal attempts.

Half an hour later, whistles shrilled, calling the team to the three coaches standing on the sidelines.

Coach Call Helder stepped up to his team. "Sit down, men; we need to talk."

The team dropped to the ground. Some sat cross-legged, some stretched out with their head propped on helmets.

Coach Helder turned to his coaches behind him. The backfield coach spiraled a football to him. He snatched the ball out of the air, then tossed it in the air, spinning it expertly, gripping it in a single giant hand it as it landed.

"Men. This is known as a football." He thrust the ball out toward his audience. "Balls like these are used in an activity called a football game. The point of this game is to carry one of these balls over a designated goal line while preventing your opponent from doing so. This game is normally played by groups of men who are highly disciplined, well-organized, and strongly motivated. Those groups are known as teams. Therefore, football is considered a team sport. Now, while it is a team sport, those teams are made up of individuals—individuals who elect to set aside their personal preoccupations in order to dedicate themselves to the support of their team. It's an activity requiring focus and dedication to a common goal. Men who can do this make the game of football a thing of beauty, grace, and balance. Such men are called winners."

Coach Helder tossed the football into a near-bye trash can, turned, and walked away from the seated assemblage. His staff followed wordlessly.

Monday morning The Group—As they had come to call themselves—assembled in front of the school, waiting for the bell. They watched as Gent pulled into the parking lot in his Kia. He and his passenger got out of the car and headed toward them.

The boy with Gent was a slender African-American who stood only an inch taller than him.

"Ladies and gentlemen," Gent said. "I want you to meet your new best friend, Ali Jackson Jones. Ali-Jack, these are the slackers I told you about." Names were passed, hands shaken, and greetings given. "Ali-Jack is a transfer student from West Virginia, where he tells me they play football from time to time. His father is a new professor of sociology at the college, and they've moved next door to me. Ali-Jack plays halfback, and runs the forty in 4.2. He was honorable mention last year in West Virginia." Gent let this soak in before he continued. "He's fast, catches everything I throw his way, and has the moves. Gentlemen, we have an offense."

By the end of the week Ali-Jack was well on the way to membership in The Group and was assured of a work-out in the game coming up.

That Friday, High Country won by their largest margin ever. Ali-Jack scored three touchdowns—two running, and one pass reception. Train scored one, and Bryce passed to Council for another. Loren was called on for kick-offs and extra points. The rest of the time she warmed her end of the bench.

Coach Helder called for a Saturday practice; the first ever. He came with a DVD of the game.

The mood in the locker room was ebullient. The team had been told to keep their street clothes on because "Coach has something to say." They were trading wisecracks and horseplay, but when Coach Helder entered the room he was not smiling. The mischief stopped.

He began. "Last night we won. We won because we were playing a weak, ill-prepared team that was made up mostly of sophomores. If it had been Wilkes or Caldwell they would have beaten the socks off us. The poor offensive line performance was masked by Ali-Jack's quickness off the ball. If he hadn't been so quick and fast we would have gotten sacked about every third play. I'll demonstrate this to you as we replay last night's tragedy. Our quarterback got sacked four times, we turned the ball over three. It's not accurate to say that we won last night. What actually happened was that the other team lost. When you boys go to church to-morrow—and you should—say a word to the Big Boy. A word of thanks. It's been said that good fortune favors the prepared. Last night was no exception. You played and beat a team that was less well-prepared. Go to church."

"Coach, we won with the biggest margin ever."

"I know that, Ellis. It's how we won that bothers me. You let your man through at least four times last night. Where were you?"

The big offensive tackle blushed with the awareness that his coach was right. He started to say something but was silenced by the Coach.

"Defense. Our defensive line is worthy of a lawsuit. The only thing that saved them is the fact that the linebackers did their job. Seems like they realized early in the game that the line wasn't going to do theirs, and they rose to the occasion." Turning to his cluster of defensive backs he said. "Thank you. You probably saved the game. You should send a bill to the defensive linemen." Coach Helder stopped and looked out over his team.

The horseplay had long since evaporated and the team sat completely silent and motionless. Each player was focused on a place on the wall or floor that was utterly fascinating to them at the moment. The only sound was a dripping shower head.

"I'm going to ask Coach Sunders to review the DVD with you. I've been up nearly all night with it, and I don't want to see it anymore." Before walking out of the room he turned to his assistant coach and said, "Coach, roll the cartoon." He quietly closed the door as he left.

High Country High won its next game the following Friday against a strong, well-disciplined Avery High. Then it beat Wilkes County. Spruce Pine put up a good battle but was unable to break through the 'High Wall,' a name that even opposing teams used to describe High Country's defensive line. Ali-Jack was unstoppable. No one could catch him when he got up to high gear. Gent scored on a bootleg play that Coach Helder said was worthy of an Oscar in deception. He kept the ball after pretending to hand off to Ali-Jack, causing Spruce Pine's linebackers to chase the wrong man down to the goal line. You could hear Spruce Pine's coach screaming to his team all the way across the field. "The quarterback's got the ball." Gent, in a characteristic display of panache, almost walked into the end zone, an act that earned him a mini-lecture.

High Country was scheduled to meet Watauga High, the other, and older, high school in their county, for the first time. Previous scheduling commitments had kept the rival teams apart until now. It was a grudge match from the first, and would remain so for decades to come. Watauga scored on the kick-off. High Country took five plays to respond with a score. The remainder of the game was played between the thirty-yard lines. The score remained 7-7 for almost four quarters. Finally, Watauga fumbled and the ball was picked up by Ollie Miles, who lumbered down to Watauga's twenty yard-line before getting brought down. A short pass over the line to Council was off the mark and almost intercepted.

Train made three yards down the middle, and was stopped by a stocky Watauga linebacker known by teammates as Badger in recognition of his ability to stay low and burrow past offensive blockers. He rarely went through a game without sacking the quarterback at least twice. Badger had already taken Bryce down twice and

Gent once. He was everywhere he was needed. Short, stocky, with powerful legs he was a force unto himself. When he hit an opponent, the opponent knew he was hit. Losing or quitting were not words found in his vocabulary. Defensive linebacker positions were made for men like Badger.

On third down Ali-Jack did a wide end-around to the left that was good for another three yards. Fourth down, four to go. Twelve seconds remaining in the game.

"Land."

"Yes, Coach."

"Win the game." Helder motioned Loren to the foray with a head bob.

Loren jogged onto the field during her team's last time out. Council nodded to her, knowing what was expected. Bryce set the snap sequence, spoke briefly to a couple of the linemen. They waited for the whistle.

At the whistle they lined up, each man moving crisply to his position. Each player knew that if he did his job they would win the game. Loren was not going to miss.

Loren paced back to her position, waiting for the snap. The ball came out high and wobbling. It passed over Council's waiting hands, bounced once and fell into Loren's arms. Council turned to her, rising and pivoting counter-clockwise, he immediately assessed the situation. In a flash of eye contact he barked, "Follow me." as he spun to the right and sprinted into a protective lead. Loren followed. Council was able to fend the first startled defender with a stiff shove. Loren continued behind him. At the five yard line Council took out a defender with a body block that left them both on the ground. He spun to his feet just in time to see Loren do two things: Cross the goal line in control of the ball and receive a head-on hit from Badger two steps inside the goal line. He heard what sounded like a dry branch cracking. He was the first one to reach Loren, who was lying on her side clutching the football; she didn't move to get up to hear the referee's whistle blow the end of the play, or to see him signal a touchdown.

"You speared him, you bastard," Ollie shouted as he gave Badger a vicious elbow to the throat, and then slammed him to the ground. It quickly turned into a melee with players from both teams piling on. Council was crouched crab-fashion over a prostate Loren in order to protect her in her helpless state. Bryce dropped to his aid.

In less than a minute the players were sorted out, a touchdown signaled, and Ollie sent to the bench. Badger was helped off the field, clutching his neck. While Loren was being attended, the referees assessed a fifteen-yard penalty against High Country. Loren had not moved.

Two doctors and a nurse appeared from the stands. A stretcher was brought out, then a gurney, and finally, a plate for Loren's still body. She was very carefully moved onto the plate, and then lifted to the gurney. A small crowd followed as she was carried to a waiting EMT vehicle.

Ali-Jack attempted a wide end-round for an extra point try. Its failure ended the game with a High Country victory, 13-7. The crowd sat quietly with little cheering at game's end. The EMT siren had put a damper on the fans' desires to celebrate. Quickly and silently the crowd left the stadium and made for the hospital.

The hospital double-decker parking lot was filled within an hour after the game. A large crowd gathered outside the emergency room entry. Police were posted at the doorway to prevent unnecessary entry.

It was one o'clock when Coach Helder came to the entryway. He was obviously a man in distress as his voice choked. "Lorne is okay." A low sound of approval escaped from crowd who knew better than to make a loud noise. Then the questions began, followed by Helder's curt answers. "Probably a broken rib—he's sleeping right now—I don't know—We'll have to wait and see—no, the X-rays don't show any other injuries." For nearly fifteen minutes the crowd passed the news around, and then began to thin. By one-thirty the parking lot was emptying of the last few cars heading home or to post-game celebrations. So few people attended the post-game dance that it closed down early.

A sedated Loren slept the night in a hospital gown. Fields sat awake in a recliner beside her bed. He fell asleep just before dawn.

Chapter 42

"She's waking up." Fields and Coach Helder moved to stand on respective sides of Loren's hospital bed.

"Loren. Loren, it's Grandpa, can you hear me?"

Loren tried to sit up but was stopped by the pain, and by Fields' gentle touch on her shoulder.

"Lie still, Gal. You've got a broke rib."

Coach Helder moved closer. "Loren, stay still. The doctors have wrapped your rib cage pretty tight."

"Did we win?"

Helder smiled. "We won, but we didn't have anyone to kick the point after and we had to try a ground play. Seems that our kicker was incapacitated at the time."

"I'm sorry. I didn't know what to do, and Council said to follow him, so I did. Did I make it over the goal line?"

"You scored a touchdown, Gal." Fields said.

The second use of the word "Gal" registered with Loren's clearing mind. She glanced at her coach, eyes wide.

"He knows. I reckon by now everybody knows."

"Coach…"

Helder touched a finger to his lips, shaking his head. "We've got other concerns right now. We have to make sure that you are doing well and will recover soon. That's what matters, Lor—Loren"

"What day is it?"

"It's Saturday, just after two. You've had a long snooze. I guess it was the sleeping meds they gave you. How do you feel?"

"I hurt. I feel like I've been run over by a truck. What happened?" She looked around the room. There were flowers everywhere. "The flowers. Who?"

"Seems you're well liked." Fields surveyed the room. "We got flowers on every flat surface, on the floor, and spilling out into the hall."

As he spoke, a delivery man came in with two more vases of flowers, nodded at those in the room and left after setting the vases on an extra table brought in by nursing staff.

Loren scanned the panoply of color in her room. She shook her head in wonder. "No one has ever… I've never…"

Fields placed a gentle finger on her lips. "Just sit back and enjoy all this care sent your way, Gal." Coach nodded his agreement.

She took Fields' hand. "Will you have the nurses spread them around the hospital? Others will enjoy them. Some likely need 'em."

Fields looked away and choked slightly. When he turned back his eyes were wet, and tears starting down his weathered cheeks. His voice was thick and turgid when he answered. "I'll see to it, Gal. Now see what you've gone and made me do. I've got a good name to hold up, and I can't do it if I go about blubbering like—like an old woman." He wiped his eyes, then trumpeted his nose into a tissue.

Coach Helder looked down at his shoes with a small smile. "I doubt your manhood is in question, Fields." He picked up a card from one of the floral displays. He turned it over and wrote something on the back. "Let me suggest that we pull the cards before the flowers are distributed. We'll write what the flowers were on the back of the card—if it doesn't already say so on the front."

"He's right," Fields said. "There's thank you notes that want sendin.'"

"Let me do it then," Loren said. "I don't want to send any away until I see who sent them—it's personal like then."

A stocky figure appeared in the doorway and rapped softly on the frame. It was Badger.

"Come in, Thomas." Coach Helder said. The boy approached the foot of the bed.

"Loren, this is Thomas Comers. His team members know him as *Badger*."

Loren raised a small wave. "Hi."

"Hi." The boy was obviously in distress. He shifted from one foot to another while holding the metal bed frame in a death grip.

"I—I'm sorry. I'm so sorry. I didn't mean…"

"Stop that now," Loren said. "It was a game, and I'm sure you wouldn't want to hurt a body on purpose. No need to apologize."

"There is. You don't know my pa. And he says that…"

"You tell you're pa that I'm okay, and I don't hold it against you."

"Anyway, I just wanted to apologize and let you know that if there's anything I can do to make it up to you I will. I didn't mean to hurt you." He paused briefly, "Leastways, not *hospital* hurt."

Coach Helder had a grim face while the boy spoke.

"We're okay, you and me, Thomas." Loren said. "I tell you what—will you do me a small favor?"

"Sure. Just name it."

"See that vase of pink glads over there on the dresser?"

"Yeah."

"Would you take them to your ma? Tell her they're a goodwill sign from me that I don't hold with no grudges."

Badger looked at Coach Helder, who gave him a slight smile and a nod of approval.

"I'll do it. I'll do it for sure. Ma will love these flowers." The boy gathered up the vase and headed for the door. "Can I come back and see you tomorrow?"

"I'm counting on it—Badger," Loren said.

Badger stopped in the door. "I didn't know you was a girl and all."

"No one did."

Badger nodded. "Well, all I can say is, you're sure some kinda Wonder Woman."

"I guess that's a compliment."

"It sure is." He was gone.

Loren realized that Fields was holding her hand. "I guess the jig's up, Grandpa."

"It is that, Gal."

"Coach, I'm sorry. I didn't mean to deceive you. You didn't know I was a girl, and I lied to you. When it all comes out, I hope you'll understand why."

"Girl? You're not a *girl*. You're a Fire Newt, and you're my kicker. I never was one to be prejudiced against a person because of the shape of their skin. We've got to get you well, and we've got games to win. It's just that..." Helder stopped to inspect his fingernails. "next time you find yourself with the game ball in your hands—fall to the ground and cover it."

"You've got my word on that, coach. My halfback days are over."

Wednesday morning Loren returned to classes and to a mixed student response. Some were accepting, and some resentful of the subterfuge. The Group was waiting in their usual place when Loren and Bryce got out of his pick-up and walked up to the shaded park in front of the complex.

"Welcome back, Hammer." "Great score." And finally—a phrase she was to hear in the hallways: "You the man, girl."

After the boisterous greeting by her friends, it was Gent who broke the ice.

"Well, you've really surprised us all. I mean, no one would have guessed that you were a girl—Man. We've all talked it over, and we want you to know that nothing's changed—you're still considered the weakest member of the team."

"Thanks, Gent. It's good to be out of that hospital. You mean they kept the team together without me? I'm impressed."

"That's okay," Gent answered. "Just don't go hittin' on me. I'm pretty much spoken for."

"Thanks again. That takes a load off my mind. I was considering asking if you wanted to go steady, but I guess I'll have to give you up to one of the cheerleaders."

Then Ollie surprised everybody, "We thought about breaking up, but coach remembered that I know how to kick the ball, so we decided to go ahead and try to make it to the next game anyway."

After the laughter and guffaws subsided, Jo Mae said, "There was this weird old man hanging around yesterday. He talked with the principal and a couple students. He was asking about you."

"What did he look like?"

"Looked old. Gray slick-back hair. Gray suit. He was slim but had a belly like he was plumb pregnant. I think his name was Herman or something."

CHAPTER 43

The courtroom was filled and over-flowing. The bitter January weather could not keep away the folks from Piney Flat, nor the supporters from Watauga County.

Judge Edythe Tilson had planned to have a quiet hearing in a small side room, but she changed plans when she arrived at the courthouse and saw the packed parking lot.. Fortunately, the main courtroom was open for the day, and she gave instructions to have the hearing there. She also made sure that several deputies were on hand for the hearing. Her clerk informed her that there were no less that six reporters waiting.

"I need to speak with Aldrich Herms before I begin the proceeding," Tilson said to her clerk. "Locate him and tell him to come to my chambers." The clerk nodded and left as the judge began putting on her robes.

She glanced out the window at her car in the parking lot below. An inch of snow had covered the vehicle since she arrived. The wind had dropped and snow was falling in earnest. She was considering cancellation when the clerk re-entered.

"Aldrich Herms is not here, Your Honor. Alexis Card, the department head, is here in his place. Will you see her?"

"No. I wanted to ask Mr. Herms some specifics regarding his conduct in Watauga County. Thank her for coming, and tell her that if she wants to see me before the proceedings I'll talk with her. Are all the witnesses here?"

The clerk reviewed the folder he was carrying. "Yes, everyone ordered has reported in except Mr. Herms."

"Give him some time. This weather has slowed everyone, I'm sure. Pass the notice that we are going to delay thirty minutes."

A deputy appeared at the doorway and knocked gently. "Your Honor."

"Yes, Deputy, what is it?"

"Three more news vehicles have entered the parking lot. It's turning into a traffic jam out there."

Judge Tilson looked up from the files on her desk. She rose and walked to the window. The snow was piling on the parked cars.

"Deputy, can you take care of the parking problem?"

"Yes, ma'am. I can move the sheriff cars and park the news vehicles in their place."

"Do it then—and Deputy?"

"Yes."

"Don't go out there without warm clothes."

"Yes, ma'am."

Turning to her clerk, Judge Tilson said, "Make that delay one hour instead of thirty minutes."

"Okay, Judge. Anything else?"

"Make sure that those waiting are comfortable and out of this weather. Pay special note to the elderly and children. I don't know when I've seen such a crowd in the courthouse—you'd think it was a murder trial."

"The court house is filling up. With this weather... You want to cancel, Your Honor?

"No, it's early in the day. If we can dispose of this case quickly it will give people plenty of time to get home. Better call Evan's Garage and ask them if they can come blade our parking lot. Also, we'll want to have a wrecker handy in case someone needs a tow or to have their car jumped. No loose ends, Billy."

"Yes, Ma,am."

Edythe Tilson turned her attention to the paperwork on her desk, perusing the records and accounts of Loren Creek's case, one more time. In a few minutes her clerk was back.

"Your, honor, Ms. Card has asked to speak with you."

"Send her in."

Alexis Card entered the judge's chambers and took the chair that Judge Tilson pointed to. She was a heavy, large-boned woman wearing a tailored brown suit. Her beefy legs were encased in glistening panty hose. Judge Tilson glanced at the tightly crossed legs and the short snug skirt.

"You wanted to speak with me, Ms. Card?"

"Alexis will do, Your Honor. Yes, I need to clarify some points regarding Miss Creek's disposition as pertains to the jurisdiction of this court. I believe that Mr. Herms has over-looked a point of law that needs review."

Edythe Tilson leaned over her desk, steepling her hands before her face. "Enlighten me, Ms. Card."

Thirty minutes before the case was to be heard, Judge Tilson rang her clerk.

"Billy, I want all of the news reporters and Miss Creek's attorney in my office, now."

In two minutes the clerk returned with a mob dressed in a motley variety of burdensome clothing, including one in a three-piece suit. The group filed in and quickly quieted.

"Gentlemen. Ladies. I'll be brief." Pencils scurried. "Judging from the size of the crowd and the number of news media, and what I've seen and read in the news, this hearing has captured the attention of many beyond the jurisdiction of this court. It is also likely that the issues in this hearing will not be settled today or possibly in the next couple of meetings. The reason I've asked you here is to request that you respect and maintain courtroom decorum. I hope we can avoid the sensationalism that so often accompanies proceedings like these we have before us today. I think we all want this to be settled quickly, fairly, and in a just fashion within our system of law. Are there any questions?"

"Your Honor?"

"Yes?"

"Graves Atline from ABC out of Knoxville. Could you describe sensationalism for us?"

"No, Mr. Atline. All I can say is that it's like pornography. I can't define it, but I know it when I see it—and I don't want to see it."

"Thank you, Your Honor."

"Any more questions? We are on a tight schedule here."

The group was silent.

"Okay, you will be warned once. The second time you will be barred from these proceedings." Judge Tilson rose in dismissal. The troop turned to leave.

"This meeting was once." Judge Tilson announced clearly.

CHAPTER 44

"All rise."

The heavily muffled bodies rose as one to the entry of Judge Edythe Tilson. She took her place behind the elevated structure that spoke of the stature and grandeur of "The Law." The courtroom with its polished oak and marble surfaces was typical of hundreds of such community testaments. Travelers in the South will find communities of rather modest means that give their all to make sure their courthouse speaks of high regard for the Law of the Land and The Majesty of the Court. The assemblage seated with their judge.

Edythe Tilson began. "This is a hearing. It is not a trial. This was to have been a small gathering to deal with the issues surrounding the disposition of an orphaned minor.

We can see that the anticipated small gathering is simply not to be. I have cautioned the media people to avoid sensationalizing these proceedings. We are dealing with a minor, here and are determined to protect her interests and privacy. Any violation of those standards will be harshly dealt with by this court.

"I have also been informed by a representative of foster care that this issue is outside the purview of this court because it has already been adjudicated and is therefore in the hands of that office. I would point out that I was the adjudicator of the case in question and, due to a series of recent unfolding events, have elected to re-open this case.

"In a previous decision this court assigned the juvenile in question to a foster care placement from which she fled. It was the third such attempt for this youth, and as such makes it incumbent upon this court to place her in a facility that will secure her until she comes of age.

"This court will hear from representatives of Miss Creek, who takes issue with the imperatives of the court. A further note: This court is informed that, in the state of North Carolina, Miss Loren Creek is known under her false identity as Mr. Lorne Land. In this court she is Loren Creek, a female minor in of the state of Tennessee.

Loren's attorney stood in response to Judge Tilson's request.

"Richard Franklin, Your Honor."

"Yes, Mr. Franklin."

"Your Honor, it is our contention that Ms. Creek's demonstrated maturity and many accomplishments qualify her to be considered an adult for purposes of her living disposition. We ask that the legal course normally taken in response to the needs of a minor be set aside in order to permit this exceptionally capable young lady to continue living in the very responsible manner she has demonstrated for over two years."

Judge Tilson leaned back in her swivel chair. "I'm listening, Mr. Franklin."

Franklin realized this was code for *show me the evidence*. He removed the top of a large cardboard file box that had been placed on his desk.

"Your Honor, I have paperwork in the form of cancelled checks, signed by Ms. Creek, paid bills and notes, and signed agreements that demonstrate that she had been the de facto head of household since she was twelve years of age." Franklin carefully removed the paperwork from the file box, and stacked them in neat piles which were labeled by category.

"I have seen these documents, Mr. Franklin. They make an impressive case. I took them into consideration when I last determined that Ms. Creek would be best served by placement in a foster home."

"I respectfully submit, Your Honor, that those very documents contradict that conclusion at the most, and at the least suggest a need to reconsider."

"The court acknowledges your assertion, Mr. Franklin."

"Thank you, Your Honor. I have a number of people who wish to testify on Ms. Creeks' behalf."

Edythe Tilson refrained from pointing out to Franklin that the courts were acting on Loren's behalf, and nodded permission for him to proceed.

Fields Gragg spoke first. He told of how he and Loren met, and how they came to the agreements that enabled Loren to live in the community and attend school as a teenage boy. He carefully described the disciplined and responsible lifestyle that Loren demanded of herself. He was followed by Coach Call Helder, who spoke of Loren's work ethic and how it led her to make invaluable contributions to the football team.

Coach Helder's assertions were mirrored by High Country teachers and an assistant principal. After the math teacher had related how Loren had turned around a female student who was on the path to self-destruction, there came a stirring in the back of the courtroom. The High Country football team rose as a group and filed to approach the bench. They stood as a group before Judge Tilson who cast an inquiring look at attorney Franklin, who responded with an unknowing shrug. The young men were all wearing their football jerseys. A stocky sandy-haired boy stepped forward.

"Your Honor, my name is Ollie Miles. I'm on the football team and want to ask you to let Lor—Loren stay where she is and finish high school with us."

"This is an unusual demonstration, Mr. Miles, and I am this close to having all of you locked up for a day or two."

"I'm sorry, Your Honor. We ain't demonstratin'. We're just askin' you to not take her away from us. She's one of us, and we need her. And—and, Your Honor."

"Yes, Mr. Miles."

"We—we love her, Your Honor."

Loren blushed beet red when she heard those words from a boy who had done little but give her a hard time for two years.

"Your Honor. The first time I met Loren she knocked me on my—knocked me to the ground 'cause I deserved it. I didn't like her for a long time, but I came to know her and like her. When we got wind of—of her bein' a girl and all, some of us were mad at her for pretending to be a boy when she was really a girl, but we got over it after we heard her story and why she tricked us. We all like her, Your Honor. And she's one of us. If I had a sister, I'd want her to be just like Loren. She's smart, and there's nothing she can't do. But most of all, she's just plain good. I'm proud to know her."

"Thank you, Mr. Miles. Is there anything you wish to add?"

"No ma'am—Judge. That's all. Just don't take her away."

"Thank you. Please return to your seats." The boys filed to the back of the room and quietly sat down.

"Mr. Franklin, do you have any more surprises?"

"Your Honor, I had no..." He was silenced by a waved hand.

"It is getting late, and I am going to..." Judge Tilson was interrupted by the entrance of Aldrich Herms into the back of the courtroom. He was accompanied by a tall, slender man wearing a sport coat, jeans, and cowboy boots.

"Your Honor."

"Mr. Herms, how good that you see fit to join us."

"Your Honor, may I approach the bench?" Judge Tilson waved him forward.

"Who is your companion, Mr. Herms?"

"His name is Virgil Richards, Your Honor. He is a resident of Reno, Nevada."

"What bearing does Mr. Richards have on this hearing?"

Mr. Richards is Ms. Creek's father, Your Honor."

The courtroom that was already muted became dead silent. Over one hundred people sat unmoving as Judge Tilson absorbed this last bit of information. Aldrich Herms continued. "Your Honor, I was..."

"I will see Ms. Creek and her attorney in my chambers. Mr. Herms you and your companion will come with us. There will be a thirty minute break in these proceedings." Judge Tilson rose and swept from the room. The bailiff escorted those ordered to the Judge's chambers.

CHAPTER 45

"What is this, Mr. Herms?" Judge Tilson waved her visitors to seats.

"We just arrived in Knoxville airport this morning."

"Begin at the beginning, Mr. Herms—and be brief."

"Yes, Your Honor." Herms opened a folder and laid it on the judge's desk with a look that requested permission. Glancing at his notes he began to speak to the judge. "An anonymous phone call alerted me to the possibility that the girl I was looking for was posing as a boy identified as Lorne Land. I went to the hospital the day she was released and verified that Lorne Land was, in fact, Loren Creek. My attempt to quickly return Ms. Creek to Tennessee was blocked by Mr. Fields Gragg and Attorney Van Riper. In the time it took to extradite Ms. Creek, I came to know her, and to know of her accomplishments as Lorne Land. I was so impressed with her character and abilities that I began an investigation into her background. With the help of some of Ms. Creek's friends in Piney Flat I was able to track down Mr. Virgil Richards, her biological father. I contacted him two days ago, and flew to Reno to meet with him. We determined that we needed to come to Tennessee immediately. And here we are. We would have been here last night, but for the snowstorm that blocked us from landing any nearer than Knoxville. I tried calling you at your home all last night, but the line was busy."

"Mr. Herms, how did you convince the state of Tennessee to foot the bill for your expenses? Round trip tickets to Nevada aren't cheap, and I have to count every penny I spend in my office."

"I paid for the ticket, Your Honor."

"You paid for it?"

"Yes Ma'am. I used my leave time to make the trip, so it didn't cost the state nothing."

Judge Tilson thumbed through the folder that Herms had laid on her desk. She laid the folder aside, took a deep breath and became lost in thought for what seemed a long time to those on the other side of her desk.

"Mr. Herms," she said evenly. "I have to ask you why? I mean, I've been made aware of how assiduously you pursued resolution to this case, and I've wondered why you were so motivated to locate Miss Creek. Do you have an answer you could share with the court?"

Aldrich Herms squeezed a cupped hand over his mouth a couple of times as he considered the judge's question. Then he spoke softly and with an apparent careful choice of words.

Your Honor. I was a foster child. Me and my sisters were bounced separately from pillar to post through the system. We were abused in more ways than I care to say in public. When I turned eighteen, I went and found my sisters and set about makin' a home for us. It wasn't easy. We all worked, scraped, and saved. We started out in a give-out trailer and, slow-like, worked our way up into a better trailer, then to a run-down shack that was only a little better than a trailer." Loren sat watching Aldrich Herms with widened eyes. Her lips were parted slightly and she seemed not to breathe. Herms continued. "To make it short, Your Honor, we now own a good home in a nice neighborhood—it's all paid up and our'n. My sisters worked and put me through community college, and one of my instructors found me work with the foster care people—I owe a debt to her on that account. I was able to work and finish a four-year degree. It took some doing, but we're not strangers to hard work—Your Honor." He paused as though seeking permission to go on.

Judge Tilson leaned forward, elbows propped on her desk, and her chin resting on her clasped hands. She nodded for Herms to continue.

"I took to my job like a duck to water. I didn't want any child to go through what me and my sisters had. I reckon I've got one of the best placement records in the state—I'm not bragging. What I done I done with hard work and long hours—no brag." Judge Tilson nodded.

"I took up this job so I could work with people, not with paper. I do my paper-work by night, and my people-work by day—this makes for long days but it gets the job done right, and keeps my desk top clean. I purely hate that paper-work, but I hate more that it would take away from my people-work if I's to let it do so. I work long days, six, sometime, seven days a week. But I got a record I'm proud of, and that's something nobody can take from me." Herms stopped, took a long a deep breath, and then turned to nod toward Loren. "Miss Creek here was a blemish on my record. You'd be right to name it pride if that was the all of it, but there's more. I failed in two placements with Miss Creek. It was my failure, nobody else's, and that hurt. I finally found what I'm sure is a good Christian home of loving, decent folks, and I placed Miss Creek there. Your Honor, I'da give anything to have had such a home when I was—was…" His face showed tell-tale signs of a struggle to remain composed.

Judge Tilson sat erect. "That's enough Mr. Herms, I think I'm beginning to understand."

Herms shook his head in small jerks. "No Ma'am, there's more—can I go on?" Tilson nodded.

"I think there are any of a dozen families in Piney Flat that would take Loren in if she's to let 'em. But she wouldn't give in to bein' what she told them was a charity case. When I first started askin' her neighbors to take her in, they right away agreed to it. But as Miss Creek found out, she paid visits to them, and I started getting phone calls telling me of their change of mind, giving long, reasonable-sounding excuses. Word passed quick that Loren didn't want foster care service, and her neighbors closed up agin' me and agin' the State of Tennessee—they don't cotton to government interference anyhow, and Loren's way was easy for them to accept. They's Mountain through and through."

"Thank you Mr. Herms—for the clarity." Tilson said softly.

"There's more."

"Continue."

"Well, Your Honor. That gal's *stubborn* just stuck in my craw. If she'da just bent a little, she could have had pretty much ever thing she wanted and been able to stay surrounded by lovin' neighbors who'd knowed her all her days. But no, she had to have it just the way she wanted or not at all. At first I was real angry with her, but as I got to thinking on it, and talking with them that knows her, I came to a good respect for her, and wanted to come up with a solution better'n what had been made before. Then I hit on the idea of trying to find her father. No one had even considered him in all our comin's and goin's in this case. It was like he didn't exist. But he does, and here he is." Herms gestured toward Virgil, and then he leaned back in his chair. "And that's the all of it, Your Honor."

Tilson picked up the folder again and resumed a study of its contents. She took up a small pad and scribbled a couple of notes before closing the folder.

"That's quite a story, Mr. Herms. I think that you and I need to get our heads together sometime in the near future, but right now we need to deal with the matter at hand."

"Yes, Ma'am."

Tilson turned to face Virgil Richards.

"Mr. Richards, are you Ms. Creeks' biological father?"

"Yes, Your Honor, I am certain of that."

"What evidence exists for this?"

Herms opened the folder on the Judges desk and quickly produced a certificate of birth that showed Virgil Richards as the father of Loren Creek.

"Your Honor, I did not know of the existence of this certificate until Mr. Herms showed it to me yesterday."

"Mr. Herms?" Judge Tilson lasered Aldrich Herms against his chair.

"Your Honor, I was able to track down Mr. Richards from the information on Miss Land's birth certificate. I couldn't have done it without help from some of Miss Land's neighbors in Piney Flat who, once they realized that I was only interested in helping Miss Land, were glad to be of assistance. You'll notice that is a certified copy. It is correct."

"Miss Land, did you know of the existence of your father?"

"No, Ma'am."

Judge Tilson studied the small square of paper in front of her as though she might find something missing, or something that might change her ruling.

"Mr. Richards, do you have a legal claim that you wish to make?"

Virgil Richards glanced at the slender girl sitting erect in her chair, and who had not made eye contact with him since he presented himself before the judge.

"Yes. Loren is my child, and I have no intention of standing by while she is placed in a foster home of strangers who more than likely don't care one iota for her welfare. I want to help my daughter if she will let me."

"Miss Creek?"

"I don't know this man from Adam's housecat. I don't care who he is or what he wants, and I don't intend to become his daughter after he betrayed and abandoned me and my Momma. I don't want to have anything to do with him." Loren gave Virgil Richards a level stare. "He is not a father to me. He is someone my Momma tried to forget and put behind her, and I feel the same way my Momma does—did, Your Honor."

"Mr. Richards?"

"Your Honor. I didn't know I had a daughter." He was looking at Loren. "Loren's mother and I were living together—it was the sixties and we were caught up in the peace movement of the times. We were deeply in love with each other—and with what we thought was a daring and free lifestyle. We agreed that someday we would marry, but right then we wanted to feel free and rebellious. I had a small rock band that was popular, and making good money. We had friends, fans, and a future. There were record contracts, regional television and radio shows, and concerts. It was just a matter of time before we would break through on the national scene. Sarah and I were in love with *us* and with life. I remember it as the most joyful time of my life." Richards looked away, took a deep breath and returned to his statement. "But I ruined it all in a stupid mistake. I thought our modern open-minded lifestyle, would allow Sarah to understand and eventually forget about it. I was wrong. Not so much wrong about what happened but what I assumed would be understood. Sarah was furious. I'd never seen her like that—livid rage best describes how she reacted to what she thought to be a dalliance. She packed and left that night at two o'clock in the morning. I didn't even try to stop her. I was angry because she was angry with me. I thought we would get back together in the next couple of days, talk things over, and get back with our lives." Richards stopped, leaned forward and stared down at the floor.

"Apparently, that's not what happened," Judge Tilson said.

"Yes, judge. That's not what happened." He answered with a slight smile. "Several days passed, and I started making phone calls. I called our friends and associates. I called Sarah's folks. I called her friends in Tennessee. A couple of weeks passed. No Sarah. I flew to her parents' home in Piney Flat where I was met at the door by her mother and father. I was not permitted to enter but was told that Sarah was not there, and that even if she did return to them, they did not want me to come to their house again, or to call or try to contact them in any way unless it was acceptable to Sarah. They had always resented the fact that Sarah had dropped out of school to go away with me. I would say they were bitterly resentful. As I've grown older, I've come to understand their position." Richard looked levelly at Loren when he said, "Your Honor, I didn't know that Sarah was pregnant, and I never knew of the birth of our child."

Loren found her tongue. "Why did you stop trying to find us?"

"I didn't know there was an *us*, Loren. I sent dozens of letters that were returned unopened. After nearly a year, your mother wrote to me saying that she had married a boy she went to school with and that she wanted nothing to do with me. She asked that I respect her wishes. I sent a short note in response to that, and never again attempted to contact her." Richards lifted his briefcase to his lap and opened it. "I kept the unopened letters in a box. I still have them and I want you to have them. Perhaps, from them you'll begin to understand how much I loved your mother. I was a hollow man after she left me. It took years for me to recover from that loss. In fact, I never have. I still love the Sarah that I knew. There's hardly a day that goes by that I don't find myself reflecting on the moments and days we shared. I remember the long walks we used to take, the times we went swimming in streams and pools we found in the country side. I remember moonlit nights, sunrises, sunsets, music, meals and wine. I remember what we ate and how it tasted. Those memories are all I have left of your mother. Sometimes, on down days, I think that's all I have left, period. I loved your mother, Loren. I see you in her, and I want the chance to love you. I would like to somehow make up for what I did to hurt her."

"Well, you'll not use me to make yourself feel good about your mistakes." Loren shot back. She heard a breath caught short behind her, and turned to find Aldrich Herms, red-faced. He was wiping his face with a large blue bandana. She turned back to see a hard-eyed Judge Tilson staring at her.

"I—I'm, I'm sorry. I didn't intend to be mean," she said softly.

Tilson's face softened visibly. "This is very difficult for you and for Mr. Richards. He has stated his contrition for his past mistake, and regret over his ignorance of your birth. You have had some sixteen years without a father you needed and wanted. Both of you are deservedly confused and distraught. I submit that it is time for us to sit back, calm down, and try to make as much sense out of this thing as possible. You both have much to gain and much to lose by the choices you embrace and the subsequent decisions coming from those choices. Mr. Richards, I would caution you to go slow here. You appear to be eager to push yourself into the life of a person who is a veritable stranger to you." Tilson stopped a moment to jot some notes on a pad. "Miss Creek, please try to set aside your tendency to judge, and listen to what Mr. Richards is saying. I believe he is trying to reach out to you." She pushed a button on the side of her desk that brought the clerk of court to her door.

"Announce a recess of one hour to the courtroom. You know the drill; see to it that the people are as comfortable as can be expected under the circumstances."

"Your Honor."

"Yes, Loren."

"I would like to have some time with Meredith and Tara. I need to talk with them."

Judge Tilson wrinkled her brow in thought.

"I've come to know your daughters these past two months and I respect their opinions and advice." Loren added in a careful attempt to conceal the fact that she and the two sisters had been close friends for over two years.

"Yes, of course you can talk with them. Do you require a room?"

"That would be nice."

Judge Tilson and the clerk of court exchanged nods. Loren followed him out of the judge's chambers.

Edythe Tilson continued. "Mr. Richards, I'm going to need a lot more information than you've given me so far. Are you prepared to answer my questions?"

"Yes, I am, Your Honor. I've brought documents that testify as to who I am, where I live, and how long I've lived there. I've also brought copies of my IRS records for the past three years. I'm self-employed as a song-writer and an entertainment agent. My records will show that, by some standards, I'm a wealthy person.

I can assure you that, among those with whom I have dealings, my income and life-style are considered quite modest."

Out of the corner of her eye, Judge Tilson saw her daughters pass in front of the partially open door to her chambers.

Tilson looked at Virgil Richards, "One of Loren's issues is that she doesn't want to leave the region in which she was born and raised."

"That's no problem with me. I can live here. I can exercise my profession nearly anywhere there is an Internet connection. If she will have it, I would want to come live here with her, at least until she is in college or embarked on a chosen profession."

"We have to respect that she may not want that. If that is her choice, to refuse your offer then I would have to place her in a facility until she is of age. I'm very much opposed to that idea, but I have little choice in the matter."

Loren's attorney interjected, "I can think of at least one other alternative."

All heads turned to listen.

"If Loren were to accept Mr. Richards as her father and legal guardian, it would allow a condition to exist whereby he could permit Loren to continue to live where she is—under the supervision of Mr. and Mrs. Fields Gragg. Nothing would have changed in fact, but there would be a de jure change that would allow Loren to continue her independent manner of life. My client would get what she wants, Mr. Richards would put himself in the position of becoming established as her father, and would have time for a relationship to develop if it is going to. Lastly, I am sure that Mr. and Mrs. Gragg would be delighted to continue their relationship with my client. They adore her and regard her as their grandchild—an understanding that my client both accepts and wants."

"Thank you, Mr. Franklin. Mr. Herms, what say you?"

"Your Honor, I can't speak for the State of Tennessee, but I assure you that I will do everything in my power to support such an agreement were it to come about. People have written dozens—no hundreds of letters and e-mails to the Governor, and to our office asking—demanding an intelligent decision favoring the needs of Ms. Creek. While I also can't speak for the Governor, I wouldn't be at all surprised if he supported such an agreement. Your Honor, I do know that my office wants to bring this issue to resolution."

"Thank you, Mr. Herms." Turning to Loren's attorney, Judge Tilson said, "Go to your client and determine if she is ready to return to chambers. I don't want us to discuss this any further without her present." She pressed her desk button again, bringing the clerk of court.

"Announce to those waiting that we will reconvene after lunch." The judge turned to the three men in her chambers. "Gentlemen we have work to do."

CHAPTER 46

"All rise."

Once again the heavily-bundled audience rose for the judge and sat back down as she seated on the bench.

"Thank you for your patience, ladies and gentlemen. The issues at hand are complex, and require reasoned, patient discussion. However, we have arrived at a resolution and decision."

The courtroom assemblage once again grew perfectly silent, and seemed to breathe in unison as one animal.

"The court is satisfied that records show Mr. Virgil Richards to be Loren Creek's biological parent." The courtroom animal murmured softly. "As such, Mr. Richards will be given sole responsibility for the welfare of Ms. Creek, with the following understanding: That Ms. Creek continue to reside at her residence of the past two years adjacent to Mr. and Mrs. Fields Gragg, who have agreed to accept responsibility for day-to-day supervision of Ms. Creek. Mr. and Mrs. Gragg are to report to Mr. Richards on a weekly basis. The Foster Care Agency of Tennessee will submit a monthly report to the court on the progress of this arrangement. Unless there are issues or discussion of this agreement from members of the courtroom, this hearing is considered closed."

Judge Tilson paused in mid-stroke as she looked over the assembled body of citizens. She waited, looked, and then, her gavel fell.

As Virgil Richards gathered his paperwork to leave, the bailiff approached him. "Mr. Richards, Judge Tilson wishes to speak to you in her chambers." Richards looked at Aldrich Herms.

"Don't worry, Mr. Richards - she's thorough but fair."

"I was wondering about transportation—the rental car's in my name, but you're welcome to take it."

"No need. My house is not far, and they's any number of folks here who'll see me home. You best go to the judge. Just tell her as it all happened—she don't take to bein' misinformed."

"Thanks for all you've done. I owe you a great debt—and I pay my debts."

"No debt, Mr. Richards—just doing my job." Herms turned and walked from the courtroom.

The bailiff stood waiting for Richards. "Her Honor said that you and she could eat lunch in her chambers—she'll call in the order."

CHAPTER 47

It was late summer on the meadow below Fields' porch. The green of the pastures and trees, the sound of the birds and insects, and finally the wonderful lush scents of summer flowers and trees were not lost on Virgil or Loren. After the iced tea was served and sweetened to taste, the father and daughter sipped and rocked, almost in time with the cicadas. Virgil broke the silence.

"I haven't talked about the break-up of your mother and me these past six months because I wanted you to be ready for it. I would say it's time."

"Yes, I want to know the whole story about why I grew up without a father."

"I didn't ignore that fact. I simply didn't know about it, and that's the truth. Again, I didn't know you were born—that you existed. Your mother never told me she was pregnant. We were planning to get married that summer—and then we had our falling out."

Loren took a sip of iced tea and let her hand fall softly onto Sugar's head.

"Falling out? What was that about?" She ran her finger tips through the soft fur.

"Like I said in court, I was a singer; I had a rock group that was popular, and it was just a matter of time before we got the break we needed to make what we called the Big Time."

"Did you? Did you make the Big Time."

"No. I shot myself in the foot. I didn't mean to, but it happened because of a mistaken assumption by your mother. It was an accident."

"An accident? How'd your running around with other women turn out to be an accident?

"I wasn't running around. I was never unfaithful to your mother."

"But you said…"

"That was a quick short version of what actually took place. I later explained it more fully to Edythe—actually, that was the conversation that put the two of us on the path we've taken toward friendship." Loren's dad laughed at the startled expression on his daughter's face. "Don't be shocked. We've been dating for five months and have found that we are made for each other. We're both in love. We love that couple we've become, and we want to share the rest of our lives with each other—much like Beverly and Fields. It came and stayed as a surprise. It will be some time before we commit to a permanent relationship, because we are both so careful."

"What's the long version?" Loren asked, skepticism freezing her voice.

Virgil jerked upright in his rocker, took a deep breath and looked askance at Loren.

"I'm sorry." Loren said. "I didn't mean to sound like I don't believe you. It's just that…"

"No offense taken. You're entitled to some skepticism. You've deserved a whole family—a father and mother—all your life, and you didn't get it. I'm sorry. I only hope that somehow I can in some way, make it up to you. I'm willing to try. But then, I've already told you that—more than once."

"Yes. Yes, you have, and I want to believe you. But Momma was so angry with the ways of men that she's made me more than a little defensive. She told me to beware of people who try to get your affection by pretending to give you their affection."

"You think that's why I'm reaching out to you? You think that's why I'm risking a multi-million dollar enterprise that is going to take me years to rebuild after you've graduated and come of age? Do you really think I'm trying to be your dad in order to win you over? Six months ago you didn't even exist for me. Your mother did though. But I didn't know that she had misinformed me when she wrote that she was married. I didn't know that she never married, that you were born, lived, and grew into the excellent person you are. I was ignorant of all this—all the while suffering in my own private hell over a mistake that shouldn't have happened—that I didn't really make. I think you better re-think your position. You should ask yourself why I'm doing all this." Virgil waved his arms in an all-encompassing gesture. "I'm trying to love you, Loren, but you're not making it easy."

Loren rose, walked to one of the posts holding up Fields' porch roof. She leaned against it with the loose-limbed grace of an athlete.

"I believe I asked you about the long version?"

"I'm getting to that. But I have to say that you're showing a side that I don't like. What's saddest of all is that, if you've gotten this anger from you mother, then she must have been carrying a lot of pain. There was nothing like that in the Sarah I knew and have loved for nearly twenty years. In my mind's eye, I envision the lissome, kind, gently woman who was both strong and beautiful.

"Gently?"

"Yes. It was a pet word that we had for each other. We were gently with and to each other, and proud of it. Gently."

Loren frowned at the word she had heard her mother use so often. "I'm sorry. I was rude."

Virgil shrugged. "The long version goes like this: We were a hard-working rock band who did sixteen hour days on the road. We did this, day after day. I worked with three other musicians and a female vocalist—Abby. We were friends, close friends. We worked together, played together, wrote music, cried, laughed, and argued. We were nearly a family. Drugs and alcohol were always there in those days. Uppers, downers, gallons of coffee, and terrible food were all part of our diet.

"One night, on the road, we all piled up in our motel room after a gig. We were tired, but had to work on a new musical score for the next night. We were stretched out on the couch, in chairs, on the floor, wherever. Around three in the morning I fell asleep on the king sized bed where I was stretched out with Abby and our drummer, Elmer. I fell asleep and Elmer and Abby kept working. Finally, she fell asleep. Elmer woke up the other guys and sent them to their rooms, leaving Abby and me on the bed. Abby had her own room, but Elmer didn't want to wake her. We were clothed and sleeping on top of the covers. Elmer threw a quilt over us, turned out the light and left. It was no big thing. We'd all slept together before at one time or another. But that was all we ever did—sleep.

"Sarah was home at the time, but she decided to hook up with us. So, in the morning, she left the house we were renting and caught up with us around eleven, when she found Abby and me asleep in bed. She'd gotten the key from the morning clerk and entered the room. The lights were out, and so were we. Sarah didn't say a word. She just quietly closed the door, returned the key to the clerk and drove home. I didn't know about her discovery until later. I called home several times that day and there was no answer. I called all day, and that night I called several times during breaks. Finally, I shortened our gig that night and drove home. She was there, but had been packing and crying all day. I tried to tell her that nothing had taken place between Abby and me, but all she saw was the two of us in bed. There were accusations and denials. We both got angry and said things we shouldn't have. She left, and that was the last time I ever saw or talked with her. I tried to contact her at her parents' home in Piney Flat, but to no avail. No one knew where she was, and I was warned by her mother and father to stay away. They wanted me out of Sarah's life. In my childish anger I did just that. I went into a snit that lasted for months—possibly years, I don't know. I began having an affair with Abby. If I was going to be accused, then I was going to justify it, a childish response at best. Of course, that didn't work out. She quit and left the group—taking Elmer with her. We got replacements, but it was never the same after that. The group was dead within a year. I took to writing letters to your mother. They were always returned unopened. Finally, she sent me a note announcing that she was marrying a local boy. I respected her choice and quit trying to contact her. That's pretty much the long version."

"I don't know what to do." Loren said. "I have no reason to doubt your honesty or sincerity. I've been raised with one story all my life, and here you come along and say it was all a lie. A lie from the mouth of the person I love more than anything else, my Momma. Did she lie, Virgil? Did my Momma lie to me all those years? If she did, then why did she do it?"

"I think it was your mother's way of protecting you. Most people don't consider a lie to be an evil thing if it is done with the intention of protecting others. Your mother was deeply hurt by what she thought was infidelity on my part. So deeply that she never wanted you to feel that kind of pain. She made up a story in an effort to put you on guard against relationships with men. She wanted you to be self-sufficient to an extent that you wouldn't need the love of another to feel complete."

"Well, I'd say she got what she wanted. I don't need or want to lean on other people for help or support. I'm my own woman, and I go my own way. I don't need anybody—I carry my burdens on my own shoulders. I can outwork and out-do most everyone I know. It's always been that way, and I expect it will always be that way. I guess that's why I don't feel that I need you as a father."

"It sounds like you believe that self-sufficiency is a sign of strength."

"Yes. I do, and it is." Loren answered.

"Is that what you think?"

"Yes."

"Is that what you think you've done here?"

"Yes."

"All that support you've received from your Grandpa Gragg, and all the help Meredith and Tara gave un-asked for was just you being independent then."

"Well, I…" Loren blushed and her mouth tightened.

"Do you think for one minute that you could have made it without Mattie Hooks' love and care? She saw to your money, lied for you, protected you, she helped Fields fetch Alice, and would have risked jail time rather than see you hurt. That was you "carrying your own burden" I suppose."

"That wasn't what I meant." Loren said softly.

"Well, what did you mean—that you didn't need anybody? You think that's being strong? That's not strength—that's weakness. That's the path that cowards take—the mask that those frightened of commitment hide behind. Please don't tell me that's you."

"No, I'm not." Loren was weeping openly.

They thought in silence and rocked. Virgil broke the silence. "The Russian novelist, Leo Tolstoy, wrote a little-known work titled *What Men Live For*, a slim volume containing a parable. In the end he points out that men live to be loved. The implication of that thought is that the imperative to love is more important than everything else, and this obligates us to love others because that is what they want, and that is what we want."

Virgil rose and went to Loren. "I'll leave you with that thought—and one more—my own. Only the strong can love and be loved. The weak cannot love—or be loved." You think about it, and let me know when you are ready for love." He walked down the steps, got in his car and drove off.

Chapter 48

The giant newt-shaped banner flamed over the stage at the end of the cavernous multi-purpose room. Teal letters over an iridescent tangerine background—the colors of the Fire Newt and of High Country High. Truly ugly tones that the students loved and wore with defiant pride. The football uniforms were invariably a source of derision when, at the beginning of the game, the team stormed onto the field. Tangerine with teal trim or teal with tangerine trim—either combination was wonderfully visible to the quarterback looking for receivers.

Large fans were set to blow over the outrageous banner, making it waffle in the wind—setting it ablaze. The banner was designed and executed by the cheerleaders—not knowing that fifty years in the future it, or a clone, would still preside over dances, festivals, and some competition events and ceremonies. It even had a name: *Newt*. We've got to hang Newt this afternoon—be there! Newt needs a good cleaning. Newt's starting to fray on one corner, bring needle and thread. Newt was loved.

"Well, boys and girls, it's almost over." Gent said over his plastic glass of Newt Sweat—a blend of tangerine and lime juice, sporting a slice of kiwi. "I mean, we've got only one more year together, and then we'll blow out of this tree and go our separate ways—some of us never to be seen by some of the others. Only a memory, never to return to these hallowed halls."

Jo Mae responded with: "Hallowed Halls? Are you crazy? The school is only three years old. You don't hallow in three years. Our grandchildren can do a little hallowing', but we can't. Hallowed Halls, indeed," she scoffed. "You're right, though, a lot of us will find homes elsewhere—though I can't imagine why. I mean, why leave paradise?"

"Not me," Ollie quipped. "I'm stayin' right here. I'll go to school at Caldwell Community College and App State. Y'all will always know where to find me. The folks have cut out ten acres for me. I'm gonna build on it, marry a good ol' mountain gal and raise a passel."

"Well, there you go now," Gent replied. "Ollie's probably the smartest one of us. He's certainly the bravest for telling us what's dear to his heart. We all ought to follow his lead. I'll start it off." Gent looked down the length of the table at his cluster of friends. "The only rule is that no one seriously laughs at, or puts down, any one else. Okay?"

"You want us to pour our hearts out to this bunch of no goods?" Jo Mae asked in mock dismay.

"That's right—heart pouring."

"Oh. Okay then. Pour away."

Gent took the floor. "If I live through next year's football season, I plan to graduate and go to pre-law at whatever school is crazy enough to take me in. I want to be a lawyer for an environmental non-profit." He shrugged his shoulders in a dismissive gesture.

"That's it? That's pouring your heart out?" Jo Mae asked. "I mean, you nearly moved us all to tears with your heart-rending disclosure."

"Well, I left out the part where I was going to marry you and raise a dozen kids." This effectively silenced a blushing Jo Mae Butler.

Council cleared his throat and leaned forward. "I'm negotiating with Virginia Tech for a track scholarship. I'm going to major in bio-chemistry. Though I doubt I'll amount to much as a runner without having Loren pushing me till I throw up. I'll miss you guys, but most of all, I'll miss trying to make Gent and Bryce look good catching those wobbly passes they challenge me with."

Bryce and Gent groaned out loud.

Bryce said with a toothy grin, "I'm countin' on you guys making me look good this fall. If you do, I have a shot at a football scholarship, but it's not likely I'll take just any offer because I have my cap set for Duke. I don't rightly know what I'll major in but Mr. Griggs says I'm a natural for math. He says I'm a solid student in his classes, and he's willing to help me go as far as I want with math this year. He said I should look at a career in statistics." This was greeted with sighs and groans.

Tara took her turn. "As you-all know, Jo Mae has stolen Gent away from me, so I'm just going to sulk around broken-hearted until I can find another feller." Jo Mae flashed a grin at the girl who had become her best friend. "Mom says I've got to go to college, so I might major in home economics or some such thing.—maybe just straight economics." More groans.

Tara said, "Virgil wants me to consider theater. He says I'm a natural, and he's helped me a lot with school plays. I believe he knows everything about acting and actors and everyone in Hollywood. He took Mom to Hollywood last month for some kind of awards ceremony. She says he introduced her to half the actors there. I didn't know that agents were such important people." She looked around and smiled. "I think that Meredith and me are going to be bridesmaids sometime this coming Spring." This brought sounds of approval along with a round of applause.

"After that crack about a dozen kids," Jo Mae said, "I'm giving Gent back to Tara. So I expect she'll be plenty busy. Too busy for play-acting."

When the laughter dwindled, Meredith followed up her sister.

Meredith added, "I've never seen anyone stake out a claim as fast as Mom did on Virgil. The poor guy didn't have a chance. As things go, it looks like Sis and I are going to add a sister, and I can't tell you how happy it makes me to finally have a sister with some sense." Tara made a face for this. "Anyway, I'm going to go to med school and become a doctor so I can take care of you sick souls in your old age."

Loren was the last one to speak up. "If I had a choice of fathers, I don't think I could have chose better than Virgil Richards. He's hit it off with Grandpa and Beverly. Heck, even Sugar accepts—no, adores—him. I've never seen that dog make over a body like he does Virgil. Fields says he's spoiled forever—says he's lost a good watch dog. Our female is ready to make more Sugars, so I'm taking orders.

I got no idea what I want to major in. I'm going to college to find out what I should do. My future stepmother has told me not to hurry. That I had the first two years of college to make up my mind, and that's just what I plan to do. I might want to major in human relations—I want to find out more about love." A BEGINNING

ACKNOWLEDGMENTS

Ms. Lora Anne of Sugar Grove, NC provided inspiration for the character of the protagonist in this story. I have tried to capture her personal qualities of integrity, strength, and intelligent resilience that so characterize the Appalachian Mountain People. It is people like Lora Anne who have given this country its greatness, and perhaps the growing difficulty in finding such people is the reason behind the story that follows.

Those who are adamant that writing is a lonesome activity are guilty of myopic insight. At my elbow are scores of boys and girls, then men and women, who whisper in my ear—at times they shout. Yes, I would like to credit myself with cunning and wisdom, but the simple fact is that much of that which I call *me* comes from others—who in turn got it from others. It's an unbroken chain that goes back decades in my life—and decades beyond that: My mother who admonished, "Learn to listen because you'll never live long enough to make all your own mistakes." A tee totaling grandmother who, during prohibition, made home-brew for her guests' use because she didn't think the government had the right to tell people they couldn't take a drink. Uncle Frank, who invited me to watch a Salvation Army street corner event, which included a small band and chorus, and an inspirational speaker. We stayed through the whole thing, and when we left he told me that he disagreed with their beliefs but would fight and die for their right to stand on that corner, beat their drums and shout their message. A father who was so proud when I shot my first squirrel at age six. I still have the shotgun, and am skilled in all manner of firearms but I haven't killed game in over five decades. As with each of us, the list of those for whom there is a debt is long and fading into the mists of memory. To forget the contributions from those souls would be inexcusable. The following tale is as much from their combined efforts as my imagination.

Closer to home - and nearer to now - are those who will read these words and get satisfaction knowing that I'm aware of them—and thankful. Collectively, they are the members of High Country Writers of Boone, NC, whose dirty little secret is that they are indeed "High"—on Life. Along the path of our decade of association they have encouraged, prodded, poked, questioned, doubted, laughed at, laughed and wept with each other, themselves—and me. Were I to someday achieve recognition as a writer, theirs would remain a debt so inestimable as to defy payment. I identify some of the guilty parties: Sandy Horton, editor, who after telling me what a good writer I was, proceeded to help me correct the hundreds of mistakes. If the reader should enjoy this book—it's her fault. Wendy Dingwall, publisher who took a risk. Peggy Poe Stern—I know of no milkmaid who is a better writer, or critic, of thangs country. Nora Percival, author, just for being who she is to her fellow writers—a study in the grace of excellence. Bill Kaiser, a Rock in the midst of the muddy maelstrom of our writerly shoutfests that sometimes degenerate into meetings. Ree Strawser of the red-hair. Photographer and friend, who has steadfastly resisted the urge to strangle me—all the while encouraging my attempts to write. Her photo of me graces the back cover—should I sue? After a loving family, I guess our greatest wealth is that of good friends. My wallet bulges.

I remember two pieces of advice from army buddies; SP4 Gary Highland, in the 82d Airborne, who told me, "Don't sweat the small stuff." And then there was the Sergeant Major, veteran of WWII and Korea who said of Gary's advice: "He's right. Just remember—there is no small stuff."

In that vein, the reader perusing book shelves will casually pick up an author's blood offering, glance at it, and either return it to the shelf, or tuck it under her arm to give it a new home. Her choice will depend largely on the efforts of a graphic artist, and of those skilled in book design and lay-out. If the book is selected and enjoyed, the writer is credited—but rarely the artist or book designer. Like as not, it was their efforts that sent the book into the shopping cart. A Stephen King or John Grisham could publish on a blank white cover showing only their name under a title, and their work would sell. However, the majority of writers have no such name recognition and are dependent almost totally on the vagaries of artistic expression. For such expression I'm indebted to Joe Burleson, a wondrously talented artist who bent his eye to a presentation of this cover. To Aaron Burleson, kudos for cover design and book layout. Joe—Aaron, the success of our book depends as much on your shouted skills as it does my penned. The reader doesn't know me from Adam's housecat, and is taking a risk—but she can *see* your artistry at a glance.

Finally, the first person to address the making of the cover of this book was Dalton Babcock, who, at the time was thirteen years old. This bright young man took my brief description of what I wanted on the cover and assembled photographs into a scene that was later rendered as a painting. Dalton, stay the course of your uplifting spiral into a promising manhood.

Thank you all.

Bart Bare
Winter 2010

Bart Bare received his AA from St. Petersburg Jr. College, in St. Petersburg, Florida, his BA from the University of S. Florida and his MA in psychology from Appalachian State University in 1974.

He taught psychology at Caldwell College for 27 years, and part time at ASU. Bare has a wealth of diverse experience. He was a Sergeant in paratroopers at Fort Bragg and Germany. He was a community organizer in the mountains of NC during war on Poverty, worked in construction, retail sales, bulldozers, raced sports cars, landscaping, and operated a shrimp boat. He is an active member of High Country Writers, Watauga County Beekeepers, NC Beekeepers, American Chestnut Foundation, and the National Associate Fruit Growers Exchange. He is a resident of Blowing Rock, NC, currently retired, and recently widowed after 43 years of marriage.

Girl is Bart Bare's second novel, his first, *Satan's Bargain*, was published in 2007. Also coming in 2010 are *SS Jew* and *Wadmalaw: A Ghost Story*.